playing
it safe

ALSO BY BARBIE BOHRMAN

Promise Me

BARBIE BOHRMAN

playing it safe

Montlake
Romance

Text copyright © 2014 Barbie Bohrman
All rights reserved.

Published by Montlake Romance, Seattle

www.apub.com

Amazon, the Amazon logo, and Montlake Romance are trademarks of Amazon.com, Inc., or its affiliates.

ISBN-13: 9781477825464
ISBN-10: 1477825460

Cover design by Mumtaz Mustafa

Library of Congress Control Number: 2014907965

Printed in the United States of America

To the best friend, the bestie, the BFF, the confidante, the wingman . . .

There are a few people in my life who fit this description—some of you I've known for as long as thirty years, and some I've known for far less. But the amount of time of our friendship does not at all lessen the impact you've made in my life.

So this one's for you, with love.

CHAPTER ONE

I'm sitting across from a Dick.

No, really. His name is Dick, and he won't shut up. I think he may love the sound of his own voice or something because he hasn't stopped talking for the last twenty minutes. I know this because I've been able to eat my entire meal without uttering a single word.

It's a fine art pretending to be enthralled in a conversation with a person you have absolutely no interest in speaking to normally. Almost like an acquired skill. Apparently, I possess said skill set in spades. This can be a blessing and a curse all rolled into one. It's a blessing because not really saying much other than the occasional *"Really?"* or *"I understand completely,"* along with a varied selection of head nods, you can get away with making it appear like you give a shit, when in reality you don't give a shit whatsoever. Unfortunately, these same reasons are why it's a damned curse. Because the other person takes your feigned interest as an indication that you *are* interested. And this is how and why I currently find myself in quite the pickle.

Sitting across from me at this very fine Italian restaurant is my date, Dick. Yes, I'm aware the name alone should have been enough of a warning for me to run in the opposite direction when he asked me out the first time a couple weeks ago. What can I say? It made me laugh to know that I was or would be dating a "Dick," further proving my closest friends' theories that I have the sense of humor equivalent to that of a thirteen-year-old boy. So, foolishly or hard up, haven't decided on which one of those applies to my lapse of better judgment, I agreed to the date, and he was . . . nice. That right there should have been indicator number two. He was just plain old nice. Maybe that's why I agreed to this second go-round with him because he kind of duped me into a false sense of security with his "nice" routine.

This time, though, as we sit in this upscale dining room that only fits about thirty to forty people, and it's so exclusive that there aren't even any menus—the chef will prepare items based on your likes and dislikes—he's far from nice. He's been rude to the wait-staff, a pet peeve of mine, and he's made it more than obvious that he's expecting a little something in return at the end of the evening, an even bigger pet peeve of mine. I could lower my standards for the night and sleep with him, because the fact remains he's not too hard on the eyes, and as I've previously mentioned, I'm a little hard up. But there's hard up and there's desperate, and I'm nowhere near the level of desperation required where I'd want to knock some boots with Dick. There's nothing exciting, enthralling, engaging, or even the slightest bit fascinating about him. In fact, he's the polar opposite of all those things. He's boring, irritating, and uninterest-ing. In short, if Dick were any more of a dick, he'd be, well . . . a *total* dick.

"Julia?"

Dick's voice is grating on my nerves and snaps me out of the task of trying to count every single polka dot on the dress of the woman sitting behind him right now. I veer my gaze a fraction of a hair back over to his, and I can tell he's noticed that I wasn't pay-ing the slightest bit of attention to him. Hell, I wasn't even bother-ing with the aforementioned occasional nod this time. I must have gone straight into self-preservation mode over the utter boredom

I've been feeling during this date. No need to panic, because along with having the talent of pretending to be interested, I also possess the talent of covering my tracks.

Oh so casually, I smile at Dick and grab my wineglass for a quick sip. All the while his eyes never leave mine, watching and waiting to see what I'm going to say. Now, I can play this one of two ways. One, pretend I know exactly what he was talking about and take the chance that whatever lie flies out of my mouth will fit perfectly within the conversation he was having with himself while I was busy with polka dot lady. Or two, admit to not paying any kind of attention to him. This second choice is tricky and can have a high risk of coming back to bite you in the ass. But, if played correctly, you can get sympathy from your date instead of being insulted, which, if he had any clue, is exactly how he should be feeling. I have about a half a second to decide as I bring the glass of merlot down from my lips and set it back on the table.

"I'm sorry, Dick." I have to stifle a laugh; it still cracks me up. "I've been so busy with work, and this is the first night I've had off in about a week. I'm just so stressed and can't help it if it seems like my mind is elsewhere. I'm sorry."

Pitch-perfect. His brown eyes soften slightly, and his head tilts to the left in that sympathetic look reserved for funerals or sick puppies.

In a condescending tone, he says in response, "Julia, I've told you before, you shouldn't be working yourself so hard."

My spine stiffens, and I sit upright. He wanted my attention, well now he's got it. For the record, I love my job. Not many people can honestly say they love what they do, but I can. I run an event planning business that used to belong to my father until he had a health scare and retired a few years ago. He had been grooming me since college so that one day I could take over the company, and I'm proud to report that it's doing better than ever. Maybe it's the independent woman in me or my strong-willed personality, but I take offense to Dick's comment.

I put down my fork and sweep my blunt blond bangs away from my forehead. They cascade right back into place as if I hadn't done a damn thing to move them. Carefully, I forge ahead. "And what does that mean, exactly? How can I not work too hard when I own the company? The fate of my employees rests on the sole fact that I *do* work hard to ensure they get a paycheck every other week."

He puts his hands up in defense while chuckling. Ugh, I instantly regret selecting option number two; I should have just played dumb when I had the chance. "Julia, that's not what I meant. I simply meant that when you work too hard, you don't get to enjoy the other things in life. Like this." He motions his hand between us to drive his point home that he means "us."

Is he shitting me? There is no "us." I'd rather watch paint dry than be here on this date with him. Thankfully, the waiter comes before I can respond, and he asks if we need anything else. Dick doesn't even ask me; instead, he tells the waiter to bring the check. Normally, this would bug the hell out of me since it's another pet peeve to add to Dick's ever-growing list of cons, but tonight I'm glad he did it because it means I'm that much closer to never having to see him again.

After he signs the check, which he makes a big deal out of since the final tally of our dinner is somewhere above the hundred-dollar mark, I stay silent and just put on a tight smile while we walk to his car. The drive back to my house is even worse. He blasts Marvin Gaye's "Sexual Healing" over the speaker system the *whole* way home.

Seriously?! I couldn't make this shit up if I tried.

And it's right then that I have a moment of clarity. An epiphany, if you will.

Why am I putting myself through the torture of another date that never goes anywhere? I'm not a conceited person by any stretch of the imagination. I think I'm halfway decent in the looks depart-ment, pretty goddamn funny, and successful enough in my own right that I could afford several dinners that this prize just paid for on my behalf like he was doing me a favor.

The answer sneaks up on me just as he pulls into my driveway. I don't need to put up with guys like Dick over here, ever. In fact, I don't think I need to bother with men at all. Maybe what I need to do is take a complete and total break from dating. They do say when you're not looking for love is when you'll find it magically appearing on your doorstep. He'll appear with a pretty red bow on his beautiful, perfectly coiffed head. Mind you, nobody knows exactly who "they" are, so this theory is still up for debate. But still, I think it's worth a shot.

"So, are you going to invite me in?"

I turn in my seat to face Dick, who is trying his damndest to grin in a sexy way. Instead of being sexy he looks more like an over-eager twit.

"Thanks for the date, Dick." Still funny. "But yeah, um, I don't think so."

He actually has the nerve to look surprised. "Come on, Jules. The night doesn't have to end so early. I can make it worth your while."

Rule number one that I should put out as a disclaimer for everyone who meets me: never, under any circumstance, call me Jules. Anger infiltrates me to the point that I'm *this* close to smack-ing him upside his head for calling me that, especially since he knows I hate it with a passion.

I have to take a deep breath and exhale before I say anything back. "Listen closely, *Dick*. On what part of this date, or the one before it, did I lead you to believe you were going to ever get inside my pants? Did you think that just because I agreed to a second date that I was a foregone conclusion? A sure thing? Better yet, did you think because you paid for dinner that it gives you the right to assume I'd let you inside my home to have your way with me?"

His mouth drops open to say something, but I'm on a roll now. "You are a pretentious, overeager asshole. There is no scenario in the world where this date ends with you in my bed. I'd much rather pleasure myself with my battery-operated boyfriend for the rest of my lonely existence than have you attempt to find my G-spot."

"You use a vibrator?" he asks with an obvious smirk in his tone, like he didn't hear anything else I just said to him.

"Good night, Dick."

"Wait! I just meant—"

I don't even wait to hear the rest of what he just meant. Opening the car door as he's still bumbling to form a coherent string of words that would closely resemble a sentence, I make my way to my front door. Once inside, I slam it behind me and turn the dead bolt for good measure. I heave a sigh of relief that that's all over and done with, and this new phase of my life can immediately begin.

One thing to know about me, I'm pretty big on lists. And this occasion lends itself to a list for the ages. Feeling resolved in my newfound singledom, I kick off my heels and toss my purse and keys onto the floor before making my way to the kitchen, because this list calls for a big-ass glass of wine.

"Ha! I can't believe he actually thought he was going to get some," I say out loud to absolutely no one. Ever since my old roommate and best friend, Sabrina, moved away about a year ago, sometimes I forget that there is nobody here to listen to me rant. We keep in touch often and Skype frequently. So much so that her boyfriend, Tyler, thinks we're completely and utterly nuts. I miss her like crazy, but I'm so happy for her because she's found the love of her life, and more than anyone I know she deserves it.

But back to my current dilemma. The list. Yes, the almighty list that will help me focus on the important goals and any other bullshit I can think of while the wine seeps into my bloodstream.

1. Focus on career.

2. No more dating losers because of number one.

3. ~~Try to take a pottery class.~~ Yeah, probably not something I want to do . . . ever.

I sit back and stare at the list while taking a sip of wine. Not my finest, most detailed list in my whole twenty-nine years of list making, but I like it. It's short, to the point, and serves its purpose in reminding me of my goals. To drive the point home, I go one step further. I sprint for my laptop that's on the coffee table and log on to my Match.com account to disable it before I chicken out.

There, I feel *sooooo* much better. Like a weight has been lifted off my shoulders. I'm sure the alcohol has something to do with it, but who cares? I kick my feet up, feeling empowered by my new sense of self, and turn on the TV to unwind before going to bed. Glancing at the clock, I do a little fist pump when I realize I'm not too late to catch another rerun of my favorite comedy. I hurry and change the channel before relaxing back into the couch, ready to laugh for a little while before calling it a night.

"Make me laugh, Jerry."

Yeah, I might need to work on this talking out loud stuff . . . I'll add it to the list tomorrow.

CHAPTER TWO

"*Niña, estas de madre,*" my assistant calls out to me while walking into my office.

That's Lisette, my Girl Friday, telling me, in no uncertain terms, that I'm a hot mess. I don't speak fluent Spanish, but I've lived in Miami my entire life. I know the basics, and of course over the years I've learned a variety of curse words and phrases, so I get by . . . and she's right.

I *am* a hot mess.

I have been for the past three and a half weeks since my date with Dick when I swore off men. So yeah, Lisette pretty much just hit the nail on the head. It's not like I'm some crazed sexual deviant, but come on! Three weeks! That's one hell of a dry spell, and it might also explain why I've been lusting over the UPS guy every time he drops by my office.

From my vantage point, I have a clear shot of the receptionist's desk. Without fail, at one fifteen p.m. every day, give or take a few minutes, he appears before my eyes like a mirage in the desert. Then circa 1970s cheesy porn music starts playing in my head, and what do I have? A recipe for disaster, that's what. Because what I've left out is that Mr. UPS Guy is probably in his mid to late fifties, with a beer belly and bald. I'm not knocking bald men. Nope, not at all. Some men can really rock that look, like The Rock and Bruce Willis. But this guy isn't even close to that caliber of hotness.

Did I mention that he has really nice calves? They're like perfectly formed muscles shifting ever so slightly and sexily as he prances in front of me.

You don't believe me?

Well, trust me, he does.

"Ugh, Lisette, I know I've been in a piss-poor mood lately. Sorry."

Lisette eyes me carefully while getting her pad and pen ready for our daily afternoon meeting. As I've come to expect, her ensemble is perfect, with a smart charcoal-gray pantsuit that is complemented by a black chiffon blouse. If I didn't know her so well, I would never be able to tell she's not a natural blonde. Then again, I know she goes far out of her way to ensure that *nobody* ever knows that about her. She's a Miami native, just like me, and she married her high school sweetheart. They have twin boys who are about to go off to college. She doesn't look a day over thirty, and that's only my best guess since she keeps that kind of intel on lockdown. But whenever I get an opportunity, I ply her with drinks to see how much I can get out of her. It never works; she just ends up sloppy and drunk off her ass. Lisette is also the only woman I know who can pull off blood-red lipstick year-round. She can work the shit out of that look better than any runway model could. And it doesn't matter if you bump into her at a grocery store on a Sunday afternoon; undoubtedly she'll be sporting the red even if the rest of her looks like crap. I've known her for . . . I can't say for sure how long I've known her, since she started off working here as my dad's assistant. Needless to say, we go way back—*waaaay* back. We usually get together at least once a day to go over any loose ends on upcoming events my company is planning or hosting. These afternoon "meetings" usually consist of about a half hour of actual business, immediately followed by another half hour of shooting the shit and gossiping.

"Then do something about it," she says in a matter-of-fact tone.

"Do something about what?" I ask.

"*It*. As in, go out and find yourself a man," she answers with an expression on her face that suggests I'm a moron for not knowing what she's talking about.

I swivel my seat so that I'm completely facing her, picking the stress ball up off my desk at the same time. Lately, I've been squeezing the living shit out of this thing; fucker could burst at any moment by the way I keep gripping it. It'll pay off eventually because the next guy I give a hand job to is going to see stars.

Lisette's eyes dart to my hand as it's flexing and tightening itself, before raising an eyebrow in defiance. "Don't give me that look, Julia. You've just had a run of bad luck in the man department. Everybody goes through those once in their life before meeting their Prince Charming. But you need to actually get your ass out there to meet him and not lock yourself up in your house all weekend, doing God knows what." She immediately crosses herself, as if what she just said implies that I'm skinning cats or some crazy shit like that, and that the power of prayer is going to absolve me somehow.

I clench my fist around the stress ball and roll my neck around like a prize fighter getting ready to do battle before I hear it crack. "First of all, I've been busy redecorating Sabrina's old room." This is such bullshit, although I have given it quite a lot of thought while watching an exorbitant amount of television. I can't help it if I have to catch up on Jax Teller, but she doesn't need to know this. "Secondly, do I need to remind you of the long list of losers that I've had the pleasure of dating over the last year?"

"It wasn't that bad," she says, dismissing me quickly, even though she damn well knows it totally was.

I chuck the stress ball onto my desk, and it lands smack-dab on my keyboard. A distressing amount of beeps sound off in the background while I stand up and plant my hands on my desk, ready to remind her of just how bad it really was.

"First, there was Jack, who told me he was into 'alternative films,' which really meant he liked to watch porn all day. Then there was Dave, who apparently thought I looked *so* much like his beloved ex-girlfriend that when we finally had sex he shouted her name when he came. Then there's Ryan, who told me on our very first date that he didn't have a bank account, had never filed taxes, and had worked on a drug farm. Let's see, oh! Then there's Vincent, who—"

"*¡Por favor!* Stop, I get it. You've had some bad luck."

"Bad luck?" I say with a mocking laugh. "Bad luck is more like not winning the pick six by one number. Or when you get a flat tire. Or getting your period while you're at the beach. This is so much worse than bad luck. This is just . . . Jesus, I don't even know what you call this, but I sure as shit can tell you it's not just bad luck!"

Lisette is trying to stifle her giggle fit by covering her plump, red-coated lips with her hand and looking everywhere but at me. Between her sputtering laughter, I sit down again and calmly pluck the stress ball off the keyboard and being to massage it, hoping that it will help me center my chi, or whatever you call that nonsense. After about ten seconds of squeezing it to death, I give up and throw it back onto my desk, where it lands with a loud thud, barely missing my coffee cup.

"You need to work on your aim," Lisette says while still snickering.

"I need to work on a lot of things," I mutter under my breath.

She stops laughing long enough and coolly announces, "You're gonna be fine. I bet your Prince Charming is right around the corner, and when you least expect it, he'll swoop in to save the day. Girl, I can just feel it. He's coming."

"His Garmin must be telling him to come by way of Bumfuck, Egypt."

"You know what I'm going to do," she goes on to say, ignoring me completely. "When I get home tonight, I'm going to *encender una vela* in your name to *Santa Bárbara*."

I roll my eyes because Lisette has been lighting so many candles to one saint or another in my name for years that by now it seems like a waste of a perfectly good matchstick. Not once have I seen anything come from it. However, if it makes her feel better and gets her off my back about my pathetic love life, fine.

"You'll see," she chirps, "it's going to work, *chica*."

With a loud *pfft*, I turn my attention back to the computer and pull up the coming week's schedule. Three events are lined up: a grand opening of a new restaurant/bar in Coconut Grove, an engagement party at a home in Key Biscayne, and finally, at the end of the week, an opening at the Art Gallery here in South Beach.

That last one, the one at the Art Gallery, should be a cakewalk considering I've been handling their events and openings exclusively for the better part of the last year. And that would be thanks to Alex Holt, the owner.

Alex is kind of an enigma. Well maybe not, but there is something about him that I can't quite put my finger on. My best friend Sabrina worked for him at the gallery before moving to Philly. At some point, he made it clear that he had the hots for her, but she was already in too deep with her boyfriend, Tyler. Well, not technically, but deep enough that Alex didn't stand a chance.

Sounds like a fucking soap opera, right?

Anyway, the shit hit the fan, then yada, yada, yada, she moved away. But not before I made a deal with him that I still had to repay him for. I kind of told him that I would do any event of his choosing, free of charge, if he got Sabrina's résumé to the right person at the Philadelphia Museum of Art. He did, she got the job, and almost a year later, he still hasn't collected on my debt. He hasn't even brought it up to me once, and I see him quite regularly. And we've become good friends.

Well, *good friends* is a bit of an overstatement; *good enough* is probably more of an accurate depiction. It doesn't help that he's hot as hell either. I'm not going to lie; the man is sex on a stick. He is gorgeous with a capital *G*. If Josh Holloway is ever in need of a stunt double, well look no further, because Alex should be the first and only person he would need to call. Our "friendship" could be described more by saying we playfully argue and exchange one too many flirtatious comments that drive me crazy. I didn't even say anything yet about those dimples of his. Sweet baby Jesus, it's just not fair.

"Julia, what the hell is wrong with you?" Lisette asks in a concerned voice, while I'm still conjuring up images of Alex's dimples.

"What? Nothing's wrong," I say a tad too defensively, playing it off with a shrug of my shoulders. The last thing I need is for Lisette to drag out my daydreams of Alex in any way, shape, or form. "Just thinking about how crazy the schedule is for this week."

"It's not that bad. We've done three events in one week before. You can do this with your eyes closed and your hands tied behind your back."

My mind goes straight to the gutter. Thoughts of being blindfolded and bound to a bed, at Alex's hands and completely at his mercy, start whirling around in my head. God, it would be good . . . *soooo* good. Like earth-shattering good. Like speaking in tongues good. And I'm not even that into being tied up. But for Alex . . . damn, I'd haul my ass on over to Home Depot and buy the rope myself.

You know how I know he'd be amazing? Because there are some men—and when I say some, I mean a select few of the species—that the first thing you do when you meet them is picture how many sexual positions you can recreate from the *Kama Sutra*. Alex, without a doubt, is one of those men.

Okay, okay, so *maybe* I have a little crush on him. I don't think I would act on it, though. The guy did boldly go where no man has gone before, or at least he tried to with my best friend. That would be like sloppy seconds, right? Maybe incestuous in Bizarro World since she's like the sister I never had? Eww, so gross! I really need to come up with another way of looking at this whole situation. There are times, however, that it feels like he wants something to happen. Like he's waiting for me to make a move. Goading me even. These instances are becoming more frequent to the point that I'm constantly questioning the parameters of our friendship. But the second I teeter on the brink of doing something about it, I reel myself back in.

"Earth to Julia! Come in, Julia!" Lisette's hands are cupped around her mouth when her voice snaps me back to reality.

Shaking off the mental hopscotch I just played, I get back to the business at hand. "Sorry," I quickly answer. "Was just thinking about all the redecorating I'm planning on doing this weekend. Where were we?"

Her cackle fills the room instantly. "*¡Por favor!* You were not thinking about redecorating."

"I was! I was thinking of color palettes."

She narrows her eyes at me and says, "You forget how well I know you. If you don't want to share, fine. But remember, I've got my eyes on you." Then she lifts her two fingers and points them toward her eyes, then at me, and then back to herself again.

"Whatever."

"Yeah right, whatever," she says, mimicking my dismissive tone. "Fine, can we discuss the Grandersons' party then?"

"Yup, hang on a second while I pull up their file."

A few strokes of the keyboard later and the details of the party we're planning at the Grandersons' home in Key Biscayne this

Wednesday night are up and ready for review. I do a quick scan of the particulars before turning my head to face Lisette again, but not before I take note of the time on the corner of my monitor: 1:12 p.m.

"Lisette, sweetie, can you move your seat over to the right just a hair, please? The glare coming from the window behind you is killing my eyes."

She smiles and does as I ask before going into details about the party. Everything seems to be in order, and then like clockwork, my eyes feast upon a vision standing at the receptionist's desk. There he is. Mr. UPS Guy in all his UPS uniformed glory.

Bow chicka bow wow . . .

CHAPTER THREE

It's like Africa hot in this tent, or oven—whichever way you want to refer to this plastic, white-walled room of heat. Even though it's mid-September in Miami, if you're in a tent at any time of the year, it's the equivalent of a sweat lodge. As for me, the secret to Secret deodorant is to not sweat like a pig. Which completely defeats the purpose since your secret is out of the bag, as evident by the giant rings of perspiration currently gracing my white pintuck blouse. It's a classy look.

I tried to talk them out of using this thing, but there was no use. Mr. Granderson, my client, refused to hear anything to the contrary. His only requirement for me was to make his baby girl happy at her engagement party. And his baby girl wanted a tent, so whatever baby wants, baby gets.

Speaking of "baby," the few times we spoke during the planning stages of her engagement party she'd sometimes get a dreamy, faraway look in her eye. As if the mere thought of her betrothed would incapacitate her ability to hold a conversation. I can't lie. I'm jealous. I want that for myself. I want to meet someone who robs me of speech, makes my pulse race, and loves me beyond measure. It might be a pipe dream at this point in my life. I'm barely holding on to the hope of finding "him." And as I stand to the far side of the sweat tent observing the guests congratulate "baby," I picture myself in her shoes.

People raise their champagne-filled flute glasses until someone clinks theirs with a spoon to quiet the crowd. "Congratulations, and may you both live in the glow of love for years to come. To Julia and . . ."

Damn, even in my daydream I can't muster up a make-believe name for the faceless man I'm supposed to be engaged to. If that's not pathetic, I don't know what it is.

A defeated sigh escapes me as I scan the crowd again, looking for the groom-to-be. I never got a chance to meet him since "baby" said he was out of town on business. I think I spot the back of his head finally just as I catch Lisette heading my way from the corner of my eye. By the determined look on her face, my first thought is something happened with the caterer, which always seems to be the case at these things. But I quickly realize it's much worse than that by the one word that spills out of her mouth as soon as she reaches me.

"Aiden."

My voice catches in my throat when I ask, "Aiden, what?"

She chews nervously on her bottom lip because if there is one rule in regards to my personal life it's this: never speak of Satan, a.k.a. Aiden. However, I'll make an exception this one time and give you the abbreviated version.

Aiden was my boyfriend right after college. We were together for two years, five months, and sixteen days. But who's counting? Um, this jackass, that's who. I put up with so much bullshit from Aiden, it was sad.

For example, he had this "I'm finding myself" phase where almost every day for a good four months he was all about trying to get in touch with his inner Aiden, whatever the hell that's supposed to mean. He started out by devouring every self-help book he could get his hands on. Then he changed his eating habits to a macrobiotic-type diet. This didn't bother me too much because I could always fend for myself come dinnertime. But when he started talking about going to get his-and-hers enemas, I was done. It got to the point where whenever he said he was "working on Aiden," and yes he would refer to himself in the third person, I would tell him to just look in a goddamn mirror and call it a day. Then there was his "I'm a gamer" phase where he would tune the whole world out for hours at a time, sometimes entire weekends, just so he could cultivate his video-gaming skills. Because according to Aiden, he was going to "get the gold at the next World Cyber Games." For the record, that never happened.

That's just a couple of the things he did over the course of our relationship that I dealt with. And why did I put up with it? Mostly because I was young and naïve and very much in love. *And* because he would tell me that I was his girl and that we were going to get married and have lots of babies and a whole slew of garbage that I ate right out of the palm of his hand. That is, until the day he called and said that he never wanted to see me again.

"Yeah, that's really funny, Aiden," I had said to him.

He was dead serious because the motherfucker had up and left for California that morning to shack up with some broad he had never met in person. Thank you very much, World Wide Web.

Long story short, ever since him I've been extremely wary when it comes to men and letting my guard down. And as luck would have it, I've had the worst pick of the litter since him.

"He's here," Lisette says.

"Here," I repeat. "As in at *this* party?"

My eyes canvass the crowd, darting from face to face until Lisette stands in front of me to block my view.

"It's worse than that," she says.

Before I can ask her how that's possible, I peek over her shoulder and see him.

The years have been kind to the devil incarnate. Aiden looks better than ever, to my utter disappointment. I'd been wishing he would have developed a deformity à la Hunchback of Notre Dame by now, but no such luck. He still looks male-model worthy with his cropped black hair, piercing blue eyes, and what I know is a lean, muscular physique hidden beneath his dark suit. The bastard could still give David Beckham a run for his money.

Lisette snaps her fingers within an inch of my nose. "Hey, are you okay?" she asks.

"Yeah, yeah. I'm fine."

I'm not. In my head there are alarm bells going off, and all I can think of is why the hell is he here?

"Did you know he was going to be here?" I ask while trying to sneak another peek over her shoulder.

"No! How can you ask me that?" She sounds appalled that I would even entertain the idea for a second. "Did *you* know he was going to be here?"

My shocked expression along with my eyebrows flying up to my hairline is enough of an answer.

"Relax. I just meant that since the name of Sophia's fiancé was Aiden, you might have asked about it."

"Who's Sophia?"

"Julia, that's the bride-to-be," she deadpans.

"Oh! You mean 'baby,'" I answer.

"Who's 'baby'?" Lisette asks.

"Never mind," I grumble under my breath. "Wait a minute, what did you mean you thought I would have asked about Sophia's fiancé's name?"

She gently grabs my arm and tries to move me, but I don't budge. And that's because I finally put two and two together as I see Aiden take "baby" in his arms and kiss her as if she's the last woman on earth.

"Julia, come on," Lisette says softly. "Let's get you out of here."

"You have got to be shitting me. He's engaged to 'baby'?" I ask her in a deathly quiet voice.

It's too late to leave because I've been spotted. Sophia, "baby," or whatever the hell her name is, is pointing me out to Aiden and leading him by the hand to where I'm standing.

"Dammit, they're coming over here. What do I do?" I ask Lisette through clenched teeth.

She steps to the side and whispers, "Act natural."

"Easy for you to say," I say under my breath just before they reach us.

With each step the look on Aiden's face is priceless. He obviously had no idea that I was the party planner. And when he's finally standing right in front of me, close enough for me to kick in the nuts if I were so inclined, his eyes quickly move between me and Sophia in disbelief. She's completely oblivious to the potential shit-storm brewing right in front of her. Honestly, I feel bad about how she'll react when she finds out because she's a genuinely nice person and I'm sure she won't want to know how much of a dick her fiancé is.

"There you are," Sophia says happily. "I was looking all over for you. I wanted to introduce you to my fiancé, Aiden."

"We already kn—"

Aiden speaks over me and cuts me off. "Met."

Sophia looks confused, and I'm staring at Aiden with the phoniest smile I can muster.

"You two know each other?" she asks.

"No," he tells her. "I mean we met earlier tonight."

Sophia seems reassured and smiles at him. "Awesome! Didn't she do an amazing job, honey?"

I'm too shocked to say anything, and my mouth drops open as a result. Lisette pokes me in the ribs with her elbow, and I turn to see her give me a chiding look. I mouth *What?* to her, and she plasters a fake smile across her red lips. When I turn my attention back to the lovebirds, they're staring at me expectantly. Well, Sophia most definitely is. Aiden looks more like a deer in the headlights.

"So will you do it?" Sophia asks.

"I'm sorry," I answer her. "I didn't hear what you were asking me."

She laughs. "I was wondering if you'd be willing to help plan the wedding."

Hmmm, let's see . . . help plan the wedding of an ex who I thought would be the man I would be marrying someday. Um, that would be a big no.

"When is the wedding?" Lisette asks.

She can't be serious. It's my turn to poke her in the ribs, but she doesn't even flinch.

"April fifteenth," Sophia says with a lilt in her voice.

"Oooh, I'm sorry, Sophia," Lisette responds with just the right amount of regret in her tone. "But we're solidly booked from here to next summer."

Wow! I'm impressed with Lisette's lie, and I grin from ear to ear in approval as she tilts her head to acknowledge me.

"That's too bad," Aiden says while hugging Sophia from behind.

"Yeah, too bad," she agrees with a sad smile. "I really would have loved to have you do it."

"I would have loved to help," I finally say even though I want to laugh like a lunatic at the absurdity of the situation. Of course, that would be after I kick Aiden in the nuts. And maybe stab him in the eye with a dull knife.

"Sophia!" someone yells from the far side of the tent.

"Oh, I have to go," she quickly says and then extracts herself from Aiden's embrace. "I'll catch up with you later. Okay?"

"Sure thing," I answer with a curt nod.

And then there were three.

"I'll leave you two to talk," Lisette abruptly announces and walks away.

And then there were two.

We stare at each other for a few seconds as if in a standoff; there are so many thoughts swirling through my head that I can't pluck just one out. But if I know Aiden at all, which I really don't, as proven by his disappearance and sudden reappearance, he'll have some crap to say about all of this.

"It's great to see you, Julia."

"It's great to see me?" I try the words out slowly. The feel of them on my tongue tastes as bitter as I sound. I hate that I'm still affected by his dismissal of me after all these years. I hate that I'm that girl: jealous and unforgiving and yes, still heartbroken.

He sighs and runs a hand through his short hair. Looking around nervously, he smiles sheepishly at me before taking a step forward. "I don't know what else to say, but it *is* great to see you."

"You don't know what else to say to me?"

"Did you turn into a parrot since I last saw you?" he quips with a laugh. "The Julia that I knew would at least have something to say."

I take a moment to gather my thoughts, opening and closing my hands into fists at my sides. I tilt my head to the side when my mind clears and the right words are finally at the ready.

"You no good, son of a bitch, assclown have the balls to think this is cute, don't you?"

He raises his hands in defense.

"It's not a question I want you to answer, Aiden." I roll my eyes. "And as for 'the old Julia,' she's gone. But the new and improved Julia has a ton of things to say to you. Shall I start at how I faked every orgasm? Perhaps I should start with how you disappeared five years ago, never to be seen or heard from again?"

The faking orgasm bit is a total lie. The man knew how to make my body sing like no other has been able to do since, but it gives me a glimmer of happiness to say it anyway. Does that make me a vindictive bitch? Probably. Do I care? No.

"Okay, okay," he says and reaches out with his hand to grab my arm. He pulls me along to the corner of the tent while whispering, "Do you mind keeping your voice down?"

We come to a stop, and I look down in disgust at his hand still gripping my arm. "Get your fucking hand off of me."

Aiden does so immediately and looks over his shoulder. Thankfully, Sophia still hasn't noticed our little tête-à-tête.

"I guess the idea that you could look past this was just a pipe dream, huh?" he asks.

"You know what, Aiden? After tonight I'll never have to see you again, so why don't we forget we ever saw each other, and you can go back to whatever rock you crawled out from under."

I turn on my heel and walk as briskly as possible to the nearest opening in the tent, leaving Aiden behind. The idiot in me who's a sucker for punishment forces me to look over my shoulder at him. He's still standing where I left him with a grin tugging at the corners of his mouth. God, what I wouldn't give to smack that look off of his face. But instead, I keep walking, desperately in search of Lisette or alcohol, whichever I find first.

Luckily, she finds me first and gives me a quick once-over. She tells me in no uncertain terms that I am to go home for the night and that she'll talk to me tomorrow. I'm not going to disagree with her for once either. So with only an hour or so left at this engagement party from hell, I decide she's absolutely right and leave Lisette in charge.

Walking through the wall of humidity and trying my damndest to not think about Aiden, I finally reach the front of the house and hand my keys off to the valet to wait for my Land Rover to be brought around. While I wait and still not think about Aiden, which means I'm totally thinking about him, I rummage through my purse to find a ponytail holder since my long blond hair is sticking to the back of my neck.

Gathering it all in my hands, I make a messy knot on the top of my head and instantly feel cooler. The night breeze off the ocean only a couple of miles away is finally making itself useful. It would've been nice if it had shown up about an hour ago, but you can't have it all. I cannot wait to get home and wash away the sweat and stink off of me. My signature scent is Christian Dior's Miss Dior Cherie, but right now it's more like a mixture of perfume and body odor and not at all pleasant or alluring. And oh my God, don't even get me started on the swamp ass.

My purse is ginormous, so I can probably find more than Mary fucking Poppins in this thing. I pull out a loose piece of paper to create a makeshift fan and then begin fanning myself as a shiny, cherry-red BMW pulls up to the valet. I snort rather unattractively at the sight, because whoever the hell is arriving to the party is almost two hours late. This I have to see.

A second valet attendant, not to be confused with the one who is currently out searching somewhere near the Sphinx for my vehicle, steps forward to open the passenger-side door. Out unfurl two very nicely shaped, tanned, long legs attached to a rather good-looking chick, if I do say so myself. Brunette, guessing about average height, on the skinny side, wearing a Marc Jacobs pleated dress that is color-blocked in black and white, showing off a lot of skin—tastefully, of course, and as only Marc Jacobs can because the man is pure genius. I was eyeing the same dress last week at Nordstrom's. Lucky bitch.

Whatever, like you wouldn't be thinking the same thing.

Trying not to attract any attention to myself while I stare longingly at her outfit, I scoot to my left and try to blend in with the plant life. The driver of the BMW steps out. Lo and behold, there he is, Bruce Wayne himself. Or as I know him: Alex.

Really? Now, here, of all places, when I look like shit on a shingle and I'm feeling like a complete scatterbrain thanks to Aiden?

I duck my head before he can notice me, but as luck would have it, the expedition to find my car finally ends, and it appears directly behind his. The attendant gets out of my car and starts looking for me at the same time Alex decides to walk around the hood of his car to hand his keys over to the other attendant. My sorry attempt to hide can't last much longer when the valet guy finally spots me and whistles to get my attention.

"Dude, I can totally see you. Whistling is *so* not necessary," I say quietly while clenching my teeth. Especially since everyone is now looking in my direction, Alex included.

Oh well, here goes nothing.

Craptastic fan in hand, I step out of the shadows and walk over to my car like I own the joint while keeping my eyes trained on the "Whistling Dixie" valet.

"Julia?" I hear Alex's deep, velvety voice loud enough that I can't even think about pretending that I don't.

Turning my head as I unwillingly hand over a tip to the valet, I see Alex already making his way over to me in a few elegant strides. Yes, that's right, I said elegant. The man practically glides when he walks. It's lovely, and obviously I've paid too much attention to it before to be able to categorize it as such. And dear Lord, he looks delicious. He's wearing what could only be a tailor-made black suit, but no tie, and the top button is undone on his crisp white dress shirt.

He flashes me his dimples when he steps right in front of me, crowding my personal space. "Were you really not going to say hello to me?"

"Alex! Oh my God, I'm sorry. I didn't realize that was you," I say, doing my best at feigning ignorance.

"Bullshit."

"Like I would ignore you? Please, what kind of person do you think I am?"

"The kind of person who was ignoring me," he quickly answers.

"Did I hurt your feelings?"

His crystal-blue eyes light up in amusement, and he leans in an inch so that he's a little closer while putting one hand over his heart. "I'm crushed."

With him being so close, I take in the wonderful smell that is Alex: a cocktail of perfectly blended amounts of sandalwood and the beach and something else that eludes me. Whatever it is, it's heavenly. Then it hits me—I'm sure the stink emanating from me is infiltrating his nostrils, so I take a small step backward just as I hear a woman's annoyed voice coming from somewhere behind him.

"Alex, what are you doing?"

His smile vanishes, and he smoothly pulls back to stand up straight and turns around to face the direction of the woman he arrived with. She's far too young to be with him, and yes that might be jealousy rearing its ugly head, which when added to the stress of facing my ex again makes me more testy than usual.

"Do you know her?" she asks, clearly bothered by his actions. Can't say that I blame her. If I were her and my date was all up in some other woman's grill, I'd be a little peeved too.

"Marisa, this is Julia, a very good friend of mine," Alex clarifies for her. Then he turns his attention back to me and says, "Julia, this is my friend Marisa."

Oh, Alex, you have no idea the mess you've just made. If Miss Teen USA has any sense, she would have picked up on the fact that he said "good friend" when he spoke about me and "friend" when he described his relationship with her. Although, I have to admit, I find it to be rather intriguing that he would identify us like that for her benefit—or maybe he did it for mine? See what I mean? He's totally an enigma.

"Alex," she coos while wrapping herself around his arm, "I thought I was your good friend."

Yup, she picked up on it without missing a beat.

She giggles, and I swear the sound makes me want to vomit. Alex, in turn, has a tight smile on his face and looks uncomfortable while shifting his weight from foot to foot. Me? I just want to get the hell out of Dodge.

"It's nice to meet you," she says with a bright smile and way too enthusiastically before extending her hand to me.

I grab it and give it a firm shake. "Hi, Marisa, it's nice to meet you too."

Her eyes scan me from head to toe and back again dismissively as if she were Joan Rivers from *Fashion Police*. With that move, she's officially made it onto my shit list.

"So," she says, "how exactly do you know the Grandersons?"

"I don't."

"Then why are you here?"

"Because."

I know I'm being purposely evasive, but now I'm having too much fun making Alex more uncomfortable by the minute. Plus, I don't like her knowing too much about me. Call it women's intuition, but something about her just rubs me the wrong way.

Marisa lets out a dry laugh. "My, my, aren't we mysterious?"

"I could say the same about you. Alex has never mentioned you before. Have you, Alex?" Turning my gaze back to him, he tries to hide the smirk that is threatening to crack the corners of his mouth.

He clears his throat before saying, "Marisa is an old friend of the family."

"An old friend? Well, now you're just being silly, Alex," she says, trying to play it off like he didn't just diss her right in front of me again.

"Alrighty then, you two kids have a great night and try not to be too silly with each other. I've gotta get on home. It was nice meeting you, Marisa. Alex . . . I'll see you Friday night."

I couldn't help myself; I had to throw that last dig out just to see if she'd catch it. By the look of irritation on her face, I'd say she did and is currently trying to figure out why the hell he's going to be seeing me on Friday night.

As I walk around the hood of my car, I can tell she's whispering something to him, but when he answers her back, I can hear it clear as a bell. "I'll tell you later, Marisa."

Throwing my jumbo purse haphazardly onto the passenger seat before slamming the door, I shoot one last glance over at Alex, who is trying to steer Marisa toward the party. He runs his hand through his dirty blond hair and then looks over his shoulder in my direction while sporting a devilish grin.

Such a flirty bastard. Ugh . . . and I'm a total sucker for it every single time.

Not more than five minutes into my drive home, my cell phone dings, alerting me of a text. While stopped at a red light, I fish it out of my purse and unlock the screen to see a new text from Alex.

Payback's a bitch, you know?

I quickly shoot off a text back, playing it off like I'm clueless. I love this little cat-and-mouse game with him. It's entirely too much fun. Not to mention that it takes my mind off of Aiden.

Payback for what?

Just as the light turns green, my phone beeps again with another text from him.

You've been a bad girl, and I'm going to have to teach you a lesson.

When I reach the next red light, I grab the phone and stare at the screen in a daze because that right there might have crossed into the point of no return. You don't see me complaining, but I'm kind of surprised and not exactly sure how I should answer him. What the fuck does he mean, "teach me a lesson"? Is he going to put me across his knee and slap my ass with a ruler? Is it wrong that the thought of that has me so turned on right now that I want to turn my car around and climb his body like Mount Everest?

My phone beeps again while in my hands with another text from Alex.

Cat got your tongue?

With my heart racing and my stomach doing a somersault, I type out an answer. Two can play this game.

No, I'm just looking forward to it . . .

My high is short-lived when he responds so quickly this time, it's scary.

I know you are ;)

Well played, Mr. Holt, well played. For the first time in God knows how long, I'm left speechless. Now I'm just wondering what the hell I've gotten myself into.

CHAPTER FOUR

Standing before my full-length mirror, I take one last look at myself before heading to the Art Gallery. It's taken me almost a whole hour just to decide on this dress. It's a halter, fifties-pinup-style dress in a deep red, very reminiscent of Marilyn Monroe's famous white subway dress. So the front dips down a little to show off some of the goods. My hair, which has taken me the better part of the afternoon to finish, is in waves and pinned to one side so that most of my bare back is exposed. I don't even want to delve into why I'm all of a sudden so worried about how I look tonight. Okay, maybe I do. I'll give you one guess. His name starts with the letter *A*.

No, not *him*. I don't even want to discuss or think too much about *him* . . . Aiden. Because as much as I hate to admit it, the guy has been in the back of my mind since I saw him a couple of nights ago, buzzing around like an annoying fly. And what gets me even more irritated is that the more I think about Aiden, the more I come up with better things I should have said to him when I had the chance the other night. Don't you hate that? The best one-liners always come to you after you actually need them.

Anyway, enough about Aiden since the *other* guy whose name starts with the letter *A* is the reason why it's taken me this long to get ready.

Yeah, yeah, yeah, I'm so busted. I must be crazy, because first of all, there's still that whole mess Alex had with Sabrina last year, but now there's this new thing with Marisa. But flirting is harmless, right? I mean, it's not like anything is going to happen between us, so why not just play along and enjoy the ride? If anything, it will provide me with at least a fuck-ton of fantasies to hold me over until I decide to get back into the saddle again. At least that's what I keep telling myself as I adjust "the boys."

"The boys" are what I affectionately call my breasts, and I currently have them showing off some nice cleavage in this dress. Well, the right amount of cleavage and in a totally tasteful manner because I'm not trying to look like a hooker walking the streets. It's a well-proven fact that men fall under one of two categories: tits or ass men. I felt it was time I find out which one of those two categories Alex falls into. My money is on tits, hence the cleavage.

The opening itself doesn't start until seven, but I always arrive at an event I'm handling about an hour earlier to double-check that everything is in place. When I pull into the gallery parking lot at just past six o'clock after dealing with Miami traffic—and if you haven't had the pleasure of dealing with Miami during rush hour, consider yourself blessed—I'm already in a bad mood.

It would be important to point out that I have not spoken to Alex since we had that super-flirtatious text exchange a couple of nights ago, so I'm not sure what to expect. We've flirted and had witty repartee countless times before, but I'm still not sure how what occurred the other night will affect our friendship. Plus, when you throw Miss Teen USA into the mix, well, I could be facing a clusterfuck of epic proportions.

I walk in through the back door of the gallery and make my way toward the front of the building where most of the action is already taking place. Sidestepping some of the catering staff and some of my own, I see Lisette talking to Sarah, the gallery's receptionist. Before

I reach them, both of them look up and spot me walking in their direction. Lisette has a grin on her face as she takes in my "look" for the evening, while Sarah lets out a low whistle.

"Holy shit, Julia! You look amazing!" Sarah says loudly.

"Thank you, girlie. You don't think it's too much?"

"Um, no. You're totally going to be getting digits tonight."

I glance over at Lisette, who's still grinning from ear to ear. "What? Why are you grinning at me like that? You're freaking me out."

"*Niña*, with that dress, you're going to be finding more than Prince Charming tonight. You look fabulous!"

I roll my eyes, trying to play it off like I don't care what they think, but let's be honest, *every* woman wants to hear they look good. Especially when you've put half the goddamn time I did into this ensemble.

"So," I say, changing the subject quickly and jumping into organizing mode, "how is everything coming along?"

In unison, they answer, "Good."

I chuckle and shake my head. These two together always give me a good laugh. And when I get them both at a happy hour, I might as well be wearing adult diapers from laughing so hard. Which, by the way, I can neither confirm nor deny that that's actually happened before.

"Good. I'm going to do a walkthrough anyway. Lisette, can you come with me?"

She grabs her iPad from Sarah's desk, and we head off to double- and triple-check the hell out of this thing before it's go time. About forty-five minutes later, and after being completely satisfied that things are all good, I duck toward the back of the gallery to use the ladies' room so I can freshen up. When I'm done, I quickly sashay back to the front of the gallery, where guests are already starting to file in. Normally, I don't drink at any of these things, but when I'm working an event at the gallery, I do imbibe on occasion because

I've handled so many events here that it usually runs like a well-oiled machine with little to no assistance from me. I stop in front of a person from the catering staff and grab a champagne flute off the tray. I spot Lisette at the far end of the room, then lift my glass in a salute and watch her laugh before heading off to keep an eye on everything.

Turning into one of the far rooms of the gallery, which is almost like an alcove that only a few people can fit in at a time, I finally spot Alex.

Alone.

Just me and him in this tiny space.

He's dressed impeccably, as usual, in a pinstripe suit and a light blue dress shirt that perfectly accentuates his eyes. He's not wearing a tie again, but that's good for me because I get to look at his throat while his Adam's apple bobs up and down while he talks. I know I'm being ridiculous, but something as insignificant as that is so very sexy to me in a really hot guy.

"What are you doing in here all by yourself?" I ask him before bringing the glass to my lips to take another sip. "Are you hiding or something?"

He smiles and ever so smoothly brings his line of vision down my body and back up again, but not before lingering a moment too long on "the boys."

I knew it! Alex is a tits man, and I feel so vindicated it's not even funny. In my head I'm doing the Running Man to the tune of Salt-N-Pepa's "Push It" and giving myself a pat on the back.

"Why would I be hiding?" he asks.

"I don't know, why would you be hiding?"

"Why do you care if I'm hiding or not?"

"Why do you answer every question with another question?"

Alex takes a step forward, and there he goes again crowding my personal space, but I'm standing my ground this time. He raises an eyebrow at my stance and says, "Maybe I like getting you all worked up."

The double meaning in that is *so* not lost on me, and just like that, we went from zero to sixty in no time at all.

"Maybe?" I ask innocently while gazing up at him.

"Now look who's answering with questions."

His masculine chuckle resonates through me, making my toes curl while he takes the upper hand again. I seriously cannot keep up with this much longer. I'm either going to throw him against the wall and rub myself all over him like a slutty cat on a scratching post, or I'm going to douse myself with a bucket of ice-cold water.

"For your information, I'm not hiding . . . at least not from you," he explains. "Just like the quiet sometimes."

"Huh. Always figured you for the type that was into parties and shit."

"That would imply you're thinking about me," he says without missing a beat.

"You'd like that, wouldn't you?"

He takes a step forward and moves to my side to leave, but not before ducking his head closer so that I feel his warm breath fan across my ear. "That's a good question. Are you ready for the answer?"

And then he's gone, disappearing behind me back into the gallery's exhibit, while I ponder what just happened, kind of pissed off that the son of a bitch just answered me with another goddamn question. Even worse though, I'm so incredibly hot for him right now over his toying with me that I don't know what to do with myself!

Frustrated in more ways than one, I turn on my heel and blend in with the crowd that has accumulated since I've been competing in the Flirting Olympics with Alex. Standing off to one side while I stare out in space with my now-empty champagne flute in hand,

I feel a nudge on my side and turn around to see Lisette and Sarah looking worried.

"What's the matter?" I ask quickly.

They turn to look at each other and then back at me while they debate who is going to be the sacrificial lamb who tells me whatever the hell the problem is.

"Guys, someone speak up and soon."

"Sarah has something to tell you," Lisette throws out.

Sarah gives her the stink eye before turning her attention back to me. "Okay, well . . . see . . . there's this woman who's going off on the catering manager, saying something about this not being what she ordered for the event. He called us over and said he doesn't get paid enough to deal with brats—his words, not mine. Anyway, he's threatening to pull his staff if someone doesn't get that lady away from him."

I'm already walking with them over to the catering manager, who is stationed in the back of the building, as she's finishing the explanation. I swing the door open to the warehouse portion of the gallery, which is where the catering staff has all of their prep stuff set up and where they replenish hors d'oeuvre and drink trays. Joey, the catering manager, who is the nicest guy, by the way, is probably freaking out over having to deal with some random woman complaining about the order. This, for the record, is news to me. Lisette and I only deal with Alex or Sarah at the gallery, so this mystery lady is about to get a fucking earful by yours truly in about two seconds.

The mystery woman's back is to me as she's going off on Joey, something about how he's inept and clueless and that she demands to speak to whomever is in charge.

I tap her on the shoulder and announce, "You're looking for me?"

The woman swings her torso around, causing her pin-straight brown hair to whip behind her and almost slap me in the face.

You have got to be kidding me. Marisa, a.k.a. Miss Teen USA, is the bitch on wheels?

Her face goes through a myriad of looks while scrutinizing me before settling on recognition. Took her long enough to recognize me. Call me crazy, but I love a good smackdown. And a tip for all of you playing along at home: never *ever* let it show that they're getting a rise out of you. The key to a good smackdown is to kill them with kindness. Unless, of course, they cross the line, and then all bets are off.

"Julia, right? What are you doing here?" she asks with obvious distaste in her voice.

I smile. "I'm the person in charge. What can I do for you?"

"You?" she says with a laugh. "Well, isn't that just perfect."

"I'm not sure what you mean by that, but I can assure you that I *am* in charge, and I ask that you please stop harassing Joey and direct all your inquiries to me instead."

She looks between Joey and me as I give him the go-ahead to get back to work so I can deal with her. This is when I get a really good look at her. She's beautiful, no doubt, with her almond-shaped brown eyes and lithe figure. Too bad for her she's wearing a dress that was so last season and, worse, is coming across like a whiny baby in her mommy's big-girl clothes for a night out on the town.

"Fine, I'll deal with you if I *have* to," she says as she rolls her eyes. "This isn't the menu I wanted at this thing."

"This is the menu that was provided to me and my staff," I say, motioning behind me to Lisette and Sarah. I turn my head in their direction. "Ladies, if you don't mind, can you please bring Alex back here to discuss this further."

Marisa crosses her arms and sticks her foot out while pouting as we wait on Alex. Every minute I hate this girl more and more.

"You look different," she says.

"You look the same."

"What does that mean?"

I shrug my shoulders. "It means whatever the hell you want it to mean."

The sound of the door swinging open smoothes the look of disdain off her face. Her mouth morphs into a syrupy sweet smile, letting me know that Alex has just arrived.

"Marisa, what are you doing back here?" he asks calmly, but he looks so incredibly annoyed at the same time.

"Alex," she gushes as she rushes to his side. "I was just trying to explain to *this person* that the menu isn't what I wanted."

Did she just say "this person" like I'm some piece of gum on the bottom of her Jimmy Choos? Oh hell to the no! All bets are officially off!

I open my mouth to unleash the unholy string of curse words that are on the tip of my tongue, but I stop short when I see Alex giving me an apologetic look before directing his attention back to Marisa.

"I told you that I let Julia handle everything at these events because she's the best at what she does. I would appreciate it if you would apologize to her right now so I can get back inside and deal with more pressing matters than this nonsense."

Suck it, bitch!

She looks pained when she turns her head to me and says, "Julia, please accept my apology."

Smiling like a Cheshire cat, I answer, "Apology accepted."

Of course I don't mean it, and now I know for sure I'm going to have to watch this one like a freaking hawk. All mini-drama over and done with, Alex, still looking as uncomfortable as ever, mouths an "I'm sorry" as he guides Marisa toward the door to leave. The moment he turns his head, she shoots me a look over her shoulder and then sticks her tongue out at me.

Let me repeat. Sticks. Her. Tongue. Out. At. Me.

I don't even hesitate; I lift my hand and give her the finger with a huge smile on my face as Sarah and Lisette try to contain their giggling.

"That girl really hates you!" Lisette exclaims.

"Yeah, what's up with that?" Sarah asks.

"I don't even want to talk about it," I mumble.

"Well, we do!" she says.

I put my hands on my hips and let out a heavy sigh. "There's not much to tell. I met her the other night when she was Alex's date at the Grandersons' party. She didn't like me then, and obviously from that whole display, she *really* doesn't like me now."

Lisette puts in her two cents. "She's jealous of you."

"Yes! That's exactly what I was going to say," Sarah says.

"Jealous of what?"

They both look at each other and then back at me like I just grew two heads. I know what they're going to say, and I don't want to hear it. I feel like if someone else says it out loud, then it confirms whatever it is I'm feeling for Alex and vice versa. And maybe, just maybe, I'm not imagining that this crazy flirting between us isn't just flirting.

"That Alex is head over heels in lust with you and you're head over heels in lust with him," Sarah says so quickly that it comes out sounding like one long-ass word with a few syllables thrown in there for good measure.

"You two are nuts, you know that?" I say, rushing to deflect the attention.

"*Niña*, I have been praying to *Santa Bárbara* for this day." Lisette crosses herself while looking up to the heavens, but she's really looking at a dingy ceiling.

"I know, right?" Sarah says right behind her.

Now they're just staring and waiting for me to say something. They have another thing coming if they think I'm going to say a goddamn thing about Alex and our flirting and where it *isn't* going. I only have one way out of this mess.

"Alrighty then, I'm out. I'm leaving you two in charge. If Alex asks where I am, tell him I wasn't feeling good and went home."

"Chickenshit!" Lisette yells to my back while I gather my belongings and start to walk out the door to my car.

Whatever. Let them think what they want. Between the two of them, I'm going to get an ulcer. Then throw in the verbal fucking sessions with Alex, and this girl is sticking a fork in herself. I'm done.

I get home about a half hour later, and as soon as I get in the door, my cell phone rings. I answer without checking to see who it is while plopping myself down on the couch, completely exhausted and frustrated.

"Are you okay?" Alex asks, his voice full of concern.

"I'm fine."

"Then why did you leave?"

"I wasn't feeling well."

"Then you're not fine."

"I'm fine, Alex."

Silence. Utter silence from both of us. Not for nothing, but it's an uncomfortable silence. Like shit-just-got-real-between-us kind of silence, and I don't really know what to do with it. I hear him breathing on the phone and notice for the first time that it's quiet wherever he is. Like he's in his office or something.

"Where are you?" I ask in a rush of breath.

"In my office."

"Where's your date?"

"Why do you want to know?" he asks with a smile in his tone.

"You're right. I don't."

"Yes you do."

"You know what, Alex? The better question would be why are

you calling *me* in the confines of your cozy office, all alone I might add, when you have a date?"

He chuckles, and the sound is one that I will catalog in the recesses of my mind for future reference because it sends a chill down my spine.

"That would be the better question," he says smoothly. "Too bad you didn't ask it."

And he hangs up. The smug bastard just hung up on me!

I throw my cell phone onto the couch next to me and rub my eyes with the heels of my hands. My phone dings, and I'm almost afraid to see what it says, but curiosity gets the better of me, and I snatch it up to see a text from Alex that brings a huge smile to my face.

You looked beautiful tonight.

Swoon.

CHAPTER FIVE

She what?!" Sabrina yells loud enough that I have to turn down the volume on my laptop.

We're on our weekly Saturday morning Skype session. It's become a ritual with us ever since she moved away last year. I just finished explaining to her about Marisa sticking her tongue out at me like a child on a school playground last night and me giving her the finger in retaliation.

"This girl obviously doesn't know who she's dealing with," she says while laughing her ass off until she starts to cackle.

"I know, right? Can you believe that shit?"

"Wait a minute," she gets out in between a laugh and wiping a tear from her eye. "You've got to tell Tyler about this."

She yells out his name, and he appears on my screen a few seconds later with just a pair of sweatpants on, looking like he just rolled out of bed.

"Hey, Julia, how are you?" He gathers up Sabrina from the chair and sits down in her place. She plants herself back down on his lap, and he gives her a quick peck on the cheek.

"My morning just got way better by looking at your fine ass. How about you?"

"Julia!" Sabrina shouts in shock.

"Oh please, we're all adults here. You *know* he's fine. *I* know he's fine. Shit, I bet *he* even knows he's fine."

Tyler is trying to cover the smirk on his face but not doing a very good job of it before clearing his throat. "So, what was it that had my girl laughing so hard? With you involved, I can only imagine."

I tell him the story, but just like with Sabrina, I don't elaborate too much on the Alex part of it. I know that Sabrina is completely head over heels in love with Tyler, but I still feel funny talking to her about him.

Tyler starts to laugh and then asks, "How old is this girl?"

"I have no idea. But if I had to guess, I'd say twenty-five at most."

"Alex likes them young, huh?" he muses.

"I wouldn't know," I say, somewhat dismayed myself.

Sabrina notices my slight tone change. I can't get much past her and vice versa. I'm grateful that I have someone in my life I can share my ups and downs with. But as close as we are, I still haven't been able to fully disclose what I've been feeling toward Alex. Worse, I haven't mentioned how I had a run-in with Aiden earlier in the week and the amount of times I've replayed our meeting in my head since then. I can only imagine how crazy I would sound to her by admitting out loud just how much that has done a bit of a number on me. The best part is I'm not even sure why. You would think after all this time since Aiden that I wouldn't care, that it would just roll off my shoulders as if he meant nothing to me. And he doesn't . . . kind of. I don't know. I can't even explain it to myself, so there is no way in hell that I could possibly explain it to Sabrina, right?

I feel guilty keeping things from Sabrina, and I know she'll be upset when she eventually finds out, but for now it's for the best. At least that's what I keep telling myself. Ugh, I know, I know, I'm a horrible best friend, and now I think I have to cover my tracks a bit.

"I mean, I don't know how serious they are or anything like that. It's only the second time I've seen them together. And now that I think about it, both times I've seen them together he didn't seem to be too interested in her, so I have no fucking clue what he sees in her. Maybe she has a cape flying out of her crotch with a giant *S* on it. That, or she can suck the chrome off a trailer hitch. Either of those has to be the *only* explanation, because everything else I've seen screams *see you next Tuesday*. And a huge one, at that."

Tyler is now doubled over laughing while Sabrina is shaking her head at me, covering her mouth with her hands to try to control her giggles.

"Wow, why don't you tell us how you really feel, Julia?" she gets out, while failing miserably at holding her laughter in.

Oops. I really need to try and apply a filter to my thoughts more often before they reach my mouth. So much for trying to cover my tracks. I think I just elaborated a tad too much on my assumptions about Alex's relationship with Marisa, or whatever you call that aberration.

Honestly, aren't you scratching your head on this one too? I sure as hell am. I'm a little embarrassed to report that I may have spent most of my night lying in bed having an actual argument with myself over it. Out loud.

"I'm glad I could be a source of entertainment for you guys this morning," I deadpan while they're still laughing.

Sabrina collects herself long enough to say, "I'm sorry, sweetie."

She elbows Tyler behind her to get him to stop laughing, then leans in to whisper something in his ear.

"Hey! That's not fair! Don't be whispering sweet nothings in his ear while I'm sitting right here."

When she turns her body to face the camera again, Tyler brings his lips to her neck and starts to nuzzle her until she giggles again.

"I so hate you guys right now," I say sarcastically. "Get a room, for chrissakes!"

Sabrina slaps him away and then clears her throat dramatically. "I have something to tell you."

"Oh my God! Are you PG, Sabrina?"

"PG?" she asks, all confused.

"Yes, PG. You know, like Mary with Jesus but you know who the father is," I say, pointing at Tyler on the monitor, who is practically choking.

"Are you insane? No, I'm not pregnant! And if I was, I don't think I'd be telling you that news after you *just* called someone a cun . . ." She trails off, not being able to bring herself to complete the actual word. She's always had an issue with cursing, so I'm surprised she was able to get as far as the letter *n*. Me, on the other hand . . . well let's just say that if I had one of those curse jars where I put a dollar in for every bad word that came out of my mouth, Robin Leach would be doing a segment on me on the next episode of *Lifestyles of the Rich and Famous*.

"Oh shit! Are you guys getting married?"

Both of them answer at the same time, she with a "no" and he with a "not yet."

I tilt my head, thinking that little exchange right there was rather interesting, but I decide not to jump all over it like I normally would. I'll just ask her about it another time when Tyler's not around.

"Okay, so if you're not knocked up and not getting married, then what is it?"

She flashes me a smile and says, "I kind of got a promotion at work."

"Congrats! That's great news."

"Thank you," she says.

"Wait, what do you mean 'kind of'?"

"Well, it's not official yet because my boss wants to see how I manage the next two exhibits at the museum on my own."

"I'm sure you'll do great."

"You really think so?" she asks.

"Girlie, I'm positive. You have nothing to worry about. Right, Tyler?"

He agrees and gives her a tight squeeze before shooting me a wink, which even though he's my bestie's man makes me want to swoon on the spot.

"Your boyfriend is winking at me again, Sabrina," I tease. "Please have him try to control himself around me."

He laughs as she gives him a light slap on his arm.

"All right, you two," I say, noticing the time. "I've gotta motor since I have to stop by my parents' house in a bit."

I bring my hand to my lips to blow her a kiss, and she repeats the gesture before we start in on saying how much we miss and love each other, as only true BFFs can. This tacks on a whole other five minutes to the Skype session before finally Tyler gets exasperated and just starts shutting it down on us. Good thing too, because if not, we could have easily spent the rest of the day on there talking about everything under the sun and then some.

As soon as I switch off my laptop, I move my ass into gear and start getting ready for the visit, which should be all kinds of interesting. My mom and dad love each other, no doubt about that, having been devoted to each other for the better part of almost thirty years now. But having been together for so long, they tend to get on each other's nerves a bit. I'm fairly certain it has something to do with the fact that ever since my dad retired a few years ago, he's home a lot more than he used to be, and my mom's not digging him cramping her style.

I hope to God that my little brother, Darren, will be there since my other brother, Lucas, is living out in Las Vegas. I should probably call Darren and find out what his deal is and see if I can bribe him into hanging out with me while I'm there. He's usually pretty easy to get a hold of. As for Lucas, you can never get him to pick up the phone, much less return a freaking phone call. I'm lucky if he even remembers to call me on my birthday.

Picking up my cell phone off the coffee table, I unlock the screen and thumb scroll through my contact list until I find Darren's name. While I'm scrolling, I notice that I have a ridiculous amount of people on here that I haven't spoken to in years. Like this entry right above Darren's for a person (I have to say person, because I have no clue if they're male or female) named Dale. Who the hell is Dale? And how did they get starred and categorized as a "favorite" under my contacts? I'm still pondering this Dale person when I press Darren's name on the screen just below it.

He picks up on the second ring. "Talk to me, Goose."

"What's up, Maverick?"

It would be important to note that my brother Darren stumbled upon *Top Gun* when he was a kid and became obsessed with it. Hence the nicknames for each other of Maverick and Goose. In fact, he was so obsessed with that movie that he eventually turned it into a career by joining the Air Force right after high school.

"Nothing much, heading over to Mom and Pop's," he says.

"Yes! I was hoping you'd say that."

"Why?" he asks. "Are you heading over there too?"

"Yup. You'll probably beat me there, but I'll be there sooner rather than later."

"Okay, I'll see you soon then. Later, Goose."

"Later, Maverick."

I disconnect the call, but my phone rings in my hand a second later, so I answer it thinking it's Darren again.

"Did you forget something, Maverick?" I ask while roaming toward my bedroom to get dressed.

"It's your mother, not Darren," she says in a rush. "Julia, are you still planning on coming over today?"

"Yes. I actually just got off the phone with Darren, and he said he was stopping over as well."

"Oh, thank God!" she says. "Your father is driving me crazy."

I mosey over to my closet and ask, "Is everything okay?"

"Sweetheart," she says, her voice going deathly quiet, "I love your father dearly, but if he brings out his toolbox one more time to *fix* something, I may stab him in the eye with one of his screwdrivers."

My eyes are trying to zero in on the outfit I'm going to wear when I hear my dad's booming voice in the background. "Marilyn! Where the hell is my goddamn Phillips screwdriver? I left it on the kitchen island not two fucking minutes ago!"

"Mom, did you take Daddy's screwdriver?"

She doesn't answer, but I can hear her breathing on the line still. "Mom?"

"I'm here, sweetheart, and yes I hid his screwdriver . . . and you'd better hurry," she says cryptically before hanging up.

Jesus Christ, those two are going to end up killing each other if my dad doesn't get a new hobby, and soon. Flying through what normally takes me about a half hour to accomplish by throwing on a pair of black yoga pants and an old, black racer-back tank top, I'm ready to roll. I slip on my flip-flops and gather all my hair in a ponytail while heading out the door to face whatever calamity awaits me at my parents' house.

CHAPTER SIX

I pull into the driveway of their house an hour later. Having had to deal with toll traffic on the Rickenbacker Causeway due to the perfect beach day weather, it's taken me a little longer than usual. My brother Darren's Bumblebee Chevy Camaro is already here, and I park right behind him just in case I have to make a quick getaway. Ugh, I hate that car. It's so . . . yellow. Reminds me of a school bus rather than a car that can transform into an intelligent life-form. If it was so goddamn intelligent, it should have picked a more appealing color to be seen in.

Walking toward the front door, I'm already on high alert when I hear my dad yell out a string of curses that aren't suitable to repeat, even for me. And in case you're wondering where I got my colorful language from, look no further. My dad has never been one to tone it down for absolutely anyone's benefit for as long as I can remember.

One time, when I was eight, my parents were called to my school to meet with my teacher because I had gotten myself into a wee bit of trouble. Okay, so I called another girl a bitch because, well, she *was* a bitch. She moved my chair out from under me right before I sat down. The worst part was that I was wearing a skirt that day, and as I rolled over to get to my feet that sucker flew right up and left my panty-clad ass hanging in the breeze for the rest of the class to see. Anyway, when my teacher, Mrs. Black, told my parents the story about how I used foul language, I'll never forget what happened next. My dad stood up, looked at me sternly, and asked if what the teacher had said was true. I nodded and kept my mouth shut since I was paralyzed with fear over what my punishment would be. He looked over to Mrs. Black and said, "That little girl *is* a bitch for pulling my daughter's chair out." He turned to my mother then. "Marilyn, let's go." Mrs. Black was appalled while my poor mother was hemming and hawing, watching my dad take me by the hand and drag me out of there. On the drive home, my dad said that next time I should try to say it more quietly, then proceeded to take me to Swenson's for an ice cream sundae. It was the best day ever.

As quietly as possible, I open the front door and peek my head around the frame so I can assess the damage before throwing myself into the fray. My mom, God bless her, is sitting on one corner of the long chaise sofa, arms crossed and chewing away at her bottom lip. My dad is sitting on the opposite end, in the same manner, and sporting a look that could kill directed at my brother. Darren's back is to me, and he's pointing the now infamous screwdriver at my mother, and then he snaps his attention back to my dad, saying something about both of them being in a time-out so they can think about what they did.

Good Lord, if this isn't the craziest shit I've ever witnessed. *My* parents in a time-out? I never thought I'd live to see the day.

"Julia Ann Boyd," my dad yells when he finally spots me. "Close the door and get your ass in here before you let any more mosquitoes in the house."

"Carter, take it easy," my mom pleads. "You know you need to watch that blood pressure of yours."

"Woman, if you hadn't taken away my screwdriver, I wouldn't be pissed off to begin with."

"I did it for your own good, dear," she counters.

"What do you mean my own good?"

"Well, I mean that you . . . well, you know you never were that good at fixing stuff," my poor mother says, now stammering. My dad's face starts to turn a hue of red that rivals that of a tomato before he launches into an obscenity-laced rant about how a man's tools are not to be trifled with.

"Enough!" Darren yells. "For the love of God, would you both just shut up for a minute, *or ten*, and try to be civil? Julia and I are going to be right in the other room. Don't even think about starting this argument up again while we're gone."

It's then I finally get a good look at Darren as he turns around and envelops me in a big bear hug and then plants a sloppy kiss on my cheek. Even though he's my baby brother by five years, he's huge in comparison, towering over me easily, and I'm no slouch in the height department at five feet six inches. He's built like a brick shithouse, and I'm sure the ladies all go gaga for him with his dark blond hair and sky-blue eyes, but to me he's still the little guy whose diapers I've helped change.

"Come on, I need a beer after dealing with Laurel and Hardy over here," he says, shooting a thumb over his shoulder at my parents, who are staring at their respective sides of the living room wall, ignoring each other completely.

We walk into the kitchen, and he immediately goes for the refrigerator, opening the door and pulling out two Coronas while I hop onto one of the stools. He hands me mine before leaning against the kitchen counter and taking a long pull from his.

"So what's going on, sis? Anything new?"

"Nothing new to report. How about you?"

He shakes his head while taking another sip of his beer before asking, "How's the dating scene?"

I roll my eyes. "I don't want to talk about it, Darren. Change the subject, please."

With a hearty chuckle, he steps forward and puts his elbows on the kitchen island. "Uh-uh. Tell your favorite brother *all* about it."

"Fine, but there's nothing really to tell," I get out in a whoosh of breath before bringing the bottle to my lips again. "I have the worst luck ever with men, and I've resigned myself to living as a spinster with tons of cats and a house that smells like cat piss."

"It can't be that bad," he says while laughing. "There have to be some prospects."

How sad is it that my only prospect is an occasional flirting session with a man who once tried to get into my best friend's pants? It's pretty fucking sad.

"No prospects," I confirm as I shift from side to side rather uncomfortably in my seat.

"I don't believe you. There's something you're not telling me."

"What's with the third degree?" I blurt out, trying to turn the tables on him. "What about you?"

The corners of his mouth turn up, and he raises an eyebrow. "Keeping my options open. By the way, nice try trying to change the subject."

"Whatever," I mumble.

A staring contest ensues like we used to have when we were kids. I usually win these, but I'm not feeling as confident with all the thoughts swirling in my head over Alex and just how pathetic my dating life has been in the past year. It's enough to drive a girl straight to lesbianism. Were it not for the lack of real cock on that front—not the fake ones, because sorry, they're not at all the same—the idea of it is becoming more and more appealing. I did experiment once in college but quickly realized that it wasn't for me.

Oh, please. Like you didn't make out with your sorority sister while she felt you up to make a guy all hot and bothered. I'm probably in the minority on that one. Then again, I was feeling no pain after playing a few rounds of beer pong and thought it was the actual guy and not my sorority sister. So I don't think that really qualifies as experimenting. I suck even with the ladies.

"I win," Darren announces when I dart my eyes away from him for a second.

"Yeah, yeah, yeah."

"You're losing your touch, sis. Are you sure nothing else is going on?"

I hate that he knows me so well and can hear my thoughts as if they were plainly written all over my face. And I've been trying my hardest not to think about it. About him. No, not Alex—it's much worse than that.

Aiden.

"Julia?" Darren says, concerned. "What's the matter? You know you're eventually going to tell me, so stop dragging it out and just do it already."

I let out a breath that I didn't even know I was holding and focus on the bottle opener on the table between us. "I saw Aiden the other day."

"Holy shit," he whispers.

"Yup, that pretty much sums it up."

"How did it go?" he asks.

I sigh. "Not well."

"What the hell did he say to you?"

"Not much."

"Julia, cut the shit and tell me what the fuck happened."

I put the beer bottle down and lean forward until my elbows are resting on the countertop. "Darren, he's getting married."

"Who would be stupid enough to marry that asshole?"

"Oh, the story gets better." I pause and look up at my brother, who is staring back at me in shock. "I helped plan his engagement party. As a matter of fact, that's where I ran into him."

"Jesus fucking Christ, Julia," he mutters under his breath.

"Exactly."

"So let me get this straight," he says. "You knew he was getting married and helped plan his engagement party anyway?"

"Do you honestly think that if I knew it was *the* Aiden, I would have gone along with it? Come on, Darren, give me at least a little bit of credit here. I'm not that much of a glutton for punishment."

"To be honest with you, I'm not sure."

My eyes widen in disbelief that he would think that, and I open my mouth to defend myself.

"Whoa, whoa, whoa, relax," he says quickly with his hands up in defense. "I just remember you telling me that he was like the one that got away or some sappy shit like that. So it wouldn't surprise me if you had taken on the party knowing it was *the* Aiden."

"He's not 'the one that got away' for me, Darren."

"He's not?" he asks with a raised eyebrow. "Then what's the problem? Why are you letting it bother you so much?"

What *is* the problem exactly?

This is getting ridiculous, even for me. When I've run into an ex in the past, I usually do one of two things: say a polite hello or run in the opposite direction. But I never let it bother me to the point of distraction like this. I have to wonder if there is possibly more to my unresolved feelings toward Aiden. Because there has to be more to it at this point.

I picture seeing Aiden at the engagement party again in my mind's eye. And it hits me . . . the *engagement* party. Engaged. He's engaged . . . to somebody else. Not me. And that's okay because he's a jerk. No, the answer is so simple that I almost want to kick myself for not seeing it sooner. He never had any intention of spending his life with me. I was just a pit stop for him, someone in his probably long line of women whom he strung along like a dog on a leash with empty promises of a future that would never come to fruition.

"Come on, Julia," Darren says. "Why does it bother you?"

"Because," I answer.

"That's a child's answer, Julia."

I rub the heels of my hands against my eyes in frustration. "When did you become Dr. Phil? Jeez, psychoanalyze much?"

He's smiling when I drop my hands from my face, still waiting on my answer. "Okay, fine. He's not the one. He's more like the unresolved one."

"Sounds kind of like the same thing to me," he says.

"Here's the thing, Darren," I say, taking a quick breath and lowering my voice. "He told me he was going to marry me one day, that I was his 'one.' Then from one day to the next, literally, he up and left me with not much of an explanation. For the longest time I convinced myself that it was because he was afraid to get married and settle down. And somehow I came to terms with that, or at least I thought I did. But the truth of the matter is that he just didn't want to marry me."

Darren nods as if he understands.

"What the hell is so wrong with me that he wouldn't want to marry me?" I ask more to myself than of my brother. And that's exactly what's been really plaguing my thoughts since I saw him the other night all happy and in love with Sophia. Why her and not me?

"Nothing is wrong with you," Darren says. "Did someone say there was something wrong with you? Because if they did, I'll kick their ass."

I roll my eyes at my little brother's attempt at making me feel better. "Nobody said anything, that's the problem. Why didn't he want to be with me? Why doesn't anyone that I date, for that matter, work out? What is so wrong with *me*?!"

I look down and pretend to concentrate on the condensation forming on the beer bottle. I can't believe I just confessed all my relationship issues that I've been struggling with for years but have been able to bury under the rug to my little brother, of all people.

But thanks to seeing Aiden, it's all been brought back up to the surface and is turning me into quite the crazy person.

Darren reaches across the table and tilts my chin up to look at him. "Hey," he says. "There is *nothing* wrong with you. You are one of the most amazing people I know, and I'm lucky to have you as a sister. You just haven't met your match yet."

I smile, and he lets go of my chin. Before taking another sip of his beer, he adds, "Plus, my friends won't shut up about how hot my sister is, so you've got that going for you."

I chuckle and stand up to empty out the rest of my bottle in the sink. As I move past him, something dawns on me. We've been in the kitchen for almost fifteen minutes and haven't heard a peep out of my parents in the other room. I elbow him in the ribs and bring my finger to my lips to shush him before tiptoeing out of the kitchen with Darren trailing behind me. When we reach the end of the short hallway that opens up to the living room, we find the couch empty. But what we hear next coming from the direction of their bedroom will no doubt scar us mentally for the rest of our natural-born lives.

My mom, my angelic and pure-as-the-driven-snow mother, yells out a muffled, "Harder!" This is followed by a quick succession of pounding, which I *soooo* don't want to know what the hell that is and have no intention of sticking around to find out.

"I'm going to be sick," Darren says as we both bolt for the front door. It's a race against time when we start our respective cars. He sticks his head out of his window yelling, "Go, go, go!"

I end up pulling out of there so fast that I may have left skid marks in the driveway. And if I didn't, I'm certain Darren did as he flew past me down the street in his car, easily reaching sixty miles per hour in no time at all.

When I get home, I make a beeline for the fridge and grab a beer before collapsing onto the couch in a daze. There are so many things wrong with what just happened at my parents' house I don't even know where to begin. I think the one thing that's bothering me the most is how my parents are "doing it" on the regular, which is still gross, but at least someone is getting some action. And I'm more than happy that my parents are still in love with each other as well as physically attracted to each other after all this time, but I could have easily lived the rest of my life without ever hearing it.

I kick my feet up and lay my head on the backrest, staring up at the ceiling, and then I hear my cell phone buzzing away in my purse in the foyer. I'm contemplating letting it go to voice mail when it stops ringing and then starts up again. Dammit, whoever it is must really want to talk to me, so I begrudgingly stand back up and rummage through my purse until I find my phone.

Alex.

What the hell could he want with me, on a weekend, no less? I debate with myself for a second or two over whether I should answer, but curiosity gets the better of me.

"Don't you have something better to be doing than calling me on a Saturday afternoon?" I ask while making my way back to the couch.

"That depends," Alex rasps in my ear. "Would you care to enlighten me as to what that something might be?"

My heart drops, my pulse starts to race, and even my freaking palms get clammy. It's official, I'm a slave to his torment.

"Settle down. I didn't expect to hear from you on a Saturday."

His light chuckle sets off another chain reaction in my body, but this kind is far more pleasant. I imagine him relaxed in a pair of black boxer briefs and nothing else, in bed of course. And those dimples—those dimples that can wreak havoc on me while he has a devilish look in his eyes. A look that could easily make me orgasm without him touching any part of my body, no matter how much I begged. God, would I beg. With absolutely no shame, like a dog for a bone.

"I'm glad to know that I can surprise you, but this shouldn't take long."

"That's what she said," I mutter, trying to bring some levity to the conversation.

"I guarantee that *you* wouldn't be saying that," he says with an unmistakable smile in his voice.

Do you *see* what I'm dealing with here? This has been the way each conversation of ours ends up going. It's maddening and frustrating and exhilarating and probably a bunch of other "ings" that I can't articulate at the moment.

"I was calling," he goes on to say like I'm not at all in a trance over here, "because I'm ready to cash in on our little deal we made last year."

"Really?"

"Yes, really. Are you still game?"

"Of course I am," I snap. "I never back out of a deal. What exactly did you have in mind?"

"Julia," he almost purrs, "you really need to stop leaving yourself wide open with some of the things you say."

"I could say the same about you."

A short pause follows until he finally speaks up. "How about you come over to my house tomorrow, say one o'clock, and we'll figure something out?"

"You're inviting me to your house?" I ask in shock because I've never been to his house and I'm convinced it has something to do with it being the Batcave.

"Yes, I'm inviting you to my house. I'll text you the address in a bit, if that's okay with you."

"Sure, that's totally fine."

"Good," he says. "Looking forward to it."

"Me too."

We say our good-byes, and I hate to admit it, but I kind of miss the being toyed with bit at the end of the conversation. It's becoming something of a trademark for us.

Oh my God! Did you hear what I just said? A trademark for *us*!

I get up and walk toward my bedroom, the whole time thinking to myself, *I'm not going to sleep with him*, over and over again. And to ensure that I won't, I pull out the rattiest pair of granny period undies from the very bottom of my underwear drawer. You know the ones that you keep for those four to five days every month? Every woman owns at least one pair, and I'm going to be wearing mine, holes and all, tomorrow. If that doesn't keep me clothed, then I'm fucked—in more ways than one.

CHAPTER SEVEN

Alex did end up texting me his address last night, and wouldn't you know it, the guy has been living about twenty minutes away from me this entire time. I'm taking the last winding side street in a ficus-tree-lined Coconut Grove neighborhood, wondering how I didn't know this and feeling antsy about it. Actually, I'm not sure exactly how I feel about Alex in general now that I know he's so close to me. Because I can see it now—in a moment of weakness I'll be at his door, wearing a trench coat (because everyone in Miami has one for no reason at all, but it goes with the fantasy) and nothing underneath except for thigh highs and black stilettos. He'd open the door, and I'd waltz right in with such confidence it would make him confused at first. No words would be exchanged. I would simply command him with a quick snap of my fingers to sit on the couch. Then I'd turn on the music. "Straight On" by Heart would flood our senses as a small smile played on his lips when it dawned on him what was about to happen. I'd perform my best teasing stripper dance for him while he tried to grab a hold of me. But I wouldn't let him. Not until I ended up on his lap, straddling him, would I allow him to yank the belt of the trench coat open and watch as his eyes feasted on my naked body, splayed open for him like a present on Christmas morning. At that point, I'd be so turned on by his heated gaze that I'd hand the reins over to him by leaning over and whispering in his ear, "I want you to do everything to me . . . please." Yeah, I'd add the please bit at the end with a little whimper for effect just to see how he'd react. He'd take the bait, of course, and he'd do *everything* to me, acts that might even be illegal in some states, and I'd love every single second of it.

I'm still humming the chorus of "Straight On" in my head when I pull into Alex's driveway a few moments later and stop in mid-hum as soon as I get a good look at his house. Holy crap! It's freaking huge! I do a double take at the GPS on my dashboard and confirm I'm in the right place before turning off the engine and stepping out of the car.

It's a Spanish-style-meets-contemporary-revival one-story home that sits at the end of a cul-de-sac, hidden away from the hustle and bustle of Miami. Like a little getaway vacation home that you would only see in magazines, but not little at all. The exterior looks to be freshly painted in warm beige with accents in light cream and clay-tiled shingles. The solid wood monastery-looking front door is nestled within a large archway, reminiscent of the Spanish-style architecture that is unique to this area.

I approach the front door with trepidation, feeling incredibly underdressed in my worn, hip-hugging jeans and fitted red cardigan, which I paired with a white tank top underneath. I'm wearing black ballet flats and the barest of accessories in the form of plain silver hoop earrings. I've decided to wear my hair down today, after much deliberation, in its natural pin-straight state. Why I decided to wear it down I have no clue, since I'm already pushing it off one shoulder so that it doesn't stick to the back of my neck.

Standing directly in front of his door for a few moments, I take a deep breath and fidget for a bit before raising my hand and giving it a couple of quick raps. While I wait, I can't take it anymore; I fix my wedgie from the anti-sex granny panties I forced myself to wear, just in case I decide to lose all sense of decorum and think about giving in to the carnal urges when I'm around him.

The door unlocks and opens slowly to reveal a little girl, no more than ten, if I had to guess. She has long, curly blond hair with big blue eyes and bears a striking resemblance to Alex. What the hell? He has a kid? How did I not know this? It's not a huge deal because I've dated men who've had kids in the past. Granted, it never gets far enough to actually meet the kids because they're idiots—the dads, not the kids. What the fuck am I saying? I'm not dating Alex, so why should I care if he has a kid or not? It shouldn't bother me, right? Please, someone tell me I'm not crazy for feeling like I've been kept in the dark all this time.

"Can I help you?"

Alex's daughter's elf-like voice breaks me out of my thoughts. I slide my aviator sunglasses up to rest on the top of my head, and she smiles brightly. So bright that I can't help but smile back and stare. She is so freaking pretty, just like her dad. Well, technically Alex isn't pretty, but whatever, same thing. Come to think of it, he could be pretty, I guess, given the right circumstance and correct lighting and . . .

"Can I help you?" she asks again, this time with a good-natured giggle.

"Oh! I'm sorry," I say, embarrassed that I've been caught up again in my thoughts. "I'm looking for your dad."

"My dad isn't here."

Now I'm confused, and I look at my wristwatch to double-check the time. It's only ten or so minutes past one o'clock, which was the time he wanted me to meet him here.

"Do you mean Uncle Alex?" she asks while smiling again and revealing her braces, which I didn't notice before. She's too cute, and did she just say "Uncle Alex"?

"Um, you're not Alex's daughter?" I ask nervously.

"No," she says with a giggle. "I'm his niece, Jocelyn, but everyone calls me Josie."

"It's nice to meet you, Josie. I'm Julia."

She extends her small hand out to me, and I take it in mine to give it a firm shake just as Alex appears behind her.

First of all, I have never seen him in anything other than a suit or a variation of a suit before today. I almost wish I hadn't seen him like this, because now I'm going to have a more difficult time trying to remember that I have granny panties on. Speaking of which, thank God they have a couple of holes in them to get some air in there because I feel an instant rush of heat between my legs over the sight of him.

He's wearing tan cargo shorts and a white linen button-down shirt that has the first few buttons undone and the sleeves rolled up around his elbows. It's doing wonders to show off his muscular frame and his perfectly tanned forearms. Personally, I have a thing for forearms on men. It's kind of my kryptonite, along with them wearing backward baseball hats. So if he pulls out a baseball hat, I might just die and go to heaven right here and now. His hair looks to be slightly wet still from a recent shower, with a few dirty-blond locks falling onto his brow. He's not wearing shoes, and Jesus, even his feet are perfect. He looks absolutely delicious, like I-want-to-lick-him-from-head-to-toe delicious.

"I see you met Josie already," he says while putting his hands on her shoulders. She looks up at him with a huge smile on her face, and he bends down to quickly kiss her on her forehead.

"Julia thought I was your daughter," she says with an innocent laugh.

Alex brings his eyes back to mine and chuckles when I clarify the mix-up. "Honest mistake. She does look a lot like you."

"I get that a lot when we're out together," he answers, then motions with his hand for me to come inside.

The foyer is a small one, but it opens up after a few steps to the rest of the main living area in an open floor plan. The living room has a large, worn-in, and inviting dark brown leather couch with a matching chaise longue that faces an entertainment unit that houses a huge flat-screen TV. To the right of it is an equally big kitchen with oak cabinets and dark granite countertops. Straight across from me are a couple of sets of glass doors that lead to what looks to be a perfectly landscaped backyard with a swimming pool and furnished patio. Everything is in its place, and the accents and decorations are masculine with just a touch of color here and there for effect. And this is what I can see, because just off to the left of the living room there is a long hallway that leads to a few other doors that I'm dying to open.

"I'm going to watch some TV," Josie announces, and bounces away into the living room.

"Please don't watch anything that will make your mom upset with me again," Alex says to her back.

"What did she watch that got you in trouble?" I ask.

He smiles sheepishly and takes his hand to rub the back of his neck. "The ID Channel."

"You let her watch TV shows about serial killers?"

"Don't let her fool you," he says with a laugh. "She can be really sneaky when she wants to be."

"That, or she has you wrapped around her finger," I say, taking a guess at the dynamic between the two of them.

"That would probably be a better way of putting it. I know my sister would definitely agree with you on that one." He grins and puts his hands in his pockets while sneaking a quick glance into the living room. "So . . ."

"So," I mimic with a matching grin. "By the way, your house is beautiful, Alex."

"Thank you. I'm glad you like it," he says. "Did you have trouble finding it?"

"Not at all, especially since you don't live that far away from me," I say while reliving the stripper fantasy in my head.

"What are you thinking about?" he asks, grinning.

"Nothing at all," I say quickly.

"Would you like something to drink?" he asks.

"Sure."

He lets me walk just ahead of him and places his hand on the small of my back for a brief moment to lead me toward the kitchen. The contact, as fast as it was, brings a shiver down my spine, and I hope that he didn't pick up on it.

"Have a seat." He pulls out a stool from the kitchen island for me and then goes to the refrigerator. "Beer, wine, juice, or water?"

"Water is fine, thanks."

Grabbing two bottles, he walks over and sits on the stool next to mine before handing me one. I regret wearing jeans because his bare leg rubs up against mine as he brings his chair closer, and I would've loved to have felt it without something in the way. Then I remember there is a child present, not twenty or so feet away. With that, I decide to get into professional mode, because if not, I'm afraid for not only myself, but what I may do to him, child be damned.

Out of my oversized purse I take my iPad, a notebook, and a pen, and I efficiently lay them out on the countertop in front of me.

"So, you said yesterday that you're ready to cash in on our little deal. What kind of event is it? Another opening? A specific artist's exhibit? A private showing?"

It's then that I turn my head to face him and confirm what I've been feeling the entire time I've been talking and setting my things up. He's staring at me. But not any old stare, it's with a smile that showcases his dimples while he's casually leaning back in his chair. It's as if he's sizing me up, and even though his eyes never waver from my face, I feel it everywhere. I'm not exaggerating when I tell you that there is a distinct energy between us. Whether it's purely sexual in nature, I don't know, but it's there and it's making me rather uncomfortable.

"Why are you staring? It's freaking me out," I say quietly so his niece can't hear me.

He slowly leans forward and brings one hand to the back of my stool, trapping me in so that there is barely any room between us. "None of the above."

"Excuse me?"

"It means none of those kinds of events," he clarifies. "I have something else entirely in mind for how I want you to repay me."

Well, if that doesn't get my mind going into all sorts of dirty territory, I don't know what will.

"Care to enlighten me?" I ask and start to gnaw on my bottom lip nervously.

Alex's eyes zero in on my mouth before he says, "I'd be happy to."

We stare at each other for a moment too long for it to be anything but friendly. I'm great at staring contests, with the exception of yesterday's little slipup with Darren, but I'm not going to let Alex beat me today. It's apparent that we both have a thought or two running through our heads that may or may not involve whips, chains, and blindfolds . . . well, at least mine involve that. As for him, I don't know what he's thinking, but whatever it is it's good, as in *bad* good.

"Alex?"

"Yes," he answers, all amused and darting his eyes quickly to my mouth again.

It's my turn to crank up the heat. "You said you were going to enlighten me."

He chuckles and dips his head so that his lips graze my ear. "I will, but not today."

That threat or promise, whatever you want to call it, has my insides in a full-on frenzy. It's like the Macy's Thanksgiving Day Parade in there, and if it wasn't for me already sitting down, I'm sure I would have had to excuse myself to take a seat so I could regroup.

Having turned me into somewhat of a mute, he takes the opportunity to call his niece over. I shift in my seat and do my best I'm-pretending-to-be-busy impersonation by opening my notebook and turning on my iPad.

"Julia," he says, "I want you to plan a party for Josie."

"Really?" Josie and I both say at the same time, me in complete shock, she in complete adoration of her uncle. Alex smiles at her, and wouldn't you know it, my heart melts on the spot.

"Yes, really."

She throws her arms around his neck and gives him a big hug while she squeals with delight. I'm not a "squee-er," but even I can't help but feel all giddy inside seeing this reaction. You'd have to be dead inside not to.

"It's going to be Josie's tenth birthday next month, and I'd like to throw a big party for her and her friends," he says. "Obviously, some family members will be invited as well."

I start to rattle off a few questions. "Any ideas of what you had in mind, theme-wise? Or are we just talking a straight-up party? Oh, and any thoughts on the venue?"

"Venue will be here," he says. "Everything else I'll let the birthday girl here go over with you personally."

Alex stands up and pulls the chair out farther for Josie to sit down and take his place. She's a ball of energy, ready to burst with excitement at the proverbial keys to the kingdom she's been given. Her happiness is infectious because I'm all excited now too.

"So, let's start with something simple: theme or no theme?"

"Theme, for sure."

"Okay, did you have something already in mind?"

I don't get the sentence out completely before she blurts out, "Harry Potter."

"As in 'Undesirable Number One, Harry Potter'?" I ask teasingly.

She giggles and nods yes. "Can you do that?"

"*Pffft*, I can have this whole house looking like Hogwarts in a few hours, no problem."

"Are you a Harry Potter fan?" she asks.

"Girlie, I'm totally Team Slytherin."

"Slytherin? Oh my gosh, are you serious?" she asks.

"Totally," I say with a smile. "I do love me some Professor Snape. How about you? And don't you dare say Hufflepuff. I can deal with Ravenclaw, but I draw the line at Hufflepuff."

"Gryffindor, of course," she says while laughing.

A quick glance over her shoulder and I find Alex shaking his head with a grin. "If you need me, I'll be in my office," he says.

He disappears down the hallway into one of the rooms I was curious about earlier, leaving me and Josie on our own to go over the details with a fine-toothed comb.

"Okay, so theme, check. Venue, check. Date?"

"Um, I don't know. Should I ask Uncle Alex?" she asks.

"Well before we do that, how about you tell me when your actual birthday is. That way, I'll look at my planner and see if there is a weekend it's close to that we can use."

"Oh, I already know my birthday actually falls on a weekend this year," she says. "November ninth."

My finger scrolls the calendar on my iPad forward to November. "It's a Friday, so how about the next day, Saturday the tenth?"

"Uncle Alex! Is Saturday the tenth okay with you to have my party here?" she yells out to him.

"Yes," he yells back.

We look at each other and smile. Mine probably looks more devious than hers as the wheels in my head are spinning with all sorts of ideas for this party. Josie starts rattling off a guest list while I furiously take notes, trying to keep up with her. On top of that, I'm mentally chastising myself for worrying about coming over here today when this is what Alex had in mind all along.

How clueless can I be?

And to think I wore the granny panties, which, by the way, are chafing my undercarriage like nobody's business.

CHAPTER EIGHT

A couple of hours and many discussions later about whether or not Harry should have ended up with Ginny or Hermione, Josie and I have pretty much ironed out most of the details of what she wants for her birthday party. I've also been able to obtain valuable intel on Alex, specifically his relationship with Marisa.

Turns out she's not his girlfriend, though she wishes she was—Josie's words, not mine—and it took all of me not to laugh at the dramatic eye roll she threw in for effect as she said it. Marisa's all of twenty-four years old and has a degree in being an idiot—again Josie's words. Her parents and Alex's parents have known each other for many years, which would explain the whole "old friend of the family" bit he gave me the other day. The one piece of information Josie revealed that I found to be really intriguing is that if her mom, Alex's sister, doesn't like one of his girlfriends, the chick is usually doomed. She wouldn't elaborate much more on that other than to say how Alex and her mom are super close.

Now I know what you're thinking, and I hear you loud and clear: *Julia, why do you care so much about Alex's love life when you're still grossed out about his thing with Sabrina?*

I wouldn't say I care so much as wanting to be fully informed, because you never know when having the right intel could come in handy in the future.

All in all, I'd say my little powwow with Josie was all kinds of fun. I would have never guessed spending my afternoon with an almost-ten-year-old would be so enlightening. Her honesty and innocence is like a breath of fresh air from my daily dose of sarcasm. I almost wish that I could hang out with her more often, which is funny given my penchant for not being too kid-friendly. But this kid is pretty effing cool.

See, I'm already censoring my foul language!

"Girlie, if you weren't nine years old—"

"Ten," she cuts in.

"Okay, okay, if you weren't *almost* ten years old, I'd say let's go grab a drink and hang out this weekend."

Josie's eyes go wide in awe. "Really?"

"Totally. I've had more fun with you than I've had in a *looong* time. Maybe you can be my new best friend. What do you say?"

Her brow furrows in confusion when she asks, "Don't you have a best friend?"

"I do, but she moved away and left me all alone and bored."

Josie starts to laugh as she puts out her hand for me to shake on it. "Deal."

"Deal," I say immediately after her with a matching grin.

"This can't be good," Alex groans, making his way back into the kitchen where we're still sitting. "What are you two shaking on?"

"Julia just asked me to be her new best friend," she explains excitedly.

He stops on the opposite side of the kitchen island and plants both his hands on it before giving me a funny look. "Don't you have a best friend?"

I open my mouth, but Josie's voice fills the room first. "She said she moved and left her all alone and bored. And I'm going to be her new best friend that she's going to take out this weekend for a drink and to hang out."

"Did she? I wonder what your mom is going to say about that when she gets here in five minutes to pick you up," he says with an amused chuckle.

Josie turns in her seat to face me. "Oh my gosh, you're going to love my mom! She's super cool like you."

See what I mean? This kid is all kinds of awesome.

"So long as we don't tell her about the going out for a drink part, I'm sure we'll get along fine. That reminds me, Alex, did you tell her all about this? The party, I mean."

He smirks. "You let me worry about my sister."

I start to power down my iPad and put away my notepad, feeling uncomfortable from the curious look on Alex's face while he watched my exchange with Josie about being best friends. Plus, his sister is on her way here to pick up Josie, and that's definitely my cue to start getting out of here myself. The last thing I want is to be sized up by the big sister who, given all the information I've come to know about her, has a pretty big say in Alex's personal life. What I wouldn't give to know what she has to say about Marisa. Dammit, I should have asked Josie about it when I had the chance. I'm sure she would have been more than happy to give up that intel if I had asked her in a roundabout way.

As if on cue, I hear the front door slam shut, and I look over in that direction to see what could only be Alex's sister walking toward us. She's tall, curvy, and has long, naturally wavy dark blond hair that I would kill for. She's dressed in a pair of fitted dark-wash jeans, a vintage Rolling Stones concert T-shirt, and a pair of black Havaianas—I like this chick already.

Josie goes flying off of her stool and wraps her arms around her mother's waist before she's able to reach the kitchen. It's so fast that she nearly knocks the wind right out of her.

"Mom, I want you to meet someone," she demands.

She walks her mother over to me and says, "Mom, this is Julia,

Uncle Alex's friend, and she's going to throw me the best birthday party ever!"

"Hi, I'm Vanessa, it's nice to finally meet you. What's this about a party?"

My face must look as confused as I feel by her saying the word "finally," but I extend my hand anyway because I wasn't raised in a barn.

Her blue eyes roam over me quickly but not in an "I'm better than you" way. More like a "so this is Julia" kind of way. Which actually isn't much better either, just less invasive, and it only serves to make me think she knows more about me than the other way around. Which, in turn, leads me to believe Alex has told her about me. What the hell would he tell her about me?

"It's nice to meet you too," I say, "and you'll have to ask Alex since he's the responsible party."

Vanessa smiles and sneaks a peek at her brother, who is standing on the other side of the kitchen island with an impish grin still on his face.

"Alex," she warns, "what did you do?"

"Nothing."

"Um, maybe I should leave you two to discuss this party thing." I start to stand up and make a dash for it.

"Julia, stay put," Alex commands while keeping his eyes on his sister. "I'm having a party for Josie here at my house for her birthday."

"You're what?"

"Seriously, guys," I try to say as unobtrusively as possible. "I'll just be going now."

Alex points to the stool I was just sitting on and directs me to sit down again. What's scary is that I don't even hesitate; I sit my ass back down. Vanessa and Alex are now going back and forth about how he spoils Josie something stupid while Josie is watching them closely.

Meanwhile, I'm thinking about how he grinned at me when I followed his command to sit back down. My heart skipped a beat or two, and my pulse started to race just from pleasing him. Does that make me a sub? You know, like those women who get off on men telling them what to do inside and outside the bedroom? I may be jumping the gun, but the thought of pleasing Alex—in any way, shape, or form, inside, outside, on the couch, against the wall, on this countertop—gets me really hot.

"Right, Julia?" Josie asks. What is she asking me? I have no clue as I was in the middle of having a very vivid fantasy.

I fall back on my skill of being able to say something that will hopefully work within the conversation the three of them were having while I was starring in a Skinemax movie in my head. "Absolutely."

That was just pitiful, even for me.

Vanessa gives Alex a worried look. What was that for? Oh jeez, did I just put my foot in my mouth with my piss-poor, one-word response to Josie's question?

"If you're sure you're okay with doing all of this," she says before glancing down at her daughter, who looks ready to burst at any moment, "I guess I have no choice but to go along with it."

Phew! Josie is jumping up and down, Alex and Vanessa are smiling, and I feel like my answer was close to handing them the entire Publisher's Clearing House Sweepstakes grand prize.

"Mom, can I go out drinking with Julia?"

Did you hear that? That was the sound of a needle on an old-school vinyl record being scratched right off the turntable. Where there was sunshine, unicorns, and rainbows a moment ago, there's now a shocked expression on Vanessa's face and Alex almost choking from laughing so hard.

"Um, it's not what you think," I sputter. "I swear, I would never give her any alcohol."

"She didn't mean it like that, Vanessa," Alex says after clearing his throat.

"I swear I didn't. It's just that Josie is pretty damn . . . ugh, sorry, I mean, darn . . . anyway, she's pretty darn cool, and I had a lot of fun just hanging out with her."

The corners of Vanessa's lips are trying to contain a smile, but she bites her lip to keep it in as she watches me squirm a little.

"It's okay," she confesses. "I know what you mean, and I think she's pretty darn cool too, if I do say so myself."

I dodged a bullet on that one, so I decide it's best that I start to get going for real this time. Vanessa sees me getting ready to stand up with my belongings in hand and gives a funny look to Alex. "Don't get up. Josie and I are heading out. It's a school night, so I have to get her fed and to bed on time. If not, this 'cool' little girl will be like the walking dead tomorrow."

"How about you bring Josie to my office one day this week to go over more party details?" I offer while pulling out one of my business cards.

I hand it over to Vanessa. She eyes it and smiles. "Sounds good."

It's then that I notice she doesn't have a wedding ring on. Nowadays that usually doesn't mean much either way. But something tells me that Josie's dad isn't in the picture. We spent the afternoon together chatting up a storm, but she never alluded to her father, not once. So it would make sense to assume that Vanessa is divorced.

"Julia," Josie chimes in as Vanessa is saying good-bye to her brother, "so I'll see you again soon to go over more party stuff?"

"Don't you worry, girlie, we'll definitely be getting together soon."

"Awesome!"

Josie scurries over to where I'm still hovering between sitting and standing with my purse in my hands, and she gives me a big hug. Her tiny arms release me, and she motions for me to bend down so she can tell me something in private.

"My mom likes you, I can tell," she whispers in a rush. "You're totally in now with my uncle."

The little sneak bounces away to kiss Alex good-bye, leaving me speechless. When Vanessa says good-bye to me, I barely manage to say anything back to her, still in shock over what Josie just said. Although a part of me wants to laugh, because I have to hand it to the kid, she played it beautifully. As she's walking to the front door with her mom, she throws me a smile over her shoulder with a thumbs-up. I shake my head, chuckle, and start to follow them so I can finally head home myself.

"Where are you going?" Alex asks, stopping me from walking any farther toward his front door.

"Home."

"No you're not. You're staying for dinner," he says loud enough for everyone to hear him.

"I think Uncle Alex is going to enlighten Julia now, Mom," Josie says out of nowhere.

I want to die of embarrassment. I think Alex is even blushing now. We turn our heads to find Vanessa covering her mouth to keep herself from laughing out loud and Josie with a huge, satisfied smile on her face.

"Isn't that what you said you would do, Uncle Alex?" she asks.

"Um," Alex says.

I don't think I've ever seen him at a loss for words. It's pretty damn funny. So I start to laugh a little until he gives me a look that screams, *Help me out here*, and I shut up.

I clear my throat and say, "Um."

"Good one," Alex whispers by my ear.

"Come on, sweetie, we should be going," Vanessa says, ushering

Josie out the door. "Julia, I'll give you a call tomorrow to set something up. Alex, I'll talk to you during the week."

She's still chuckling when she closes the door behind her, leaving Alex and me alone. He runs his hand through his hair and then rubs the back of his neck. "Sorry about that," he says. "Josie is a little . . ."

"Perceptive? Precocious? Sneaky? Funny?"

"Yes," he says with a smile.

"Yeah, I kind of noticed."

"So," he says and puts his hands in his pockets. "About dinner."

"What about it?" I ask.

"You're staying."

"Why should I?"

"Because it's a good idea," he says.

"Is that right?" I ask, trying my hardest not to grin.

"Yes, it is," he says confidently. "I know you want to stay, Julia, so just say yes and get it over with."

A slew of thoughts hits me, none of which are all too unpleasant either. But the one that rises above all others is that there is no way I can do this. I know myself, and granny panties be damned, this could spell trouble. And do I really want to ruin whatever this friendship is between us? Granted, I tend to believe in the whole *When Harry Met Sally* theory that men and women can never truly be friends because the sex part always gets in the way. Still, whatever it is we have that is a semblance of friendship, I don't want to lose that either. Damn Nora Ephron and her stupid wise words that I've memorized for totally being a buzzkill right about now.

"Alex . . ."

"Julia . . ." he mimics, amused at my discomfort.

He steps into my personal space, and not for nothing, but if there is one thing I've noticed about Alex recently it's that the guy likes to get all up in my grill. Worse is that I never back away, so this technique of his is obviously paying off in the long run.

"Before you say anything about what a bad idea it is, because I know that's what you're thinking," he continues, "stop thinking so much and tell me the first thing that comes to your mind when I ask you again if you'll stay for dinner with me."

"You didn't ask me the first time."

He smiles, and dammit if those dimples aren't the key to breaking through my last bit of resolve. "Fair enough. Would you please stay and have dinner with me?"

"Um . . ." I know, that's top quality answering right there, but that's how tongue-tied he makes me sometimes.

"*Um* is not an answer. Whatever comes in your head first is the only answer I want to hear come out of your mouth."

His eyes dart to my mouth for a moment before bringing his gaze back to mine. The look in them is somewhere along the lines of amused and sinful. It's a dangerous blend, especially for me since I do love me a good challenge. I may regret this later, but what the hell, right?

"Yes."

"Good answer."

Alex walks away to lock his door, keeping me inside before I can change my mind. If it wasn't for the gratified expression on his face, I might be running for the hills. But obviously I'm thinking with my nether regions, and they are begging to come out and play. And if I listen closely, I can hear them too. It sounds like those freaky-looking British twins in *The Shining*: "Come and play with us, Alex . . . forever and ever and ever."

Yeah, I think it's safe to say that when my vagina starts speaking to me in creepy voices, that can only be a sure sign that things have taken a turn for the worse.

CHAPTER NINE

Right off the bat, I've learned a couple of things about Alex after being sucked into staying for dinner with him. One, he doesn't cook. And two, he knows how to make me feel like the center of attention but not at all in a disturbing kind of way.

Once I agreed to stay, it took us a few minutes to decide what to order for dinner. He said he knew a really good Chinese place that would deliver, and I agreed because everybody knows good Chinese food is hard to come by. He asked if I wanted to look over the menu, but again, everybody knows all Chinese restaurants have the same exact menu, so why bother?

I rattled off my order—steamed chicken and broccoli with garlic sauce on the side—without a moment's hesitation. He chuckled as he picked up his phone to call it in, and I thought it was odd that he found my order funny. That is until he ordered the same exact thing for himself. Apparently, we are Chinese food soul mates. Who would have seen that one coming?

While we wait for the food to arrive, which the Chinese place said would take about fifteen to twenty minutes, as is the standard answer for every single delivery from any Chinese place no matter where the hell you live, I feel more at ease and ask if he'll give me a tour of his house. Part of me is still dying of curiosity from the moment I got here earlier today to see the rest of it, because believe it or not, your home says a lot about you as a person. No, it's true, I saw that shit on *Oprah*. That guy, Nate something or other, was doing a room makeover in some lucky viewer's house, and he said the exact same thing. And you all know that if it was on *Oprah*, it's like the closest thing to gospel.

So off I go, following Alex as he starts showing me the rest of his house, ready to see what it says about him. From what I've already seen in the living room and kitchen area alone, it's telling me that he has great taste. Going down the hallway that had piqued my interest earlier, there are several framed photographs. They look to be of his family, but mostly of Vanessa and Josie. Before reaching the first door, there are a few photographs clumped together of Alex with a bunch of guys. Let me rephrase that so you can appreciate it more: photographs of Alex with a bunch of super-hot guys. One photo is of them on the beach, another is in Las Vegas, another snowboarding, and another fishing on a boat.

I'm staring way too intently at these pictures, first and foremost because there are a couple that have Alex with no shirt on. I can't even elaborate on how perfect he looks with the top half of him uncovered; you're just going to have to trust me on this one—it's amazing. But man oh man, his buddies aren't exactly chopped liver either.

"These must be your friends," I say, speaking up after finding my voice.

Alex smiles as he comes back to where I'm standing in his hallway staring away at the set of pictures. "We used to be fraternity brothers and have stayed relatively close over the years. Every year we try to get together for a guys' weekend."

"That's why all the pictures are from different places."

"Yes. Like this one," he says, pointing to the snowboarding photograph. "This was a couple of years ago in Aspen."

"You know how to snowboard?"

"You don't?" he asks incredulously.

I turn to face him. "Um, no. I'm a Miami girl through and through. Snow and me, we don't mix. Anything less than sixty degrees and I'd be frozen solid."

"You should at least try it once—you never know what you might be missing." He puts his hands in his pockets as I face the wall again to inspect the photographs a little better.

"So where are you guys going next?"

"We haven't decided yet. What happens is we each pick a spot, and then one of us is appointed the research guy. After all the research is done on each location, we take a vote. The one with the most votes is where we end up going."

"How very democratic of all of you," I note. "If it was me and a bunch of my girlfriends, we'd somehow end up in a tiff because so-and-so can't be in the sun for too long, and that one can't stand walking for long distances. Basically, I'd end up telling them to fuck off, and I'd pack up my shit so I could go off to an island all by myself."

"Which island?" he asks, while we make our way down the hallway toward the first door.

"Hmmm, I don't know. Somewhere that would not require me to wear much clothing and was peaceful and quiet all day and night. No cell phones, no TV . . . well, maybe some sort of TV, but for the most part a complete disconnect from everybody for a whole week."

"I know just the place," he says. "I may have to show you one day."

"That would defeat the purpose of peace and quiet, wouldn't it?"

He chuckles as he opens the first door, and I get a view of his office. It has a large mahogany desk situated in the center of the room with a dark brown leather chair. The desk faces a wall that has a pretty good-sized flat-screen TV and behind it a credenza in matching mahogany. His laptop is currently open on his desk, and there are a couple of papers strewn about, nothing messy or cluttered at all in here.

Feeling satisfied with what I've seen in this room, I brush past him on my way to the door. "Next room, please."

"I take it this room does nothing for you?" he asks.

It totally does *things* to me. All sorts of interesting things. For instance, I could tell him about the countless times I've fantasized about going to his office and locking the door so I could do all sorts of wicked things to him. But cooler heads prevail, and I shrug my shoulders and tell him no instead.

We walk to the next door, which is across the hall at an angle. He opens it to reveal a guest bathroom. Nothing much to report in here. I mean, it's a crapper with really nice fixtures that you can tell have been recently installed. Moving on, he leads me to the second-to-last door, which he opens to reveal his personal gym.

"Holy crap! You must really be into working out."

"You could say that," he laughs. "I try to get in two hours a day."

He has everything in here: an elliptical machine, a treadmill, a rowing machine, a weight machine, and free weights.

"I think I need to cancel my membership at the gym and start coming here instead," I joke.

"I don't think you'd be able to keep up with me," he says and comes up behind me as I'm eyeing some of the equipment.

I know if I turn around I'll be scarily close to him. Usually, I wouldn't be timid with my comebacks either, but I feel like if I do right now, my clothes may be off of me faster than I can say, "Fuck Bally's." Instead, I shimmy out from between his large frame and the weight machine and make my way into the hallway again. He strides toward me with a pleased look on his face and walks past me to stand before the very last stop on our tour.

Are you thinking what I'm thinking?

Bedroom.

Ding, ding! We have a winner!

Okay, let's freeze right here and assess the situation before he opens the door to where the magic happens. And let's be honest, the magic would undoubtedly happen. How do I know this? Well, besides the fact that we've been dancing around each other for months, and each time it gets precariously closer to *something* . . . I want him, plain and simple. I almost hope it's a pigsty on the other side of the door and it will turn me off rather than make me want to show him how bendy I can be.

Alex swings the door open, and what do my wandering eyes feast upon? Shit, I don't even know where to start. From the four-poster king-sized bed to the contemporary dark oak furniture that consists of an armoire, a dresser, and two nightstands—it's stunning. Directly across from me is a wall of French doors that lead to a small deck that overlooks the pool, and just off to the side is a door that leads to a master bathroom. *This* bathroom I'm definitely interested in inspecting, so I mosey on over to take a peek with Alex right on my heels. Sweet Lord above, a multi-head glass shower with a built-in stool that could easily fit three to four people *and* a separate Jacuzzi tub.

"Do you like it?"

I walk past him and back toward the bed and grab on to one of the posts to test out its durability because you never know. "I do. I like it a lot. It suits you."

He comes up to lean against the other post and grins. "How so?"

"I don't know exactly, it just does." Bullshit, I totally do, but I'm not about to go into it with him. Can you imagine if I were to say, *"It's sleek, gorgeous, and perfect like you?"* Yeah, like that wouldn't lead to any awkwardness between us.

"I'm glad you feel that way," he says.

"Why?"

"I don't know why exactly, it just does," he teases.

We fall silent, and after a moment, he pushes off the post and closes the space between us. He's so close that I can feel the heat coming off of his body in waves. I look up into his sky-blue eyes, which are dancing with mischief, and realize that all I need to do is stand on my tippy toes and I'd be able to reach his lips. It takes every bit of self-control to not jump at that impulse running through me and do exactly that. Instead, I stay put. Trapped by my own cowardice and nerves and, honestly, curiosity at what's going to happen next.

"You didn't move away this time."

"Do I win a prize?" I throw back at him. Seriously, this back-and-forth turns me on like nobody's business.

"It depends."

"Depends on what?"

"Depends on whether I think it's the right time to give you your prize," he says.

"What kind of prize is it, Alex?"

He searches my face before settling on my mouth, staring at it for a second or two, then bringing his heated gaze back to my eyes. "I think you'll like this prize, Julia. As a matter of fact, I'd be willing to bet my life on it."

"You're awfully sure of yourself," I say.

It's then that he shocks the shit out of me by taking one hand and snaking it around my waist slowly. He pulls me even closer so that my body is flush against his, and I have no choice but to steady myself by putting my hands on his biceps. When I look up at him, his eyes are fixed on mine. He brings his other hand to caress my cheek before smoothly moving it back to the nape of my neck to keep me in place—not that I have any intention of going anywhere. And he knows it, as evidenced by the devilish smirk playing at the corners of his mouth. I lick my lips in anticipation just as he dips his head, but he bypasses them altogether and heads for my ear.

"Why don't we cut the bullshit, shall we?" he says in a low voice that causes my nipples to perk up and say hello.

I don't say yes, or nod, or even move one goddamn inch; I may in fact be holding my breath while my heart is beating erratically in my chest.

"We've been playing this game for a very long time. And I'm all for playing games, Julia, but sooner or later, one of us is going to win."

I take a gulp of oxygen and pivot my head an inch so that my lips barely brush against his cheek. "Alex?"

"Hmmm?" he responds and starts to slowly trace my jawline with his lips. God, that feels good. His lips are soft and sure as they roam down to my neck, and I arch my back in his arm to give him better access.

"You should know that I'm kind of a sore loser," I whisper.

His light chuckle resonates against my neck when he moves his mouth to place the softest of kisses there. "That's the best part. Even if you lose, you win."

He continues his slow torture of kissing and nipping up my neck until reaching my chin, where he stops to hover over my lips without touching them. Holy mother of God, I might have reached an orgasm, and he's not even technically kissing me yet.

"Do you give up?" he asks in a low voice.

"Never," I say back to him and loop my arms around his neck.

"Have it your way then."

I feel the faintest trace of his smile against my lips when he finally starts to kiss me, slowly and with smooth deliberation. His tongue gradually seeks entrance, and I open for him with ease. He deepens the kiss by lightly tugging on the back of my hair so that he can angle his mouth over mine completely. It's as if he can't get enough of me, the way he's taking his time exploring my lips, caressing my tongue with his and savoring every second.

This is what it feels like to be kissed properly and thoroughly. And the only coherent thought that races through my mind is that I've kissed a lot of frogs in my lifetime, but *this*—nothing has ever been quite like this.

Ding-dong! Ding-dong!

You have got to be shitting me. The freaking Chinese delivery guy has to start ringing the doorbell just as we're finding our groove. Really?!

Alex reluctantly breaks off the kiss but doesn't budge to answer the door. It rings again, and he unleashes a gratified expression, dimples and all, while I'm struggling to make sense of what I just let happen.

"I win, and don't you dare think of running on me," he warns.

"Um . . ."

"I like you all tongue-tied—should make for an interesting evening," he says.

He lets me go then and turns on his heel to answer the door. I'm left standing there trying to rationalize how I got myself into this predicament. I steady myself on the bedpost and look in the direction of where he disappeared to, my brain going in every direction and my body still humming from the few moments of nirvana that it got to experience.

Oh, shut up! I already know, and you're right, I should have known better than to take the tour that would lead to his bedroom. Don't you think I know that I was about five minutes away from showing him the granny panties? Trust me, I do, I *soooo* do.

"Julia?" Alex calls out to me from the living room.

"I'll be right there."

Fuck shit, fuck shit, fuckity fuck shit!

Okay. I'm just going to go back out there and play it off as a moment of weakness, have dinner with him, and then I'll get the hell out of here.

I start toward the bedroom door, giving myself a quick pep talk before reaching the hallway: *Julia, you CAN do this. You will NOT sleep with him.*

Yes you will.

No I won't.

Yes you will.

"No, I won't!"

"Did you say something?" Alex asks, stepping into the hallway just a few feet away from me.

"Nope, I'm coming," I lie, quickly recovering and striding with fake confidence right past him.

You bet your ass you will. In more ways than one.

CHAPTER TEN

I'm not used to being this anxious. Men in general don't usually make me nervous. Dating has always been a natural progression kind of thing for me. Perhaps it's from growing up outnumbered in the male department that helped shape this part of me—two brothers and my dad, versus my mom and me. However I got to be so comfortable around the guys has been a blessing in the past. I've been able to hold a conversation and be charming and funny without a second thought. So this thing with Alex that I'm feeling is something entirely foreign to me.

Let me paint a picture for you.

He's sitting to my left at the kitchen island. Open Chinese food cartons are lined up in front of us, and we're eating straight out of them. When we decided that, I have no idea because I was too busy scheming in my head how I was going to get out of here unscathed. For once, I thank the Lord above that my hair can act as a veil and covers the side of my face that he's currently boring holes into with his eyes. On top of all of that, I'm having the worst time with these goddamn chopsticks, because guess what, I grew up eating with a freaking fork and spoon.

"Are you going to ignore me the rest of the night?" Alex asks while reaching over to grab an open carton.

I manage to get some rice onto my chopsticks, and it slides right off just as he's sitting back down. "Who, me?"

"Yes, you," he says.

I'm about *this close* to stabbing myself in the eye with these things, so I chuck them into the carton and put it down on the countertop. Under my breath, I let loose a couple of curse words in frustration that cause him to laugh. Oh, this is funny, is it? Actually, I'm sure he thinks all of this is rather amusing, judging by the smirk on his face and relaxed demeanor that I can see from the corner of my eye.

"I'm so glad you find all of this funny," I say.

"I wouldn't say funny so much as fun watching you get all frustrated because you're nervous. To be honest, it's quite endearing," he says.

No better time than the present to get it all out in the open between us. Because this, whatever the hell *this* is, can't go any farther than a kiss.

I pivot in my seat, and he puts down his chopsticks to give me his undivided attention.

"Alex, this is a very bad idea."

I know, so original, but it's sweet, short, and to the point.

He puts his carton on the countertop and turns so that he's facing me with a confused look on his face. When he opens his mouth to say something, which I know will be something along the lines of "You're wrong," or, "This is a very good idea," I raise my hand to get him to stop before he even starts.

"God knows we've been flirting and dancing around each other for months toward something, and by *something*, obviously I mean fucking each other's brains out. And as much as I'm dying of curiosity, I can't go there with you because I don't want it to ruin our friendship. Secondly, there's that little thing you've got going with

Marisa. Your niece did tell me that she's not your girlfriend or any-thing, and that's great news. Because I have to be honest, as your friend, she is so not your type, and you could do a hell of a lot bet-ter. But regardless of all that, *she* clearly thinks there *is* something other than friendship between the two of you, and I don't want to be the catalyst for having her figure out that there isn't. Thirdly, I don't really know much about you other than what you let me see. I mean, today is the very first time I've gotten any kind of glimpse into outside-of-work Alex. Don't get me wrong, at-work Alex is a real turn-on, and so is outside-of-work Alex for that matter, but that's beside the point. Basically, what I'm trying to say is that I don't really know enough about you to jump into bed with you."

He looks completely unfazed by my mini rant. If anything, he looks even more amused by everything that came flying out of my mouth.

"Is that all of it?" he asks.

"You know what," I add, a little irritated by his casual response, "no, it's not all of it. I forgot to mention how you once tried to hook up with my best friend. Without going into details of how strange it is to make out with someone who has made out with my best friend—yeah, she tells me *everything*—I don't want to be anyone's sloppy seconds."

After that, he doesn't say a peep. Instead, he sits there and stares rather unaffected by the myriad of reasons I've just supplied him. Beyond gratified at leaving him speechless for a change, I take the opportunity to start gathering my things and stand up to leave.

"Thank you for dinner, and I'll be in touch with you and your niece later this week with details about the party."

"And where do you think you're going? Shouldn't I get a chance to respond after your little speech?" he asks.

Sighing in defeat, because I would feel like a real piece of crap if I didn't let him speak, I wave dramatically in his direction, letting him know to go ahead with his side of the story. Then he smiles, a languid smile as if he's been waiting for his chance all along. I can't lie; I'm curious. But you know what they say about curiosity—it kills stupid-ass cats every day of the week and twice on Sunday.

"Shall I start at the beginning?"

"Sure," I offer. "By all means."

Alex crosses his arms and leans back in his chair without a care in the world. "As much as I do love your rather vivid description of 'fucking each other's brains out,' which there is no doubt in my mind would indeed be the case, your excuse of not wanting to ruin our friendship is ridiculous. Who says we can't stay friends?"

"Are you asking me to be your fuck buddy?" I ask, wide-eyed and totally thrown off by his question.

Choking on his words, he says, "No! Jesus Christ, how did you get that from what I just said?"

Before I can answer, he continues. "You know what, don't answer that. Let's move on to Marisa instead. She is not, nor has she ever been, my girlfriend. Does she think she is? I have no idea, and honestly I couldn't care less if she does. I take her out every so often as a favor to my parents for reasons I'd rather not get into right now."

"So you're saying that if by some miracle we started dating, you're still planning on fulfilling this mysterious favor and taking her out occasionally? Because I'm not cool with that, like at all. I don't share, Alex."

His full-wattage smile garners an appreciative tingle from my body that I'm almost ashamed to admit. I said *almost*, dammit. I'm still not on board with this whole thing, so my body is entitled to feel all kinds of tingles that he doesn't have to know about.

"I don't share either, Julia. Not that you would know that about me since that's part of, what did you call it, outside-of-work Alex?"

"It's true though. What do I know about you other than what I've seen here today?"

"That's something that can easily be remedied, so stop hiding behind that excuse. Moving on. Sabrina."

The name hangs in the air between us because I know everything about what transpired between them, from the making out to the almost tit-grabbing. I wasn't lying when I told him that she tells me everything. She told me every single gory detail. At the time, I was living vicariously through her because I'd always had a thing for him, but I never said jack shit about it to Sabrina. And don't get too excited about me saying I've always had a thing for him. Because if you saw this man, you'd want to be all over him like a cheap suit too.

"Sabrina and I are friends, that's it and you know it. I can't lie and tell you that at one point I wasn't attracted to her. I was. She's a beautiful woman, but that was a long time ago."

At that point, he stands up from his stool and starts to take a couple of steps toward me. What the fuck am I doing? If he takes one more step . . . dammit, it's too late. He's standing right in front of me now, and I did nothing to move out of his way. I suck.

"Since we're being so honest with each other," he notes while taking his index finger and hooking it under my purse strap. He slides it off my shoulder and hangs it on the back of the stool. "There are some things maybe you should know because I couldn't bear it if you continued to labor under a misapprehension. First of all, why don't you ask *me* how long I've wanted you? Better yet, ask me when was the exact moment I knew I had to have you."

He brings his hands up to cup my face and tilts my chin up so that I'm forced to look into his eyes, which are giving nothing away at the moment.

"I don't want to know," I answer him.

"Yes you do, and don't lie to me again," he says in a rough, low voice that does all sorts of things to me. He lowers his head so that his mouth grazes my ear, and the little slut that I am moves a hair to the side to give him better access. "If you ever lie to me again, I'm going to bend you over my knee and spank you raw. Do you understand?"

With almost a whimper, I muster a weak nod because in my mind I'm already thinking of ways that I can lie so that he can carry out his little threat.

"That's much better. Now, the last thing on your list was . . . I can't remember," he says playfully. "Care to remind me?"

"I don't want to be sloppy seconds."

"You're not and could *never* be sloppy seconds to anyone. Plus, who said it would even be sloppy?"

He's got me so wound up and a far cry from a few minutes ago when I was about to bolt out the door. I bring my hands up to hold on to his wrists when he starts to trail his lips lazily across my cheek before reaching my mouth. What little resolve I was holding on to is dissolving as if I were standing in a vat of quicksand.

"So what's it going to be, Julia?" he asks seductively with a raised eyebrow.

"I don't know," I rasp defiantly. A total lie. I know that I want him to fuck me so hard that my eyes roll into the back of my head and I can't walk straight for days.

"What did I tell you about lying to me? Or would you like a demonstration?"

God, yes! I would *kill* for a demonstration. But before I get an opportunity to test out Ass Smacking 101, he takes a couple of quick steps forward, and my back comes in contact with the wall. I don't have time to contemplate my next move, I don't even have time to blink, because he's on me like white on rice.

This time . . . this kiss . . . it's as if he's marking me, making me his. While our tongues are dueling for supreme ruler of the French kiss universe, he confines my movements by pressing up against me so that I can feel every ripple on his lean, muscular frame. His hands roam from my face to trail down my arms until his fingers roughly grip my waist. When I feel the hard length of him at my hip, well, all sense of decorum flies out the window. My hands weave themselves into his hair and hold on for dear life as I try to get the bottom half of my body at a better angle to rub up against it.

Alex's hands skim the sides of my hips before sliding over my ass and taking control of my body's movements. He pushes me against his erection to help me maintain the friction I need to get off. It's not nearly enough; I need to be flush with his cock. So I hop up and wrap my legs around his waist, and ahhhhh, there it is . . . perfect.

We're full-on dry humping each other like a pair of rabid dogs in his hallway now. He gently tugs on my bottom lip with his teeth as he snakes a hand up my blouse without breaking our rhythm. When he releases my bottom lip, he moves his head back a little to stare at me with a predatory look in his eyes. That look, mark my words, is going to be the death of me, I know it.

He licks his lips before saying in a gravelly voice, "I want to watch you."

A groan escapes my throat in response to the impending orgasm that is going to be off-the-fucking-charts fantastic. His fingers lightly brush my stomach before making their way to the top button of my jeans. I arch my back from the wall at the contact, waiting to see what he'll do next. I don't have to wait long. The button is undone with an unceremonious snap, and he immediately dips the tips of his fingers inside the waistband of my jeans.

"Tell me how much you want me to make you come," he whispers.

"Alex," I say, almost pleading while gripping his hair so roughly that I'm sure I may have left a bald spot.

I drop my gaze to watch his hand start to dive in until it's almost completely down my pants. Then the faintest brush of his fingers just below my navel brings reality crashing down around me as I remember what he's going to find down there.

The granny panties.

This cannot be happening to me. I'm finally about to have what will undoubtedly be the best orgasm of my life—and not even from any kind of actual penetration, which is a feat in and of itself—and I have to stop? This freaking blows.

My hand grips his wrist that is currently shoved down my pants, and I regretfully stop his movements. "We have to stop."

Alex looks as confused as you can imagine. We're both still breathing hard as if we've just run a marathon, and his hand is mere inches away from finding out that I wax regularly. "Are you sure you want to stop?" he asks.

I answer by releasing his waist, which my legs are currently wrapped around like a vise. When my feet touch the ground again, I still have to extricate his hand out of my pants with careful precision. Because the last thing I need is to have a fingernail of his get snagged in the shitty fabric and watch in horror as it unspools when he brings his hand out for air.

Like a doctor performing surgery, I wait for his hand to release a little of the tension that I can feel within my grip before pulling it up and out of my pants. He plants both hands on either side of my head, keeping me trapped against the wall while still breathing heavily.

"This isn't finished—you and I, it's going to happen, Julia. You can make all the excuses you like and try to convince yourself that this isn't a good idea, but if the last five minutes are any indication, it would be the best fucking decision we've ever made."

"Alex, I'm . . ."

He presses a finger against my lips to keep me from explaining. And no, I wasn't going to tell him about the holey underwear either; I'm not that much of a moron. I don't even know what I'm going to say to him. I'm kind of at a loss for words because I do want this. I want him. But I don't think I'm ready to throw caution to the wind just yet with him.

"Don't apologize," he says softly through a sexy grin. "Because I'm not sorry at all that just happened."

"I wasn't going to apologize," I answer quietly with my lips brushing against his finger that is still pressed against them. "I was just going to say that it's getting late and I should really get going so I can start working on this party you have me doing for your niece."

He nods, and almost as if an afterthought, he says, "I want this to happen, Julia, and I know you do too. And when it does, I'm going to make you come so many times that you won't have a chance to think about any of those ridiculous excuses you keep making up in that beautiful little head of yours."

What do you say to that? Nothing, that's what. When a man like Alex tells you he's going to make you come, not once but numerous times, you just stand there and soak it up because there is absolutely no comeback close to being worthy enough.

"As much as it would please me to no end to make that happen right now, I can tell that you need a little bit more time," he says, and removes his finger from my lips at the same time he drops his other arm that's still up against the wall.

Alex steps back and reluctantly puts both his hands in his pockets while he watches me straighten my clothing back to normal. Once I've got everything in its proper place, I snatch up my purse from where he hung it on the back of the stool and immediately take out my keys in silence. The kicker is I have so many things I want to say to him, but I don't. Can you believe the irony? Me, the girl who can't keep her mouth shut about anything, is stumped!

"Good-bye, Alex. I'll be in touch this week about the party, and again, thank you for dinner," I babble and make my way to the front door.

He follows closely behind and opens the door for me so I can walk out to my car. Just as I reach my driver's side door, he calls out my name. I turn my head to find him leaning against the doorjamb with his arms crossed at his chest and a pleased smile plastered on his face, looking as sexy as ever.

"I look forward to hearing from you," he says.

With a roll of my eyes as he's chuckling away at my expense, I hop in my car and pull out of his driveway. The whole time he's watching me. Not that I looked up to confirm, but it's one of those feelings you get when you know someone's staring at you.

Once I'm on the open road a couple minutes later, my mind is flying in so many directions. Why couldn't I go through with it? God knows I wanted to. It's not like I have much on the excuse front anymore. He very plainly explained that there is nothing going on with Marisa. He also put my mind at ease about his past with Sabrina, although I still think it's a little weird, but that's something I think I could get over in time. And as far as the granny panties are concerned, I totally could have made them work, and he would have been none the wiser.

What the hell is wrong with me? Am I that disenchanted with relationships and men in general that I'm always going to second-guess myself?

Then a thought . . . no, a person pops into my thoughts.

Aiden.

"Thanks a lot, asshole," I say out loud and turn onto my street.

It's *his* fault I'm like this. I've been trying for so long to let go of my past with him, but today is proof positive that I'm still as fucked up as ever. Dammit! Why did he have to pop up out of nowhere all of a sudden? I had my life all nice and neat and compartmental-ized. But no, he comes along and throws a monkey wrench into my emotional stability and makes me question every goddamn thing I do. And Alex seems to be the one suffering the brunt of it. Trust me, I know rationally that Alex doesn't deserve this. He's a great guy, and I'd be an idiot of the highest order if I didn't take a chance with him.

I walk into my house still reeling from the afternoon at Alex's house and the self-loathing trip I've been heaping onto myself the whole drive home. I'm exhausted, confused, and fed up. It's officially time for me to take the bull by the horns and give Alex a fair shot. How I'm going to do that I don't know yet, but he's definitely in my sights, and I'm going to sleep with him whether I like it or not.

Well, if today was any indication, I'm going to love it, but that's beside the point.

What was it that Sabrina used to say all the time? Something about tomorrow being a better day or some crazy shit like that, I think.

Whatever. Close enough.

Tomorrow *is* going to be a better day for me, even if it kills me.

CHAPTER ELEVEN

Monday mornings are not my favorite day of the week to begin with, but this morning is even worse than usual. I'm really dragging. From stopping my mother from committing murder, finding out that my parents still have sex—I just threw up a little in my mouth just thinking about it—and finally everything that happened with Alex. Seriously, my head feels like it's spinning from all the crap I have going on in there. Because I still have to figure out a way to be around him and try not to be too distracted while still planning his niece's party. And if you've ever been in the same room as Alex, good luck on not being distracted by him. It's next to impossible for me.

When I arrive at work, I make a beeline to the coffee machine and pour myself a cup before heading into my office, hoping that it will clear my head a little. While I'm waiting for my laptop to fire up, I pull out my iPad to review my notes from when I met with Josie yesterday and place it on my desk. Tapping my fingernails against my coffee mug as I'm thinking of a way to approach Lisette without it backfiring on me, I finally pick up the phone and call her into my office. She's not in the room for more than a second before she zeroes in on my mood.

"What's wrong with you?"

"That's nice. No *good morning* or *how was your weekend*," I answer sarcastically. "By the way, close the door behind you."

After she swings the door shut, she walks over and sits down. "Good morning. How was your weekend, *and* what's wrong with you? Is that better?"

"What makes you think there's something wrong with me?" I ask.

"I don't know what gave it away first, the hair in a messy bun or the bags under your eyes. Something is definitely up with you."

I put down my mug and lean back in my chair. Lisette doesn't know it yet, but she's going to help me with Alex, kind of. See, I don't want to just call him up and say, "Hey, how about we finally have sex? Does today work for you? Great! Sounds like a plan!"

I concur, that would be a bit on the slutty side.

With him, I think I need to bide my time, not just jump into bed with him. Or at least that's what I've convinced myself of, and it kept me from sleeping most of the night. Well that and having a battle with myself over grabbing my vibrator and finishing off what he started. For the record, I didn't, and that's probably why I'm even crankier. Oh, please! Have you ever been that close to coming and then not? It's like being . . . you know what, it can't be described. It sucks ass, plain and simple.

Anyway, I'm hoping that Lisette will help in being something of a buffer between us as far as helping plan this party for Josie. The way I see it, if she's around us during meetings, phone calls, and so forth, then he won't dare to make a move—or at least that's what I hope will happen. And that will buy me the time that I need to get to know him better to see where, if anywhere, this can go with him.

"*Niña*, just spit it out already," Lisette drawls out, seemingly bored at my holding up the conversation.

"Okay, what I'm about to tell you cannot leave this room," I warn.

She nods, but that isn't good enough. "I need you to swear on one of those saints you pray to or something like that."

Lisette's eyebrows shoot up so high that I'm afraid they may need to be surgically removed from her hairline. "Oh, this must be good. Fine, I swear on *San Lazaro* that this won't leave this room."

Still leaning back in my chair, I steeple my fingers together under my chin and let it all out. "I went to Alex's house yesterday. At first it was to meet with his niece to plan a birthday party for her in a few weeks. But after she left, it turned into what I think can only be described as a date, sort of. He asked me to stay for dinner, so I did. Somehow we ended up making out in his bedroom, and then luckily the Chinese delivery guy got us to stop. Then during dinner I gave him all the reasons why we can't be together, and the next thing I know I'm up against his wall about to have the best orgasm of my life with all of our clothes still on."

Lisette's movements are frozen, as is the shocked expression on her face.

"So I need your help and, as much as it kills me to say it, advice."

She's still speechless. I don't blame her. Not only would the developments with Alex be a shocker to her, but me coming out and asking for advice too? Hell may have officially frozen over.

"Aren't you going to say something?" I ask.

Her glazed-over look disappears, and she leans forward in her chair.

"Did you sleep with him?"

"No, I didn't. I couldn't," I add as an afterthought under my breath.

"And why *couldn't* you sleep with him?"

"I'd rather not say. We just stopped, and I left shortly after that."

Lisette is cursing in Spanish while she pulls out her cell phone and starts pressing some buttons rather violently.

"What the hell was that about?" I ask.

"I just texted Sarah," she answers in an annoyed voice when her phone dings in her hands. "She just said she'll be here in five minutes and not to say another word until she gets here."

"What the hell, Lisette?! Didn't I just ask you to keep this shit between us? Didn't you swear on Saint Larry that you wouldn't breathe a word of it to anyone?"

She crosses herself before letting out a long sigh. "It was *San Lazaro*, and for the record, he would be fine with it. Plus, we need reinforcements."

"You are unbelievable! I ask for your help and you text Sarah?"

"She works for the man. We—I mean *you*, need her help too," she says. "So shush! Not another word from you until Sarah gets here."

Unreal. And the best part is I'm stupid enough to sit here and do exactly what she says. I try to busy myself with checking my e-mails, but that's not going to happen while I have Lisette staring at me like a hawk. I give up and turn my seat around to face her again. She's got a funny look on her face as if she's trying to hold in a fart and it's killing her. Her movements are jerky and irritated, and more importantly playing on my last nerve.

"Fuck this noise," I announce, and go to stand up. "I'm out of here. You two can figure this out on—"

"I'm here! I'm here!" Sarah yells, running into my office and slamming the door behind her. "Did I miss anything?"

"Bloody hell," I say. "Did you run here?"

"Yup," she proudly says.

"What did you say to Alex?" Lisette asks, and I instantly sit back down because I have to admit I'm dying to know what the answer is too.

"I told him I had to run to Navarro's and buy some tampons," she says. "I've got about a half hour before I have to be back at the gallery. So what's up?"

I shoot a confused look at Lisette. "I thought you said you told her?"

"I didn't give her all the details," she says.

I roll my eyes while Lisette then proceeds to fill Sarah quickly in on everything that transpired with Alex over the weekend. When she's done, she adds, "So now this one"—she nods toward me—"doesn't know how to not screw this up."

"Hello, I'm sitting right here," I say, annoyed.

"Well it's true! That's pretty much what you said before Sarah got here."

I sigh in exasperation and cover my face with my hands. When I look at them through my fingers, they are practically bouncing in their seats with glee.

"This was a bad idea," I say quietly. Neither of them answers; I didn't expect them to. I think mostly because they can tell I'm at my wits' end.

"Ladies, how old are we? Seriously, I mean it. We're behaving like a bunch of teenyboppers. I'm almost thirty. Lisette, who knows how the fuck old you are, but I bet it's old enough to remember where you were when Kennedy was shot. And Sarah, well you're too cute to know any better, no offense."

"None taken," Sarah chirps with a wave of her hand.

"Well, I'm offended!" Lisette shouts. "I'm not old enough to remember that, but I *am* old enough to tell you to keep your skinny ass in that seat and listen to us for a change. You wanted help, dammit, so you're going to get it."

"My ass isn't that skinny," I point out while lifting one butt cheek off the seat to look at it. It's not, I swear. It's a size six, sometimes eight, depending on what store I go into to shop. You all know how that goes.

The room falls silent again after Lisette's outburst. When they start to chatter amongst themselves, I take the opportunity to grab my mug of coffee, and I notice the time. I've been at work for all of forty-five minutes and have not accomplished a single thing.

"Okay, I've brought her up to speed," Lisette says. "Now we've got a few questions for you, and you have to answer them truthfully."

I reluctantly nod.

"No, not good enough," Sarah says. "You have to swear."

"Ha! Like this one?" I laugh while pointing to Lisette. "She swore she wouldn't tell anyone, yet here you are."

"Like I wasn't going to tell Sarah about all of this? *Por favor*, Julia."

I give Lisette the evil eye and at the same time swear that I will answer their questions honestly. They look at each other and mumble over who's going to go first. "Seriously, ladies, I don't have all day. Can we move this along?"

Lisette speaks up. "I'll go first then. Do you like Alex?"

"Really? Is that the best you got? Will you pass him a note in study hall for me if I say yes?" I mock while clasping my hands together under my chin and batting my eyelashes like a lovesick teenager.

"If you want me to, I will," Sarah answers seriously. Poor kid, she's just along for the ride.

Lisette chuckles before clearing her throat. "Just answer the question for us, if you don't mind."

"Fine. I do. I like him, okay. Are you happy now?"

"Not yet," she says. "But at least we're getting somewhere."

"My turn." Sarah's voice goes all giddy. "Why didn't you sleep with him yesterday?"

"Sorry, I can't answer that. Next question."

When they finally figure out I'm not budging on this, Lisette puts her hand up as if she's in a classroom, and the idiot that I am points at her like I'm the teacher keeping these two in line.

"Then answer this one instead. Do you want to sleep with him?"

With a nonchalant eye roll, I answer as unaffected as possible. "Yeah, so? Have you seen him? I bet anyone within a five-mile radius who has a pulse and a vagina would answer that question in the same exact way. So that doesn't prove a damn thing."

"Maybe, maybe not," Lisette singsongs.

Sarah raises her hand quickly in the air, and I point at her. "Well, I for one would definitely sleep with him."

"Thank you for that information, Sarah," I acknowledge with a smile. "I'll be able to sleep a little better tonight knowing that."

Lisette smacks Sarah's arm and tells her to shut up, then looks in my direction with a determined grin. "You can say whatever you want, Julia, but we all know that there's more to this thing with Alex than you're letting on. And you know what? That's totally fine, but between me and Sarah, we're going to make this happen."

They give each other a high five as I'm bringing the heels of my hands to my eyes. I rub them hard, probably ruining my slack-ass makeup job that I did this morning in a rush to get out of the house. When I pull them away from my face, I mumble, "You sound just like Alex."

"What did he say?" Sarah asks, and they both lean forward, waiting on bated breath for me to explain.

"He said that whatever it is between us is going to happen, and then he said . . . I can't tell you what else he said."

"Bullshit, you can't!" Lisette almost roars.

"Yeah, you need to spill it," Sarah agrees.

"Fine, but I swear that if either of you says anything to anyone else, I will do everything in my power to make your lives miserable."

They both swear in unison, so I go on and tell them in an almost whisper what they're dying to hear. "He said that he was going to make me come so many times that I wouldn't have time to come up with more excuses as to why we couldn't be together."

Lisette crosses herself while Sarah says something about Jesus and how incredibly sexy that is. Seriously, if this wasn't all about my personal life, I'd be loving this little meeting of the minds like nobody's business. But seeing as it's *all* about me, I think it's safe to say I'm not enjoying myself too much.

"Well at least we know he's not a mangina kind of guy," Sarah says out of the blue.

I'm almost too afraid to ask, but come on, wouldn't you be sitting here wondering what the fuck she's talking about? I may regret it later, but I'm totally going to bite on this one.

"What the hell is a mangina?" I ask, trying to keep a straight face.

"Oh, my best friend Sandra came up with that. It's when a guy, usually a really masculine or hot kind of guy, acts like a complete . . ."

"Like a complete what?" Lisette and I both ask at the same time.

Sarah cups her mouth, and in an almost inaudible voice says, "Pussy."

In between laughs I manage to say, "Alrighty then, I'd say that marks the end of this little powwow."

"Yeah," Sarah says while standing up to leave. "I have to get back to the gallery before Alex thinks I'm never coming back. And I still have to stop somewhere and buy a box of tampons."

I'm about to tell her that she probably doesn't need to actually go out and do that because it's not like Alex will check to make sure she did. But you know what? I keep my mouth shut because it's just more fun that way. She runs out as quickly as she appeared, leaving Lisette and me all alone again.

"I hope you're happy now," I say to her after we've stared at each other for a few seconds.

"I'm not going to be happy until you get your head out of your ass and go for it. This isn't like you, Julia. Think about it. When was the last time you were such a mess over a man?"

I know exactly when that was, and thanks to that little comment, we have officially acknowledged the elephant in the room.

"Julia, he's not Aiden," she says carefully.

"I know he's not Aiden," I answer a little too defensively.

"Then what's the problem? Why do you need anybody's help or advice?" she asks.

"I don't know. I . . . I'm afraid I'll screw it up. I always screw it up."

"No, you don't," Lisette says. "And if I catch you saying that about yourself again, I will personally kick your ass up and down Ocean Avenue."

I choke back a laugh at the visual. Lisette may be mouthy and opinionated like me, but there is no way in hell she can take me.

"Don't laugh," she warns. "You've only seen pieces of my Cuban temper." She pauses and then adds, "And stop feeling sorry for yourself—it doesn't become you. So what if you saw Aiden the other day? He's a jerk and doesn't deserve to breathe the same air as you. Get over it. Don't let him be the reason that you hold back on Alex, because that's not fair to not only him, but to yourself too."

"You think I don't already know that, Lisette?" I ask. "Trust me, I do. And for the record, I'm not feeling sorry for myself."

"Oh no? Are you sure about that? Because it sure sounds like you are."

"Okay, okay," I say through gritted teeth. "Maybe you're a little right about the feeling sorry for myself bit."

Lisette stands up and places both hands on my desk and narrows her eyes at me. "Julia, you don't need help or advice. What you need is to let go and admit that you want Alex. That you want more than sex with him. Because until you do, you're going be a miserable bitch. So do us all a favor, and pick up the phone and call him."

"Gee, don't hold back on my account," I say sarcastically. Inside though, I know she's right.

Her eyes dart over to the phone at my desk and then back to me. She raises an eyebrow as if to say, "I dare you."

"Fine, I'll call him, but you have to promise to help me plan this party. I need you around to be my buffer."

"That's not going to happen. I mean, I'll help you, but you're going to deal with him whether you like it or not."

"Whatever," I grumble, annoyed over this turn of events.

"Yeah, whatever," she laughs while standing up and heading to the door. "And a hundred bucks says you're going to like it. A lot. So start dialing."

Once she's out of sight and I've come to the inevitable conclusion that my plan has turned to shit, I stare at the phone as if it's about to sprout wings and fly away at any moment.

"Don't be such a chickenshit," I mumble out loud to myself. Then I pick up the receiver and angrily start pressing buttons as if I have a personal vendetta against the phone.

Alex picks up on the second ring.

"Julia," he says. His voice is deep and lush this early in the morning, and a shiver runs through me remembering his words from yesterday: *I'm going to make you come so many times, blah blah blah . . .*

I've taken the liberty of just focusing on this piece of his threat because well, honestly, who the hell cares what else he said? It's not important.

"Julia?" he asks.

"Yes?"

He laughs a delicious low rumble from his chest. Muted, but sexy as hell. "You called me. Is there something you wanted?" he asks.

The question is laced with possibilities. And for once, I'm not going to tuck my tail between my legs and run.

"Yes," I say, trying to contain the smile threatening the corners of my mouth. "I was wondering if you wanted to get together or something."

"Are you asking me out on a date, Julia?"

"It's not a date . . . technically."

It's *soooo* a date.

"It's not?" he asks, amused. "Then what would you call it?"

"Two friends who obviously are very attracted to each other and—"

"Obviously," he interrupts. "Go on."

"As I was saying . . . two friends who are very attracted to each other and would like to get to know each other better."

"A date," he says.

"It's not a date, Alex."

"When would you like this not a date but very much so a date to happen?" he asks playfully.

I like playful Alex. Too much. But I don't want to let that show while on the phone. I'd rather play it cool, safe, and slow. It's also a bit of a torture trip for both of us, which in the long run makes the chase that much more exciting. I mean, who doesn't love a good slow burn? I know I do.

"How does tomorrow after work sound for our very much not a date?" I ask. "Fox's? Say around six o'clock?"

He's smiling when he answers. "It's a date. Shall I pick you up at your office?"

"I'll meet you there."

"Of course you will because it's not a date, right?" he asks. "Just two friends who are very attracted to each other and want to get to know each other better?"

"You're catching on," I answer.

"I'm a fast learner, Julia," he says with a light chuckle. "I'll see you tomorrow."

We say our good-byes, and as soon as I hang up I hear a slow clap coming from my office door. I turn my head to find Lisette leaning against the doorframe with a pleased-as-punch smile plastered across her face.

"Don't gloat," I say. "You shouldn't be eavesdropping."

"Oh, I'm not gloating. And you left the door wide open for anyone to hear you being all giddy like a schoolgirl on the phone with Alex, so that one's totally on you."

"Well go gloat somewhere else then," I say. "I have work to do."

She laughs. "Sure thing, boss. Question though—do you need me to be a 'buffer' at this not a date but really a date tomorrow night?"

I roll my eyes and swivel my seat to face my computer. "Very funny."

I can still hear her laughing when she walks away. As my computer begins to power up, the smile I've been trying to keep under control breaks free. I did vow to myself that today was going to be better, and so far so good. Hopefully tomorrow it will be even better. At this rate, by the end of the week I may be singing "Zip-a-Dee-Fucking-Doo-Dah!"

CHAPTER TWELVE

What was I thinking?

Me calling Alex for not really a date, when in fact it's a real date? I must have had a momentary lapse of reason. That or someone slipped a Mickey in my coffee when I wasn't looking that all of a sudden gave me a pair of really big balls.

I'm a fairly upfront, outgoing, and honest person. I tend to say whatever comes to mind. Sometimes that gets me in a little bit of trouble, but for the most part, it's a good thing. Or at least that's what I tell myself. Anyway, in all my years of being on the dating scene, I've never once asked anyone out on a date. I know it's kind of a surprise to hear, but it's true.

I've always been the one to be asked out on a date, not the other way around. I think because I've been programmed to believe that a woman should wait for a man to come to her. And that's a great way of looking at it. Nothing wrong whatsoever with it. It's laced with good intentions from both parties of the old-school romantic variety.

And maybe that's one of my problems, along with the other issues that have been dusted up recently. I'm sitting here waiting around for some miracle of a man to step out of the shadows and sweep me off my Jimmy Choos instead of the other way around. Why can't I be the pursuer for a change?

Oh, gee, that's right. I almost forgot. It's because it makes me feel like an idiot with a side of nervous wreck.

Like I do right now, for instance.

"Too late to turn back now," I say out loud to myself as I turn into Fox's. I canvass the parking lot and spot Alex's cherry-red BMW already there. Dammit! There goes my idea of arriving before him and having home field advantage.

I'm blasted with cool air as soon as I enter the restaurant. Then it takes me a few seconds to get my bearings since I'm blanketed in near darkness. Even with the overpowering 1970s decor like red vinyl upholstered chairs and the heavily lacquered bar, the place has a sensual feel due to the scattered lit votive candles. The cozy bar has a few customers already, but not enough that I can't spot Alex sitting at the corner waiting for me. A smile tugs at the corners of his mouth when he sees me. He stands up when I finally reach him, like a real gentleman and shit. He's wearing a dark charcoal-gray suit with a black dress shirt and no tie, and it makes him look sexy as sin.

He brushes his lips innocently against my cheek and pulls out a barstool for me. "You're late."

"No I'm not. You're early," I say, trying to sound cool.

With a trace of anxiety still gnawing inside of me, I sit down beside him. He slides back onto his stool with the grace of a caged panther as the bartender approaches us. Without asking, he orders for me.

"What if I didn't want to drink a glass of wine?" I ask.

He grins. "I've known you long enough to know that that's what you would've ordered."

"What if I wanted a martini instead?"

"Do you?" he asks with a full-on smile.

My face immediately betrays me without having to answer him. Don't you hate when that happens? And now he can tell I had no interest in ordering a martini and he was one hundred percent right about the glass of wine. But the smugness in his eyes makes me do the ol' cut your nose to spite your face thing. One of my most treasured habits but definitely not one of my best ones either.

"Yes, I'd like a martini," I say.

Alex's eyes roam over me for a second before he lifts up his hand and beckons me with his finger.

"Um, I'm right here. Why do I need to get any closer?" I ask.

"Kicking and screaming until the bitter end, huh?" he mumbles under his breath.

"What does that—"

"It means, Julia," he says while smoothly leaning forward and bringing his mouth to my ear, "that you're going to make this very difficult on me, aren't you?"

Alex's voice is so quiet, and his proximity rattles me. I take a gulp, and he chuckles. I think the bastard thinks he's got me under his spell. I am, but he doesn't need to be all cocky and self-assured about it. So what do I do? I decide to even the playing field a little. Because if not, I'll be jumping on top of this bar and spreading my legs faster than I can say, "Kicking and screaming, my ass."

"I think we need some ground rules," I say.

He draws back, looking like what I said amused him. I reach for my wineglass, and he raises an eyebrow, acknowledging the fact that I'm drinking exactly what I said I didn't want. So what if he was right? I'm not going to give him the satisfaction of admitting it out loud. I'm stubborn to the core and to the bitter end. So his depiction of kicking and screaming really isn't that much of a stretch.

Alex gives a flash of his dimples before taking a long pull from his beer bottle. "What kind of ground rules?"

I turn in my seat to fully face him. "The kind where we know each other's boundaries so that we don't make each other uncomfortable."

"You're not making me uncomfortable. Am I making you uncomfortable, Julia?" he asks softly.

"Not exactly."

He's not, kind of. It's more the memory of being in his arms and grinding against him the other day that's throwing me for a loop.

"Okay, so name your ground rules."

I tap my fingernail against the rim of my wineglass while thinking. "First things first. You stay in your dance space and I'll stay in mine for the time being. Second, and more importantly, this isn't a date."

He laughs. "That's it? Those are the ground rules?"

"For now, yes," I say and take a sip of my wine. "But I reserve the right to add on if necessary."

"Fine," he replies with a grin.

"Great. Now that we've got that out of the way, we can concentrate on getting to know each other better."

Alex puts down his beer bottle and leans back, looking more casual and comfortable than I do or feel. My fingers give an involuntary twitch while I watch him rake a hand through his hair because I'm dying to touch him somewhere, anywhere. I would even settle for a graze of his knee against mine. I'm that desperate and seriously questioning why I brought up these stupid ground rules to begin with when all I want is to mount him like a saddled horse.

"Go ahead and fire away then," he says in a charming tone. "I'm at your complete mercy."

"Seriously?" I ask a little apprehensively.

"You said you wanted to get to know me better, so yes, seriously, go ahead and ask anything you'd like. I'm an open book."

"Okay." I smile and pick up my wineglass. Leaning back in my chair, I try to mimic his relaxed and cool-as-a-cucumber demeanor, but I feel like it just makes me look like a grade-A jackass. So I cross my legs and let my foot dangle in between us to give off that "I haven't a care in the world" look and say the first thing that comes to mind. "Marisa."

He licks his lips quickly to stifle a smile before he says, "Going straight for the jugular, huh?"

"I try," I answer. "Plus I already know the basics."

Alex chuckles and asks, "Like what exactly?"

"Well, let's see." I pause to take a sip of my wine. "I know you're in your early thirties. You're obviously very close with your older sister and niece, who, by the way, I might just steal for myself. You own the art gallery. Although, I'm not quite sure how that came about. You obviously travel quite a bit as evident by all the pictures in your house. And last but not least, you like to work out."

His eyes glint with humor at my assessment of his life in less than eighteen seconds.

"Seems like you've got me all figured out," he says.

"For the most part," I reply coyly. "Just need you to fill in the blanks."

"I'm thirty-three. I'll be thirty-four in January, and we can discuss what I'd like for you to give me as a gift another time." He says that last part so seriously and with absolutely no room for interpretation but keeps right on talking. "I only have one sibling, whom you've met, and yes, we are very close. You'll have to go through me to steal Josie, and I'd really like to see you try. As for the art gallery, I bought it because I love art. I always have."

He takes a small pull from his beer and smiles fully as if remembering something before he goes on. "My mom might have something to do with that though. She's quite the art history buff and for as long as I can remember has been passing on all her knowledge to me and my sister, who's a bit of an artist herself. She used to take me to museums, galleries, anything and everything that had to do with art. So when it came time to go to college, I majored in business with a minor in art history. Did I ever think I'd own my own gallery? No. But when the opportunity presented itself, I took it. My dad was a little upset at first since he thought I'd be taking over his construction business. But that just wasn't me, even though I'd been working for him every summer for as long as I can remember. And as for traveling, yes, I've traveled quite a bit and try to get away at least twice a year."

"So your family is close?" I ask.

"Very. Yours?"

"Very. Are your parents still together?"

"Yes," he answers, dimples and all. "Yours?"

"Yup. Although, my dad retired recently, and I think my mom may have plans to kill him soon, so that is subject to change at any moment."

Alex tosses his head back and laughs. Watching him like this, relaxed and having a good time with no pressure of the sexual variety, makes me less nervous around him. Although, seeing him laugh like that kind of turns me on too, so I guess I'm screwed one way or the other.

"That brings us back to Marisa," I say nonchalantly and add a flirtatious wink of my eye for emphasis. "Which by the way, nice trying to get me to forget about that one."

"I wasn't trying to evade your question about her," he says while motioning the bartender to give us another round. "There simply isn't that much to tell."

"You said that you take her out as a favor to your parents. That alone is enough material to work with. Why don't you start there?"

While his upper body is partially turned to pay the bartender, I notice an eyebrow quirking up and all traces of humor leaving his face before he turns back around to face me. But it's too late. I already caught it and almost regret asking about Marisa now. Well, not really because I'm kind of nosy, but still.

"Like I said, there isn't much to tell," he answers with a forced look of impassivity about him. "Her family has known my family for a long time. She's been having a rough time lately, so my parents have occasionally asked me as a favor to them to take her out and show her a good time sometimes. That's all. There is nothing else going on, and she is not my—"

"Girlfriend," I finish for him.

He nods in agreement and then brings the beer bottle to his mouth. "Sorry, I didn't mean to sound so put off by your question."

I wave a hand dismissively in the space between us. "No harm, no foul."

"She's really not so bad once you get to know her," he says.

It's killing me not to say anything in response to that. But somehow my big fat mouth stays shut and lets it slide . . . for now.

The rest of our date but not a date goes smoothly. Even though there is this underlying energy between us that is so palpable and you would have to be blind not to see it or sense it, it's not making me as uncomfortable or anxious as before. So it would seem that my idea to get to know each other better was a success.

Before I know it, Alex is walking me to my car. His hands are in his pockets, and I steal a glance at him as I tuck a stray hair behind my ear, noticing the calmness in his eyes. When we reach my car, he holds the door open for me to climb in but doesn't say a word. I guess I'm the one who's going to have to say something since I'm the one who asked him to meet me here.

Sadie fucking Hawkins is an asshole, if you ask me. Women aren't built for this shit. I don't even know what I'm expecting to happen. I made it perfectly clear that there were to be boundaries from the get-go. So why the hell am I standing here wanting to kiss him so bad that if I don't, I'm going to punch something or some-body? How do men do this? How can they stand the not knowing of whether or not they'll be rejected? It makes me have newfound respect for the species.

Alex has one hand braced on my open car door and watches me as I toss my hobo bag across the seat to the passenger side. His lips curl up in a devilish smile that makes me want to break out in hives even more than a second ago. He's enjoying himself watching me squirm. He knows I want to kiss, lick, and nip those delectable lips of his. And he's not going to do a thing about it.

So guess what I do.

"Thanks so much for meeting me," I expel in a rush of words. "I had a great time tonight."

I thrust my hand out into the empty space between us. He looks momentarily confused and then chuckles when he puts his palm in mine. I give it a firm shake, trying to ignore the warmness sliding over me at merely touching his hand. Letting it go quickly, I slide into my car and pull the door closed just before I mumble a barely audible "good night" over my shoulder at him. Alex is still standing there when I turn back around to start my car. I know because I can *feel* him watching me, assessing me in all my absolute craziness and indecisiveness.

When my hands finally grip the steering wheel, I hear a light tap on the window. I look to my left to find Alex's head tilted to the side with a grin from ear to ear. Then he lifts up his one hand and beckons me to him with an index finger just as he had earlier tonight while in the bar.

I open the car door, and as I'm stepping back out, he comes closer and traps me into the tiny space between my open door and the driver's seat. Now there's only but a sliver of space between us. He is all I can see, feel, smell, and desperately want.

Alex brings his hands up and cups my face, tilting it up toward him slowly.

"I'm in your dance space," he says faintly.

"I see that. Are you going to ask me to dance?"

He lets out a small chuckle as his thumbs make featherlight circles against my cheeks. God, I love that. Just when I think he can't get any better, he tops himself by being a freaking face holder.

"I didn't have dancing in mind," he replies.

I bring my hands up to steady myself and grab a hold of his wrists.

"What did you have in mind?" I ask.

"Why didn't you kiss me?" he quickly asks back.

"I wanted to. I still do."

"Then do it," he says.

His eyes roam to my mouth for a second before bringing his gaze back to my eyes. They look as if they are daring me to move, to stand on my tiptoes and bring my lips to his.

It works.

I reach up and bring my mouth to his. And the moment I do, Alex immediately takes over. His lips slide over mine, barely touching and teasing until a small moan escapes me. Finally his tongue snakes out as he angles my head to the side for better leverage. The kiss spirals out of control with each deft stroke of his tongue against mine. His hands never wander from cradling my face, yet there is no question that he is commanding my entire body. It's responding to the invasion in my mouth with a huge welcome sign and begs for more.

When our breathing becomes labored and I'm this close to wrapping a leg around his waist in the middle of the Fox's parking lot without giving a flying fuck as to who sees us or not, he pulls away and goes back to rubbing circles against my cheeks with his thumbs. His eyes stay focused on mine, but they are clouded with pure unadulterated lust, and they make me want to pick right up where we left off.

"I like being in your dance space, Julia. Too much, I think," he smoothly says.

Looking up at him, I can't keep my smile under wraps at his admission, and it gives me the courage to say, "Me too."

No words are spoken and barely a breath is taken in the few seconds that follow until he drops his hands from my face and backs up a step.

"Good night and thank you for asking me out on a date," Alex lightly teases. "I had a great time."

"Good night, Alex," I say. "I look forward to our next not a date."

He laughs while I slide back into my seat, and this time I do so with an almost face-splitting grin. The feeling of being on cloud nine stays with me the whole drive home. I actually catch myself singing along to some god-awful Katy Perry song on the radio, that's how high in the moment I am. I stay that way until I check my messages. Because the last person I want to hear from is waiting on my answering machine.

"Julia, it's me. Aiden."

"No shit, Sherlock," I say and roll my eyes.

"Look, I know it was strange the other day, and if I had known you were involved in planning the engagement party, I would have come to see you sooner."

I'm staring at the machine, willing it to keep talking and at the same time wishing he would disappear off the face of the planet.

"Anyway, I think that we should meet up to talk. So call me when you get this message."

I replay it just to make sure I didn't imagine it.

No such luck. It was really him.

Seriously, of all the things to bring me down from my high from one of the best nights I've had in a really long time, it had to be him. I'm cursing under my breath while stomping toward my bedroom. After stripping off my clothes and throwing them into a heap on the floor, I change into my pajamas and fall backward onto my bed.

Bringing the heels of my hands to my eyes, I rub them so hard that I see stars. What am I doing? I just went on one of the best dates of my life, for chrissakes! Why do I keep allowing him to bother me so much?

I breathe in and out, over and over again until I'm able to think clearly and rationally. I'm going to just pretend he never called. In the morning I'll delete the message and go on with my life and never talk to him again. Hopefully he'll get the hint and leave me the hell alone. And for good measure, I'll make sure to add to my latest list one very important item:

4. Forget about dickhead and have fun with Alex.

CHAPTER THIRTEEN

No streamers. Got it," I say while scribbling it down on a note-pad. "Anything else that is a total hard limit for you?"

"Piñatas," Josie adds and sneaks a peek at her mom. "Sorry, Mom, but I hate those things."

Vanessa laughs. "Well, if I would have known you hated them so much, I wouldn't have made you suffer through them every year."

"I don't blame you," I say. "Those things explode and kids lose their ever-loving minds. It could be pretty dangerous, if you ask me."

"Tell me about it," Vanessa agrees. "See this scar?"

She points to a faint line on her forehead about two inches long that I would have never noticed had she not brought it to my attention.

"My dearest baby brother Alex was swinging away at a piñata with a baseball bat at his eighth birthday party. Instead of hitting the piñata, he hit me square on the head with the bat."

"Holy shit!" I quickly cover my mouth and apologize for cursing.

"I've heard a lot worse, Julia," Josie says while giggling.

"So what happened?" I ask.

"Nine stitches," Vanessa says with a shrug while smiling. "Wasn't so bad. My face was covered in blood though, and Alex took to calling me Carrie for a few years, that's about it."

"Right. Definitely a big no on piñatas then."

Vanessa nods in agreement and then pulls her keys from her purse. "All right, kiddo. Time to get moving so you can finish your homework."

Josie launches out of her chair and comes to where I'm sitting. She carefully wraps her arms around my neck, giving me a big hug that makes my heart melt a little, further dispelling my awkwardness around kids. Well, not *all* children, just other people's kids really. I'm sure once it's my turn to have them, I'll be fine, or at least I hope so for the kid's sake.

"This party is going to be awesome, isn't it?" she asks enthusiastically.

"Totally awesome," I say and hug her back. "I promise."

She walks away with a huge smile on her face, back to her mom, who is waiting by the door to my office. Vanessa mouths a sincere "thank you" to me before hooking her arm in Josie's and closing the door behind them.

I wave good-bye to them and get back to work, thinking I was all kinds of stupid the other day when I met Vanessa and I was a little afraid of what she might think of me. In my defense, I did want to make a good impression on her, but I really had nothing to worry about. She is extremely easygoing, and I can tell where Josie's great personality comes from.

A couple of hours later I'm about to start packing it up for the day when Lisette pops her head into my office with keys and purse in hand. "We're going to happy hour at Rio Station and so are you."

"I'm really tired," I groan. "I'll catch up with you guys next time."

"Nuh-uh. You're going. You've been cooped up in here all week, and I can tell you need a drink or two or three. Don't worry, I'll be your designated driver if you need one."

The thought of having a few cocktails does appeal to me. "Okay, you twisted my arm. Give me a few minutes, and I'll meet you over there."

Her satisfied smiling face disappears behind the door, and I rush through getting my things packed before heading over to the bar. I probably could have walked there, and I would have arrived quicker than sitting in South Beach traffic at five o'clock on a Thursday night. Because didn't you know that Thursday night happy hour is the new Friday night happy hour? Thank you to the asshole who came up with that brilliant idea. Like there was something wrong with going to happy hour on a Friday night.

When I arrive at a very crowded Rio Station, I spot Lisette and Sarah right away at the far end of the bar along with several other people from not only my office but from the gallery too. I stop in my tracks and canvass the area to see if Alex is here. As best I can tell from my current vantage point he's not, and I feel a small pang of disappointment. I start moving toward them again until they finally spot me. Sarah raises her mixed cocktail up in the air, waving it back and forth like a lunatic. Some of it spills, just barely missing Lisette, who is also waving me over, sans drink.

"You made it!" Sarah squeals loudly and pulls me into her arms for a big hug. "Yay! Lisette, look! Julia's here!"

While her back is turned, Lisette brings her hand to her mouth, tipping back an imaginary drink and pointing to Sarah, signaling that she's already tipsy.

"Sarah, how long have you been here?"

"Since four-ish, I think," she slightly slurs. "Alex let us leave early today."

"Don't worry, I already took away her keys," Lisette whispers in my ear.

"Is he here?" I discreetly ask them.

Sarah's attempt at a low voice fails spectacularly when she yells, "He's over there talking to some guy, and he's totally eye fucking you right now."

She raises her arm to point in the direction behind me, and I clasp my hand around her wrist to bring it back down. "Dude, what the hell?! Don't point at him!"

"Julia, he was already looking over here," Sarah says, defending herself. "Relax, let me buy you a drink."

Lisette moves aside to make room for me at the bar as Sarah tries to get the bartender's attention. When he finally notices us, Sarah proceeds to order a round of tequila shots, which Lisette politely declines, leaving me to drink two in quick succession. Nobody put a gun to my head, but you can't just leave free alcohol lying around. It's bad luck or something like that. With the effects of the tequila coursing through my veins, making me feel all warm and fluffy—for now, because if I do another two or three of those shots I'll be feeling all gross and want to vomit—I order myself a beer and plant myself on a barstool. The three of us hang out for a while, chatting it up about nothing in particular. About an hour and another couple of beers later, I'm officially tipsy but not sloppy just yet. It's that really good stage where I'm not going to get sick, but I'm not feeling any pain either. Either way, there is no chance I can drive home. So while I still have my wits about me, I dive into my purse and hand over my keys to Lisette. Meanwhile, Sarah, as usual, is being approached by a couple of guys. Poor bastards, they have no clue what they've just signed up for.

After Lisette grabs my keys, she leans in a little closer with a questioning look on her face. "So?"

"So."

"Please, Julia. You know what, 'so.'"

"No, I don't know what 'so,'" I answer with a sly grin.

"What are you going to do about Alex?" she asks.

I push some of my hair off of one shoulder while pretending to adjust myself in my seat. I sneak a glance to where Alex is still staring at me from across the bar. Holy hell! If you could see the way he's looking at me right now. You know how Dracula can do some freaky shit with his eyes that make you want to offer him your neck so he can suck your blood? Well Alex's stare makes me want to stand up and grab him by his loosened tie and lead him into the nearest darkened alley. It's an entirely effective look that I'm seriously considering when Lisette taps me on the shoulder.

"I'm very disappointed in you," she says in an annoyed voice.

"Why? What did I do?"

"This is not like you, sitting over here and hiding like a scaredy-cat from some guy."

Dammit, she's one hundred percent right. I do not sit and hide from anyone—usually. The only problem is that this isn't just anyone we're talking about. Even after the other night on our date I'm still not sure how to act around him without feeling as if I can't find my footing. Come to think of it, why hasn't he come over here to me? Unless he's trapped under something heavy all of a sudden, there is no reason he can't walk over to me and at least say hello. A little something is all I'm looking for, for fuck's sake! I don't think that's asking for too much.

Gah! I need to stop this hamster-spinning-on-a-wheel crap. I will not turn into a full-on neurotic crazy person because of Alex. Nope. At least not today.

Screw this waiting around and trying to psychoanalyze the hell out of this situation. I'm going in.

"You know what? You're right." I take another swig of my beer before waving the bartender over again and ordering myself another shot of tequila.

"What are you doing?" Lisette asks.

Sarah, who was temporarily detained by flirting with yet another guy, notices the shot glass being readied in front of me and claps her hands together. "Oooh, more shots! Can I have one?"

Lisette and I answer her with a resounding, "No."

She frowns. "Bummer."

"Julia needs some liquid courage," Lisette explains to Sarah.

"For what?"

I toss the shot back without a second thought. It burns going down my throat, but after a few seconds I'm okay and I stand up. I take a second to steady myself in my high heels before wiping my hands nervously on my jeans. My dad used to say if you want something bad enough, you have to fight to get it. So here I go, fighting for what I want and hoping that I don't make a complete jackass of myself in the process.

"For this," I tell her as I grab my beer bottle off the bar. "Wish me luck."

I get as far as two steps away from them when I hear Sarah start chanting behind me, "Work it, own it, work it."

God, she is the worst wingman ever, but bless her heart, she means well.

Maneuvering through this crowd is a pain in the ass. Sweaty people bumping into you by accident and on purpose are annoying as hell. The on-purpose ones are the ones you have to watch for. They try to be all Fonzie smooth about it, but it's usually a tool looking to hit on you. But all of it is worth it when my eyes feast upon my intended destination. He's casually leaning against the back wall of the bar by himself like he hasn't a care in the world. The corner of his mouth curls up in a sexy grin with every step that brings me closer until I'm finally standing right in front of him.

He slowly pushes himself off the wall and crowds my inner sanctum, sending my senses into overdrive with his proximity. "I was wondering how much longer you were going to make me wait."

His sexy as all get-out voice is already wreaking havoc on me, and I've only been standing here two seconds, three tops. And my God he smells good. Like seriously good and magically delicious.

"I was wondering the same thing about you."

His hand comes up to move the hair off my neck, and the slight brush of his fingers against my skin sends a jolt straight down to my happy place.

"I didn't want to make you uncomfortable."

"I already told you the other night, you don't make me uncomfortable, Alex."

"I don't?" he asks in a playful tone. He dips his head so he can whisper this time in my ear. "Are you sure about that?"

While he's still close and the tequila is making me brave, I exhale, and in my best come-hither voice say, "You make me anything but uncomfortable."

"Then why have you been avoiding me since you arrived?" he asks.

"Are your legs broken?"

His brow furrows in confusion. "Last time I checked, no."

"Well if they're not broken, then why the hell didn't you just walk on over there to see me?" I lean forward a little to whisper in his ear. "Maybe it's because you're the one who's uncomfortable."

Alex chuckles when he says, "Touché."

"Yeah, right," I mumble and put some much-needed space between us.

He's full-on laughing now. "You're really upset with me for not coming over to you, huh?"

I take a quick sip of my beer, thinking of something clever to say. Nothing. Totally shooting blanks here.

He leans into me so closely that I feel the stubble on his jaw against my cheek when he whispers into my ear. "Cat got your tongue, Julia?"

I can't rationally explain what happens next when Alex tries to stand up straight. It could be attributed to quite a few factors. Let's break it down, shall we?

1. *Alcohol.*
2. *He's too close to my mouth.*
3. *I haven't had sex in a looooong time.*
4. *He almost made me have the best orgasm of my life a few days ago.*
5. *Refer to numbers 1 through 4.*

All of these factors make for a dangerous blend, so instead of letting him get away from me, I lazily run my fingers down his tie with my free hand. He looks on, entranced by my movements when I reach the end and wrap it around my hand in a tight fist. I tilt my head up to meet his piercing blue eyes at the same time I give a small tug on his tie to bring his face closer to mine. I'm determined to win this tug-of-war between us just once.

"You know, Alex, I've been thinking a lot about our date the other night."

"Which part?" he asks with a raised brow. "And be very specific."

Alex scans my face and drags his teeth across his bottom lip. My eyes hungrily follow while secretly willing him via Jedi mind control to do the same thing to my lips, my neck, my breasts, my thighs—I think you get the picture. He tears the beer bottle out of my grasp and taps the shoulder of the nearest body, never once breaking eye contact with me.

"Do I know you?" a man's voice says.

"Here." Alex pawns my beer without another word being spoken to this guy who surprisingly obliges and leaves us alone again.

As I'm trying to suppress my laugh, Alex's hands sweep around my waist and pull me into all his yummy hardness.

"That was kind of rude," I attempt to say in an unaffected voice when all I can think about now is riding his dick like a pogo stick.

"Don't try to change the subject," he throws back at me. "You were about to tell me which part of our date the other night you've been thinking about."

With another light yank of his tie, I bring his head a little lower until I'm level with his ear. I lick my lips, and my tongue makes the tiniest of contact against his earlobe, eliciting a gasp of breath from him. "I've been thinking that I wish I didn't have ground rules at all between us the other night."

Alex hisses and stills his movements. I *finally* have the upper hand, and it feels fantastic.

My victory is short-lived. Because if there is one thing I'm certain of where Alex is concerned, the man likes to be in control just as much as I do. He breaks out of his stupor, spinning me around and then backing me up against the wall. My breathing accelerates into a choppy rhythm while his remains even.

"How much have you had to drink tonight?" he asks in a calm tone of voice, further rattling me.

"What does that have to do with anything?"

"Because if you've had too much to drink, Julia, then I won't attempt to find out exactly how far I can break your ground rules. I don't want to take advantage of the fact that you're even a little bit drunk because I want you to remember everything I do to you."

"Oh."

"So tell me," he demands quietly. "How drunk are you right now?"

"I'm not drunk, Alex."

Technically I'm not, but I'm definitely not sober. In addition to that, I'm turned on and there is nothing worse than being in this state and knowing that there is no relief in sight from him tonight. My fistful of his tie unfurls from my grip and falls back into place against his lean frame. I try to escape from being pinned against the wall, but his grip on my hips tightens and keeps me right where I am.

He leans in and cups the back of my neck with one hand. "Where do you think you're going?"

"Home. Alone," I snort.

"You're really upset with me, aren't you?" he asks with a light-hearted chuckle.

"I'm not upset."

I'm really not. It's more that I'm frustrated that he chose this exact moment to be honorable. I do respect that, but at the same time I wish he would forget about honorable intentions and just take me home and have his way with me.

He scans my face and lets out a reluctant sigh. "Let me take you home."

"Lisette's my DD for the night. So you don't have to worry about me."

He throws his head back and laughs. "You *are* upset with me. Now we're getting somewhere."

"No, we're not 'getting somewhere.' If we were, you'd be taking me home, and we'd be *really* getting somewhere."

All traces of humor vanish from his eyes when he drops his hands from my hips and then brackets them on both sides of my head instead. "Trust me, Julia, if you weren't drunk right now . . ."

"I'm not drunk," I quickly correct him.

"Fine. If you weren't a *little* drunk, I'd take you home and do all sorts of things to you."

"What kinds of things?" I ask breathlessly, and he grins a shit-eating grin since he knows he has me, hook, line, and sinker.

"First, I'd make you take off all of your clothes for me . . . slowly." His eyes stay locked on mine, gauging my reaction when his hand slips under the hem of my blouse and brushes against my skin. I suck in a breath at the contact, wanting so much more and wishing we weren't in a crowded bar at the moment. He continues torturing me by running his fingers lightly across my stomach and then stops when he reaches the button of my jeans.

I run my fingers through his hair before grabbing a handful and playfully pulling his head down. Lining my mouth up to his ear, I lick my lips and then quietly say to him, "Then what would you do to me? And be very specific."

Alex exhales against my cheek and says, "Then . . ."

"Um, excuse me." Lisette's voice interrupts the very vivid play-by-play Alex was starting to get into.

Letting go of my light grip of his hair, I peer over his shoulder because he hasn't moved an inch. Lisette has Sarah on her arm, who has the goofiest smile on her face and is definitely in sloppy drunk territory.

"We're leaving. Do you still need a ride home?" she asks with a tilt of her head to acknowledge Alex still crowding me.

"I'm coming," I tell her, and bring my attention back to him.

"That's exactly what you'll be saying to me—several times," he rasps, enticing me further. Immediately he drops his hands and moves to the side to let me go with them.

The smug motherfucker—and I say that in the most endearing way possible—has me drooling with lust and practically losing my balance as I take my first steps toward Lisette and Sarah.

"Good night, ladies," he calls out to us. I spin my head around to get one last look at him. He's still smiling, and worse, the dimples are out, only adding to his gorgeousness.

I think I mumble an unintelligible good night back to him, but I can't be sure because my thoughts are still between picturing taking my clothes off for him and imagining all the ways he could make me come. It's not until I get outside and the salty ocean air floods my senses that I'm snapped back to reality.

And it's a suck-ass reality. One that involves me going home alone *again* with my lady parts screaming at me for taking that last shot of tequila.

CHAPTER FOURTEEN

I'm dropped off first, thank God. Because if I had to listen to Sarah beg to be taken to IHOP one more time for French toast I was going to punch her in the face.

Why, you ask? I'm sexually frustrated beyond the point of reason, and not in the mood for company with the exception of one person, and that isn't happening tonight.

"God, I'm such an idiot."

There I go talking to myself again as I unlock the door to my house. This only serves to piss me off more since I was just starting to get a handle on that shit.

I toss my keys on the coffee table and walk to the kitchen, where I proceed to pour myself a glass of wine. Hopefully this will help to calm me down a bit before I head to bed alone. But it doesn't help in the slightest. I'm still wound up so tight that if I shoved a piece of coal up my ass it would come out looking like a diamond.

Maybe some music will help me get my mind off things. I take my iPhone out of my purse and head for my bedroom. Once it's docked in its speaker stand, I scroll through the stored music until I find something that I think will work. The beginning chords of John Legend's "Save Room" begin, and I know I've made the right choice. I have to mention that one of the perks of living alone is being able to put on music at whatever time of day or night without being fearful that you'll wake someone up in the next room. With that in mind, I start to sing along as I get undressed and ready for bed.

After I've finished brushing my teeth, I make quick work of going through my closet to pick out my clothes for work tomorrow. Once that's done, I turn off all the lights and pull back the comforter to climb into bed. It's cool against my skin, and I bring it up to my chin to snuggle with it while sinking farther into the mattress.

I lie there for a good half hour listening to music and staring up at the ceiling. What started out as a good idea is starting to annoy the hell out of me. So I lean over and pull the iPhone out of the docking station and leave it on my nightstand.

My legs are restless, and my mind is still playing over what happened in the bar tonight with Alex. It's then that I decide to do the only thing that is going to get me to sleep tonight. I've been so good too, going cold turkey for a couple of weeks, but fuck it, I need to unwind, and this is the only solution.

Leaning over once more, I open the drawer in my nightstand and pull out my vibrator. I've had this thing for a couple of years now after going to a sex toy party I was invited to by a colleague who shall remain nameless.

It was Lisette.

Like I wasn't going to tell you who hosted the sex toy party.

As soon as I saw this thing and heard the name of it, I had to have it. It's bright pink with a smiley face at the base. Just before the head, there is a bulbous part with a bunch of little colorful balls. They say it's for maximum stimulation when it's switched on, but to me it looks like a freaking gumball machine is about to fuck me. There's also this rubberish-looking claw that lines up with my clit. When that part is turned on, I'm usually climaxing within twenty seconds, thirty if I'm lazy and decide not to turn it all the way up. The very best part is the name. It's called the Wascally Wabbit. Can you believe that shit? Every time I come with this thing I want to say, *"That's all folks,"* like Porky Pig at the end of a Looney Tunes cartoon.

I kick the comforter off of me and try to clear my head from all thoughts of Bugs Bunny and back to Alex. It isn't very hard to do. Within seconds I'm already picturing him hovering over me, his mouth trailing down my throat until he finds my breasts. He begins the languorous task of sucking on my nipples with the perfect blend of pleasure and pain. After he's paid enough attention to each one, he licks his way down to my belly button. His hands spread my legs farther so he can teasingly trace the outlines of my underwear with his finger. With one swift movement, his finger breaches the side of my panties and enters me slowly.

I need to get this show on the road because I'm sure I'll break the *Guinness Book of World Records* tonight. I switch on the vibrator and go to remove my panties, but then my cell phone also starts to vibrate, scaring the living shit out of me. I'm so freaked out that I answer it without looking to see who it is first.

"Julia," Alex says with an obvious smile that doesn't help my libido.

I sit up straight in my bed, holding the phone in one hand and the vibrator in the other. "Why are you calling me so late?"

"Did I wake you?"

"No."

"Are you sure I didn't wake you?"

In a huff, I answer, "Alex, I'm sure you didn't wake me up. Care to tell me why you're calling me so late though?"

"I felt bad about how we left things, and I wanted to . . ."

"Alex?" I ask, then pull the phone away from my ear to make sure we're still connected. "Are you still there?"

"What's that noise?"

Jesus Christ, the vibrator is still turned on. I switch it off quickly and hide it under the comforter like I've been caught with my hand in the cookie jar.

"What noise?"

"There was a distinct humming sound, and now it's gone," he surmises like all of a sudden he's Sherlock Holmes.

"Nope, no noise. I don't hear a thing."

"Julia," he says in a warning tone. "What did I tell you about lying to me?"

"You said you'd spank me."

Dammit, I know I sound way too excited and breathless, because he's clearly enjoying it, judging by what he says next.

"You'd like that, wouldn't you?"

Without a moment's hesitation, I answer truthfully and blame it all on the slight buzz that's still lingering. "Yes."

We both stay quiet for a second or two. I can't deny that his sultry and assertive voice is working better on me than any Bugs Bunny vibrator ever could. I fall back onto the pillows and soak it in because as soon as we hang up I'm going to be picking up right where I left off.

"Were you doing what I think you were doing before I called you?" he asks seductively.

"What do you think I was doing?"

"If you were doing what I think you were doing, then I need you to keep going and not let me interrupt you."

"Are you crazy?" I say with a throaty laugh.

"Julia, you've got me batshit crazy thinking about you all the time, but now . . . I've lost my ever-loving mind. I need to hear you."

I bite my bottom lip and consider my options. One, hang up and get back to business. Or two, let him hear me get off over the phone. The *Jeopardy* theme music plays in my head until his velvety voice breaks me out of my thoughts, making my decision that much easier. Option number two it is.

"Were you thinking about me and what I would do to you?"

"Yes."

"Christ," he mumbles, and I giggle, thoroughly enjoying this new form of torture between us. "What are you wearing right now?"

I look down at myself in the near dark and decide that instead of making up some bullshit about wearing a corset or a teddy, I'll tell him the truth. "I'm wearing a white tank top and a pair of black lace boy shorts."

"Lose the tank top. Now."

I tear it off of me as if it were on fire and toss it across my room before lying back down.

He chuckles at how quickly I get back on the phone. "Tell me what you look like now."

"I'm only wearing the black lace boy shorts and lying down on my bed."

"Are you under the blankets?"

"No."

"Good girl," he praises. "Now tell me what you were imagining I was doing to you before I called."

God, this is weird and hot as hell.

"Don't be shy, Julia."

Tightly shutting my eyes, I take a big gulp, and in a throaty whisper I get right into it with him, describing in detail what I had been picturing in my head.

"I was imagining that you were on top of me. You were kissing and licking your way down from my mouth, stopping at my neck for a little while, then moving down to my breasts."

"And then what did I do?" he coaxes softly.

"You were sucking my nipple and pinching the other one with your fingers."

"Take your hands and pinch your nipples for me."

"Okay." I do exactly as I'm told. "Mmmm, that feels so good."

"Fuuuuck," he says, almost growling. "You're killing me, you know that?"

The position of the phone cradled at my ear is messing with our little escapade. I'm going to have to put this thing on speaker so I can play along better.

"Hang on a second."

"Wait, don't you dare hang up on me!" he shouts. His voice is blasting through my speaker phone and right by my ear since I've put it to rest on my pillow.

"Relax, I'm not going anywhere," I purr. "Needed to put my phone on speaker so my hands can be free."

"Lick your fingers," he instructs, wasting no time and diving back in. "Then pinch your nipples again for me."

If there was an award for following directions, I'd win first place by a mile. With a resounding pop from the last finger that I lick, I start rolling each nipple between my forefinger and thumb until I moan into the darkness and my back arches off the bed.

"Does it feel good?"

"Yes. So good, Alex."

"I'd lick and suck your tits until you fucking begged me to stop, Julia."

"I wouldn't want you to stop. I'd want you to suck them harder."

"Holy shit," he mutters. "Pinch them harder."

I'm squeezing the living shit out of my nipples to the point that I may not have any feeling left in them by the time all is said and done. But it's worth it while I envision Alex's mouth wrapped around one, his hooded eyes looking up at me while I writhe underneath him. Jesus, this is stupid good, and it's making me even more ballsy than usual.

"Are you hard for me?" I ask in between moans.

"As a fucking rock."

"I want you to take your cock out and stroke it so I can hear you. And don't make me beg."

An abrupt rustle fills the air while I hear him moving and doing exactly as I've requested. I might climax solely on the visual currently dancing around my head of Alex touching himself, it's that vivid and smoking hot.

"Now back to you," he groans. "Slide your hands down and take your panties off."

My hands follow his instructions to the tee. I hook my fingers inside the waistband while lifting my ass off the bed and removing my already soaked panties.

"Are they off?"

"Yes," I answer.

His voice is becoming rougher, and it spurs me on even more. "Spread your legs and imagine me licking you," he says.

"Mmmmm," I moan, picturing his head between my legs. "I wish you were really here, Alex."

"You like it when I talk dirty to you, don't you?" he says as his breathing becomes more labored.

"I love it."

"Are you ready to come?"

"Are you?"

"Fuck yes," he says with a small chuckle. "Touch yourself and tell me exactly how wet you are for me."

I take two fingers, and they slide in and out so easily it's almost embarrassing. "Drenched."

"Christ."

"Alex," I beg, unashamed now because the need is too much. "I need to come."

"Touch your clit for me, Julia."

I know the second that I flick the oversensitized piece of flesh I'll probably be yelling so loud that I might wake the goddamn neighbors. But I don't give a shit anymore. I need the relief. With a quick flick of my finger, I find the spot that will bring me that much closer to heaven. It takes all of five to six swipes before I'm moaning his name out loud and climaxing. I swear I think I see stars because what makes it even better is hearing Alex having an orgasm at the same time. God help me, it might be the sexiest thing I've ever heard.

My throat is dry, and my heart is still beating wildly in my chest. Our breathing eventually returns to normal after a minute or two of complete silence. I pick the phone up off my pillow and turn off speaker phone. Bringing it up to my ear, all of a sudden I feel nervous, knowing that we've crossed into the big unknown and there is no going back.

"Are you still there?" His voice sounds more relaxed.

"I'm here."

"Are you okay with—"

"With masturbating over the phone with you?" I ask.

"Well, I wasn't going to say it like that, but yes, since you put it that way."

"It's a little weird, but nothing about us has ever been normal. Why should this be any different?"

"Good point," he laughs lazily.

My eyelids start to feel heavy, and I yawn into the phone due to the fact that my body is tuckered out from the release I'd been holding in for too long. Either that or I'm turning into a guy who rolls over and dozes off right after having sex.

"You're tired," he says. "I'll let you go, but only if you promise me one thing."

All I can muster is a barely intelligible mumble of noises that I think resemble a yes.

"Go out with me tomorrow night." He pauses and then adds, "On a real date this time."

"Okay." I yawn again into the phone. The fight has left me; that's how good this little phone sex session was. Do I want to delve in and psychoanalyze the shit out of this right now?

Nope, not at all.

"Wow, that was easy. You're not going to fight me at all on this?"

"Hey," I say, a tad more alert but still overly drowsy. "Don't push your luck, mister. Take the yes and call it quits while you're ahead."

"Fair enough," he concedes. "Good night, beautiful."

I smile to myself in the dark at his parting words and bring the comforter up to my chin, ready to snuggle into it further. And as I drift off into dreamland, sprawled out and naked as the day I was born, I'm still smiling.

CHAPTER FIFTEEN

I wake up the next morning with the birds chirping outside, the sun streaming through my windows, and my alarm clock blaring. It's a scene right out of *Snow White* if it wasn't for the hangover. I reach over with my free hand to hit the snooze button when all of a sudden it dawns on me. My free hand? What in the name of Sweet Fancy Moses is my other hand holding on to? And why am I naked?

Afraid that I might find a horse's severed head in my bed, I gingerly lift the comforter inch by agonizing inch until a pink helmet with a smiley face comes into view. Phew! It's just my vibrator.

Wait a second.

Fragmented memories of last night start coming back to me. There was a happy hour where drinks were had and I flirted like a champ with Alex. Then Lisette drove me home—shit, I need to call her to pick me up. I go to grab my cell phone off the nightstand only to come up empty-handed. What in the blazes is going on today? My head is beginning to throb as I look for my phone until I find it buried underneath the pillows. When I unlock it and go to the recent calls so I can find Lisette's name, my face freezes in horror when I see the last name of the person who called and the time stamp. Now the rest of last night's memories are flooding my brain in all their Technicolor glory.

Don't tell me.

No, wait. Tell me that I didn't do what I think I did.

I did, didn't I?

Oh my God! I had phone sex with Alex last night!

I facepalm myself and groan out loud. The blossoming head-ache that was a dull throb has been upgraded to DEFCON level one status. Jesus, I'll never be able to face him again without think-ing he knows what I sound like when I orgasm.

First things first, I bring the comforter up to cover my body. Apparently I'm modest when I'm the only one here—well, me and the Bugs Bunny vibrator. Ugh, I'm still gripping this thing like it's the Holy Grail of vibrators, so I toss it across my bed, where it lands by my feet.

I decide to call Lisette.

"Good morning, sunshine," she says after answering on the second ring.

"I don't know about it being good," I mumble.

She laughs. "Let me guess—hangover?"

"Among other things."

"Oooh, what other things?"

"Nothing." My voice wavers slightly, and she laughs again. "Can you do me a favor and pick me up on your way to the office?"

"Of course. Can you be ready in about a half hour?"

"Yep."

"See you then."

As soon as she hangs up, I fling the comforter off of me, stum-ble out of bed, and race toward the bathroom. I take the fastest shower ever in the history of showers. All the while I'm not think-ing about "the incident" from last night. I'm so not thinking about it that I'm thinking about it, which gets me to really thinking about it, to the point of dwelling on it.

It's not the first time I've ever had phone sex. But the couple of times when it's happened before, it was in an already-established relationship after we've done the actual deed. Alex and I have just started dating or whatever you call it, and the closest to doing the deed has been with our clothes on. Not one nip slip at this point, and yet I've allowed him to talk me into an orgasm over the phone.

As I'm zipping up the black pencil skirt I had picked out for myself the night before, I freeze in mid-zip remembering something. Dear Lord, I agreed to a date with Alex tonight. I can't sit across from him and try to have a casual conversation when you know I'll be busy thinking about him jacking off over the phone. How is that going to work? Probably something like this: *"Um, can you pass me the butter, and by the way, you make the sexiest noises when you come."*

Just kill me now.

I button up my red silk blouse and grab the first pair of black high heels I can find. I rush through putting on my makeup, and I blow-dry my hair to the best of my abilities. Glancing at the clock, I see that I have three minutes to spare before Lisette is supposed to arrive. I'm darting around like a crazy person, grabbing my keys, purse, and phone when I hear her honking the horn outside. Before I make it to the front door, I turn around and run back to my bathroom, nab the bottle of aspirin for my head, and throw it in my purse—now I'm ready.

My ass isn't completely settled into the front seat when she starts pulling out of my driveway. "Here," she says and shoves a Starbucks cup in my face.

Ahhh, the sweet smell of coffee, the elixir of the gods. "Have I told you lately how much I love you, Lisette? Because I do."

"You're welcome."

I tip back the cup to my awaiting pursed lips and let it swirl around in my mouth for a second before taking a huge gulp. My cell phone starts to chirp as I'm about to take another sip. I dig it out of my purse and stare at the screen. Oh, hell no! Cursing under my breath, I ignore Alex's call and keep drinking my coffee instead. I can't face the music just yet. Plus, how can I have a normal conversation while I have Inspector Gadget sitting to my left chomping at the bit to see who keeps calling me?

"Why didn't you answer him?"

So much for trying to keep it on the down-low. "No reason," I say and shrug my shoulders. "He's probably butt dialing me and has no idea."

"Hmmm. *Muy interesante.*"

"There is nothing interesting about it, Lisette."

"If he's butt dialing you like you say he is, then that would mean your number was the last one called or the last number that called him."

Sliding my sunglasses down the bridge of my nose to peer over at her, I can almost see the wheels turning in her head. I push them back up to cover my eyes and try to change the subject.

"So how did it go dropping Sarah off last night?"

"Fine," she says like it's an afterthought. "But getting back to this Alex thing—"

"Oh my God! Really?"

She laughs again. Seriously, she's laughing. Cackling, to be more accurate, like she's really enjoying herself on my account, which only makes me irritable.

"Lisette, I'm not going to tell you what happened, so drop it."

"Aha! I knew it!"

"Knew what?" I ask in between another sip of coffee.

"I knew something happened between the two of you last night!"

I pivot in my seat to face her. "Nothing happened. That's it. End of story."

She stops at a red light and turns her head to say something when my phone rings again. *Why me?* I think to myself while looking up at the roof of the car in exasperation. I'm a good person. I pay my taxes. I donate to Goodwill. I never change lanes while driving without turning my blinker on first. So why am I being tortured like this?

"Just answer the phone, Julia," Lisette pleads before slowly inching the car forward.

"Fine. I hope you're happy," I snap.

As soon as I swipe the phone to answer his call, he doesn't even give me a chance to say hello. "Were you trying to ignore me?" he guesses with a smirk in his tone.

I suck in a breath and answer truthfully. "Yes."

"And why would you go and do a thing like that?"

"Gee, I wonder why."

Alex's rumbling laugh makes me roll my eyes. "Well you better get over that because not only are we going on a real date later tonight, you and I have a meeting this afternoon to go over some of the particulars with Josie's party, in case you forgot."

Shit, shit, shit! How do I get out of this? Then in the midst of my panic-strewn thoughts I picture sweet little Josie's cherubic face and remember that this is for her. Looks like I'll be taking one for the team after all.

"Judging by your silence, I assume you conveniently forgot about that," he goes on, delighting in his ability to trip me up at every turn.

"I didn't forget, I just—"

"Just what? And remember, don't lie to me," he chides in a naughty tone.

I sigh loudly and tilt my head, only to find Lisette craning her neck like she's Mr. Fantastic from the Fantastic Four attempting to listen in on the conversation. Covering the phone with my hand so Alex can't hear me, I slide my sunglasses down my nose to look at her.

"Ahem! Excuse me, Mr. Fantastic," I say, acknowledging her attempt at eavesdropping.

Lisette straightens her back and shoots me a *who me?* look.

"Yeah, you. Do you mind?"

"Sorry," she mumbles. "Go on."

Putting the phone again to my ear, I lower my voice. "I can't talk right now, Alex. Can we discuss this later?"

"I'll see you at one o'clock in my office," he says. "And Julia?"

"Yes?"

"Don't be late."

"I wouldn't dream of it," I tell him as sickeningly sweet as possible.

The last thing I hear is his roguish laugh when he ends the call, adding to my already crabby mood. How this man can be such a nuisance and still somehow be appealing at the same time confounds me. One minute I'm itching to be with him in the biblical sense. The next minute I have an overwhelming urge to slap him. Everything is so black-and-white where Alex is concerned. Generally, that is the way I deal with most people in my life: either I like you or I don't. But in this scenario it makes me uncomfortable. Makes me feel like I'm out of control. And God how I despise not being in control. I'd much rather be the one calling the shots.

"Do you want to talk about it?" Lisette asks sheepishly.

"Nope. And yes, I'm sure."

The few minutes left of our drive to my car is in silence. Well, not total silence since she decides to turn up the radio when Justin Timberlake's latest single comes on. Can't say that I blame her. It's quite catchy, and plus, you know, it's Justin.

When we arrive at my car, I gather up my things and step out into the blistering Miami morning sun. Not wanting to be drenched in sweat by lingering too long outside, I throw a quick thanks to Lisette over my shoulder. She drives off just as I'm climbing into my Range Rover, and I follow her back the few blocks to my office.

There is no use in pretending that I'm not distracted the entire morning at work. I'm able to power through it, but I'm edgy and having a hard time staying focused. My mind keeps drifting to the impending appointment I have with Alex. I've even tried to watch some *How It Should Have Ended* videos. Specifically the *Lost* one because it still cracks me up. But today, zilch, nada, not one crack of a smile from me. And yes, it's definitely because I'm remembering the phone conversation from last night. That right there might be the more accurate reason why it's so difficult to concentrate. It's enough of a distraction that I'm not even bothering to play with the stress ball, which has been like an extension of my own arm for the last few weeks. I can't lie either and tell you that there isn't a big part of me that is curious to see how this will go later. Because this game we so effortlessly play is part of the allure. The thrill of the chase, if you will.

But what happens when he catches me?

Wait. Don't answer that.

CHAPTER SIXTEEN

You know that feeling you get when you're strapped in your seat on a roller coaster ride and realize there is no turning back? The cars start to lurch forward, inching ever so slowly uphill while your stomach is in knots. The clanking noises of the wheels churning along the track until you get to that inevitable first drop. But at that point all you can do is scream at the top of your lungs from both fear and excitement. That's about as close as I can come to describing precisely how I feel as I approach the front doors of the gallery. I can almost hear Darth Vader's "Imperial March" in the background if I listen closely enough. Jesus, I'm going crazy because I really do hear it.

Oops! That's my dad's ringtone.

I don't know what's worse right now, having to deal with my dad or having to deal with Alex. I take the lesser of two evils, which also buys me some time, and answer the phone.

"Hi, Daddy."

"Julia Ann, where the hell have you been? You and your brother up and disappeared on us the other day without so much as a good-bye. Your mother has been worried sick about you two."

Great, just what I needed right now, a mental image of my parents being horn dogs because of a freaking screwdriver. "Daddy—"

"Don't you 'Daddy' me, young lady," he says with authority. "Just call your mother before she drives me crazy."

"Daddy, she can't be that bad. I bet she just—"

"She's gone insane, Julia! She wants me to help her redecorate our bedroom. I keep telling her to do it herself, but she says she wants us to have a bonding experience and we should do it together."

"Daddy—"

"Now I love the woman to death, you know I do, but if she thinks I'm going to Home Goods one more time just so I can follow her around like a goddamn lost puppy dog, she's got another thing coming."

I sigh loudly into the phone while I begin to pace back and forth at the entrance of the gallery. "Daddy . . ."

"Have you ever been to Home Goods, Julia?"

"Yes, I have, but Daddy—"

"Let me tell you what it's like. It's a fucking nightmare, Julia. A nightmare. It's a glorified Marshall's with no clothes."

"Daddy," I say, trying yet again to get a word in edgewise, but he's on a roll now.

"If I have to listen to your mother tell me about one more set of prints that would look fabulous in the bedroom, I'm going to lose my shit. Don't even get me started on all the choices they have for bedroom linens."

"Daddy—"

"Did you hear what I just said? I called them fucking bedroom linens. They're sheets, for chrissakes! See what she's doing to me? And that's the other thing. I—"

"DAD!" I yell into the phone. People walking by on the sidewalk stop and stare as I compose myself quickly. "I'll call her tomorrow. I promise, okay? I really have to go though."

"Oh, am I keeping you from something more important than bedroom linens?" he says sarcastically. "Welcome to my world."

"I said I'll call her tomorrow, but I really do have to go. I have an appointment that I'm going to be late for." I confirm this by lifting my wrist to double-check the time. Three minutes to one o'clock.

"Fine, go on then," he says in a huff. "I'll let her know to expect your call tomorrow. But you know what would be better? If you stopped by the house instead."

"Don't push your luck, Dad."

He laughs through his good-bye and hangs up. I'm left to wonder if my parents may need to start thinking about separate living quarters when I hear Sarah's voice behind me.

"Are you coming in finally?" she asks all bubbly.

"I was just finishing up with a last-minute phone call. Is Alex ready for me?"

She does a wiggle of her eyebrows and holds the door open farther. "Are you kidding me?" she groans. "He's been asking me if you're here every two minutes for the past half hour."

"Really?"

"Yes, really. He said to tell you to go straight to his office as soon as you arrived."

"Okay, thanks."

My high heels click across the hardwood floor as I make my way to Alex's office. Palms sweating, check. Heart racing, check. Stomach in knots, double check. Of course his is the very last door in the offices of the gallery, too. And to top it all off, it's closed. Ugh, that means I have to knock and announce myself. I don't think I can find my voice long enough to do that. But the heavens part for a brief moment when he opens the door, and then he's standing right in front of me with the most mischievous grin I've ever seen.

He's wearing black pants and a freshly pressed white shirt paired with a simple black silk tie. Trust me, I can tell that it's silk. His dirty blond hair is slightly unruly today and looks as if he's just been running his hands through it. A stray lock of hair brushes across his forehead when he bows his head slightly at my arrival and opens the door wide for me to enter his office.

"We should discuss your ground rules first," he says as I brush past him.

The only thing I have in my arsenal right now is my wry wit and cunning instincts. Bullshit. I don't know what the hell I'm going to say or do. I'm completely out of my comfort zone here, and when he closes the door behind me, I can tell I'm in for it. Don't ask me how I know, I just do. Kind of like my spidey senses are kicking into gear. Well, that and the fact that he grabs me by the wrist and swings me around so that my back is against the door.

Alex lets go of me and clicks the lock into place while scrutinizing my face. He slowly brings his hands up and slides my sunglasses off and tucks them into my purse, which he also takes in his hands. He lowers it to the ground by our feet and moves his eyes away from me for a second to do so. I take the opportunity to try and smoothly move out of this position, only to find myself turned swiftly in his arms so that I'm now facing the door. And to be honest, I'm really not putting up much resistance. I really enjoy being manhandled by him. Yeah, I'm kind of surprised by that too, seeing as how I'm usually the one in charge.

For a few seconds neither of us moves an inch. Then he steps in closer until his body is flush against my backside. I feel his arousal pressing against me, and even though I don't do backdoor action, it's still a huge turn-on.

"As I was saying . . . your ground rules." He places his hands on my shoulders and then runs them down my arms. "I'm of the opinion that they're a waste of our time at this point because there are far too many things I want to do to you. And after last night, there is no fucking way that I can stand to be away from you for one more moment."

Alex takes my hands in his and raises them until my palms are resting on the door slightly above my head. When he lets go, he swipes my hair to the side and holds it in place with one hand while the other skims down the side of my body and eventually stops at my hip. He leans in closer so that his lips graze my ear, and I close my eyes, relishing the contact.

His breath is warm and his voice gravelly when he finally speaks. "Do you want me to stop?"

"I . . ."

"Julia," he says seductively while his hand trails lower, sending shivers down my spine. He grabs a fistful of my skirt. "It's an easy question." He pauses and kisses me below my earlobe. "Yes . . ." Another kiss, this time on my neck. "Or no." He punctuates the *no* with a thrust against my ass.

I don't think I've ever been this aroused in my life. He hasn't technically done one thing to me, yet I'm in his control. Under his thumb. Damn the Rolling Stones and finally figuring out what the hell that song is really about. Christ, why am I thinking about a freaking song that is probably more than twice as old as I am when I'm about to get nailed by Alex? *Focus, Julia!*

"No," I murmur in between ragged breaths that are now coming in a rush.

Come on, did you really think I'd be able to hold up much longer? Me neither.

Alex immediately lets go of my hair and uses both hands to inch my skirt higher and higher. It ends up being bunched up around my waist, my panty-clad ass on full display for him. I give a silent prayer of thanks to the underwear gods that I'm wearing the good shit today. La Perla in the house, to be precise.

"Good girl," he whispers roughly. His hands move to the buttons on my blouse, making quick work of them until it's completely open.

His lips are nipping and kissing along my neck to my ear and back again, causing a rush of heat between my legs. I tilt my head to give him better access, and he takes the hint. But his hands aren't moving anymore. I need him to touch me. Now.

"Tell me," he demands as if he can read my mind.

"Touch me."

At once, Alex's hands are tearing down the cups of my bra and taking my breasts in his hands. His thumb and forefinger start pinching my nipples while his tongue sweeps a trail from my neck to my ear. I throw my head to rest on his shoulder and grind my ass against his dick like a cat in heat, needing more contact and arching my back in the process. His hand lets go of one breast to grab hold of my chin so that he can move it closer to his face. When our mouths finally connect, it's off to the races.

His tongue darts out to taste me, and I suck on it slowly, causing him to growl into my mouth, and oh sweet Jesus, that alone almost makes me want to orgasm. I move my hand behind his head to keep him in place, wanting to deepen the kiss. It quickly starts to spiral out of control when he slides his hand down the front of my body, causing a hot trail of anticipation the entire way until resting just above the lace of my black panties.

I feel restless and close to begging when he lightly traces his fingers along the edges, touching and teasing me everywhere but where I want him to. Alex breaks off the kiss to look at me with pure desire in his eyes at the same time his hand finally breeches the thin lace. When I feel the brush of his thumb against my already oversensitized nub, I almost come on the spot. Then he quickly follows that up by putting a finger inside of me and slowly withdrawing it.

"Fuck, you're so wet," he says through gritted teeth.

He's now full-on finger fucking me, and his thumb is rubbing circles on my clit when I moan out loud—really loud—temporarily forgetting where we are.

"If you want me to keep going, you're going to have to be quiet. Can you do that, Julia?"

"Yes," I answer, in between choppy breaths while his finger is moving slowly in and out of me at an erotic pace.

I reach behind me to press my palm against his erection, and I only get a few rubs in before he grabs my wrist and pins it against the door again.

"Is that what you want?" he asks roughly.

When I don't answer him right away since I'm on the verge of splitting in two, he stops his ministrations and gently tugs at my earlobe with his teeth. He lets go only to trail his lips across my neck while removing his hand from inside my panties. The next thing I hear is the sound of his belt buckle being undone, immediately followed by a choir of angels in my head singing, "Hallelujah."

"Answer me. Do you want me to fuck you?"

"Yes."

After a second or two of hearing his clothes rustle behind me, Alex leans in again and presses his lips to the nape of my neck before bringing his mouth to my ear to whisper, "Turn around."

I do as I'm told. His tie is gone, and his dress shirt is unbuttoned to reveal his perfectly tanned and toned flesh. His eyes covet every single part of my semi-undressed body. It feels as if his hands are touching me while he does this, taking his time to look me over, committing every curve to memory. Finally he breaks out of his spell and drops to his knees in front of me. He yanks my panties down to my ankles and over my high heels. When I try to remove my shoes, he looks up at me and says, "Leave them on."

I feel his lips and tongue inching up my inner thigh as his hands slowly move up the backs of my legs. At the first brush of his tongue against my clit, my eyes close and my head falls back against the door with a loud thud.

I'm not going to last long. I wish I could, but I know I'm not. It's like a double-edged sword. You want that sweet relief so badly, but getting there feels just as good if not better. Especially when you have a man who knows what the hell he's doing down there. God, there's really nothing worse than a guy who can't go down on you properly. Right, ladies? Then you have to give the shoulder tap and try to give directions, and who has time for that? Not this girl. But with Alex there is no question; he's hitting all the right spots. When he inserts his fingers inside of me, it takes all of me to stave off the impending explosion. But he can tell I'm close because not even a second later he takes the vulnerable flesh in between his teeth and sucks on it with the perfect amount of pressure, and the first ripples of my orgasm start to roll through me.

My hands move into his hair as I ride the wave and to keep him in place, wanting to prolong it. When it gets to the jumpy, hypersensitive part of the ride, he slows it down by removing his fingers and lazily licks me until he places a light kiss on my inner thigh. With my eyes still closed, I give a small tug on his hair to let him know I want him to stand up. He does, and I immediately start making quick work of unzipping his pants.

I open my eyes just as Alex takes my face in his hands and starts to kiss me again in an unhurried manner. I can taste the remnants of me on his lips, and it drives me further into a state of desperation than I ever was before. It's one of those teeth-scraping, tongues-battling, out-of-control kisses while my hand dives into his pants and takes his cock in a strong grip. I'm pumping away— thank you, stress ball reliever—when he breaks off the kiss and dips his head to start sucking on a nipple. His blue eyes peer up at me as it pops out of his mouth, and he swirls his tongue along the pink tip before doing the same thing to the other one.

That's it. My breaking point. I want him to bury himself inside me like yesterday. I shove his pants down his hips and look down at his dick. I take it in my hand to stroke it again. Magnificent.

Circumcised, smooth, hard enough to hammer nails with, and standing up at attention waiting to get on with the fucking. It's not often I feel the urge to drop to my knees and blow a guy until his eyes roll into the back of his head, but glancing at Alex as his breathing becomes more erratic, I instantly want to.

I start to slide down the door to do just that when his hands grip me under my arms to pick me back up. He lets me go for only a moment. Next thing I know he's lifting one of my thighs and picking me up as if I'm light as a feather so that I'm forced to wrap both of my legs around him. I feel the tip of him right at my impatiently wet entrance, teasing me as it slides up and down. On one trip down I adjust myself in his arms to better position my hips and try to trap him. The bastard eludes me and chuckles.

"Alex, if you don't fuck me right now, I'm never talking to you again," I demand in a low hiss.

"Is that so?" he asks before sucking on my bottom lip.

"Yes."

He slides the tip upward again, brushing my clit with it this time, and I moan his name out loud.

"Your wish is my command," he rasps.

His arms, which are holding me up, come down slowly to lower me onto him. It's agonizingly erotic to feel him entering me inch by torturous inch until I'm fully seated on him while he stares intently at me. I feel full and have an incredible need to start moving, but he holds me completely still. He brings his forehead to rest against mine as a rush of breath escapes him. Cupping his face in my hands, I pull him away and latch my lips onto his, wanting to have his tongue invade me while he's inside me. I grind my hips against him, and we both moan at the contact.

"Fuck, you feel so goddamn good," he says, his voice a whisper and his breath hot against my lips.

"Please move," I say back to him and grip his hair. "Now."

With that, the corners of his mouth turn up to reveal a sly smile, and he slides out of me until only the tip is left. I whimper at the loss and pout.

"Do you want me to beg? Is that it? Because I will. I don't give a shit anymore."

"Would you?" he asks. "Would you beg me to slam my cock into you?"

I lean my head forward and lick the outline of his ear and whisper, "Please slam your cock into me. Do it hard and fast and don't you dare stop."

I barely get the end of that sentence out before he thrusts into me so hard that I see stars. My back rams into the door roughly, and it sounds as if we may have made some cracks in the wood. Apparently Alex is very good at taking direction. Good to know.

"Oh my God," I cry out in between ragged breaths.

"Shh," he says and covers my mouth with his hand.

Alex spins me around with my legs still wrapped around him and carries me to the edge of his desk with his pants around his knees. I look behind me to see a couple of stacks of papers and general office supply crap.

"How important is all of this stuff?" I ask, pointing at his desk.

"Not as important as you."

With a devious smile on my face, I shove every single thing off his desk, and it all goes flying everywhere and anywhere. He pushes me back so that I'm lying down on his desk. I open my legs as wide as I can for him, and he licks his lips at the sight. I have no shame at this point, and it feels fantastic to be so reckless. I beckon him with my finger, and he obeys. Again with the directions—such a good boy. He guides himself inside me and picks up right where he left off.

It's hard and fast, just how I need it to be. I'm quickly approaching the brink again with every thrust of his pelvis. With our bodies now slick with a slight sheen of sweat and the sweet smell of sex in the air, he props himself on his forearms to look down at me. I bring my hands up to twist my nipples in between my thumbs and forefingers, and he lets out a string of curses under his breath while watching me.

His thumb trails along my bottom lip, and I take it in my mouth to suck on it. "You're going to kill me, you know that?"

I answer him by lifting my knees higher and giving him a better angle. Alex responds by taking his thumb out of my mouth and wedging it in between us to brush my clit as he continues to drive into me.

"Fuck yes!" I yell, not caring anymore who is listening to us.

My inner walls grip onto his dick as one of the most intense, mind-blowing orgasms burns through me. I faintly hear Alex say something about how good it feels before he lets loose and groans into my neck when he comes hard, and it's the most exquisite sound I've ever heard in my life. Right up there with the sound of his belt buckle coming undone.

We lie still for a few minutes, trying to get our breathing back to normal. Finally he lifts his head from the crook of my neck and kisses me, long and deep. When he breaks off the kiss, he brushes away hair that is sticking to my forehead and says, "Just so you know, we're going to be doing that again."

I'm not running anymore; he's caught me fair and square. So my answer to that is simple. "I'm counting on it."

CHAPTER SEVENTEEN

I wake up the next morning naked again, on my stomach and entangled in chocolate-brown bedsheets. Alex's bedsheets, to be exact. He's still sleeping with his arm draped across my lower back, a leg thrown over both of mine, and his head on my upper back almost pinning me underneath him. Huh. He's a cuddler. Interesting.

Oh, yeah. How did I get here?

Well, after the afternoon fuck-fest in his office, we decided that work was overrated and took the rest of the day off. We drove separately to his house, where we proceeded to get to know each other more intimately. In other words, we continued to screw each other's brains out—among other things—until the wee hours of the night when my vagina started to go numb on me.

Other things means eating a quick meal at around midnight in his bed. That meal consisted of homemade ice cream sundaes. And I guess I should mention that we ate them off each other's bodies. Let's just say Alex really, I mean *really*, likes his ice cream.

That would explain why, when I try to slide out from underneath him, parts of my body are sticking to the sheets like crazy glue. Here's the thing about using your body as a dessert plate: it's sexy and fun while it's happening, but the ugly truth is that it's not anywhere near being sexy the next day. It doesn't help that movies and books have perpetuated this illusion of glamour by having the characters suddenly fresh as a daisy the next day and not at all what you're really going to be looking and feeling like—one giant hot mess.

Right now my hair is probably a rat's nest, and from the few clumps I can see fanned out on the pillow, there are some rainbow sprinkles embedded in it that were used as a topping for the sundaes. Tack on to that the rancid morning breath I have brewing in my mouth and the not-so-fresh feeling down south, and I'd say this bright idea is downright disgusting in the light of day and makes you question why the hell you felt the need to lick food off of someone's body in the first place.

So now what I really need is a *Silkwood*-quality shower and a toothbrush, pronto.

Don't get me wrong, I rather enjoy feeling Alex's warmth all around me first thing in the morning. Especially since he's holding me under him like he doesn't want me to get away. It makes this very Grinch-like heart of mine skip a beat or two, to be honest. But if he wakes up and takes one look at me in my current state of dishevelment, he may think he woke up with the actual Grinch instead of me.

First my legs. Ever so slowly I drag them out from underneath him until they are completely free. Next, the upper half of my body. This is way trickier. Carefully, I slide to my left and make it a full inch before I'm forced to stop because a nipple is stuck to the sheet. I have to bite my bottom lip, count to three in my head, and tear it off like a Band-Aid. Here goes nothing.

Dammit, that hurts! The next time you think about doing kinky shit in bed, remember me in this very moment. But so far so good because Alex hasn't moved and is still sleeping, even though my tit needs a real Band-Aid at this point.

Okay, now I can start sliding again to my left ever so gingerly. It takes me another few moments until I'm finally out from under him. The lower half of my naked body is hanging off the side of the bed and I'm slithering the upper half along nicely when I dare to sneak a peek at him.

His one eye is open and staring back at me, and the side of his face that is visible is smiling wide enough that his dimple is flashing. Now that's just not fair. He looks absolutely edible and sexy as hell lying there on his stomach with the sheet draped just below his hips to reveal a hint of his ass.

Let me just say that I saw it last night, and it's perfection. Songs may have been written about his ass, it's that inspiring.

"What are you doing?" he asks, amused at my current position.

"Trying not to wake you up."

"I am awake."

"I can see that," I say with a smirk. "How long have you been awake?"

"Long enough."

"Why didn't you say anything?"

He chuckles. "Because it was far too entertaining watching you try to get out of bed."

In the distance I hear the familiar opening bars of Diana Ross and Lionel Richie's "Endless Love." His brow furrows in confusion while my expression is somewhere along the lines of "the jig is up." I'm sure it's Sabrina calling me to find out where I am since I'm missing our weekly Skype session.

"Is it my imagination," he says, picking his head up, "or is there a really cheesy love song from the eighties playing somewhere in my house?"

"That would be my cell phone."

"You have that song as a ringtone?" He pauses, looking me over thoughtfully, trying to piece it together on his own. "Who is it?"

"It's not what you think," I answer sheepishly with a slight shrug of my shoulder. "It's Sabrina."

"Are you going to answer it?"

"Not right now, no."

"Why not?"

"Because I'd really rather not explain this to her right now," I say, motioning between us with my hand. The song stops, and I'm positive that she's leaving me a concerned voice mail wondering where I am.

"Will you be telling her?"

"No . . . probably . . . yes," I admit. "She is my best friend, you know."

"And what will you tell her exactly?" he asks.

"I haven't thought that far ahead because all I'm thinking about is getting myself in the shower."

His playful smile comes back in full force, and he props himself up on his elbows. "Can I join you?"

Looking at him right now has me momentarily speechless; his dirty blond hair is a beautiful mess and has that morning-after-great-sex look, his crystal-blue eyes are sparkling, and his muscular and gorgeous naked body is barely covered by the sheet.

"Julia?"

"What?"

"I thought I lost you for a minute there," he says, noticing how I spaced out for a second or two.

"Nope, still here. But if you don't mind, I'd like to shower alone."

I know. I'm such a Debbie Downer, right?

Alex raises one eyebrow in surprise. "Of course, go ahead. I'll wait until you're done."

"Thanks," I mumble, because it feels awkward all of a sudden. "Do you mind turning around?"

"What?" he asks incredulously.

"Do you mind turning around? I'm naked."

"I know. I like it."

"Alex, on top of being naked, I probably look like Medusa right now."

His hand darts out and cups the side of my face tenderly. "You have never looked more beautiful to me. And as for the naked thing, you do remember last night, right?"

I blush. Can you believe it? I blush and feel a flutter of butterflies in my stomach remembering some of the things we did last night in this very bed. "So you're not turning around?"

"Nope," he says with a boyish grin. He rolls over then and puts one arm behind his head. The sheet somehow continues to cover the bottom half of his body, but the part that I can see is even better in the light of day. Much better.

I roll my eyes, and he laughs at how uncomfortable I obviously am. "Fine. Have it your way."

With the grace of a bull in a china shop, I flop my legs down until my toes touch the hardwood floor. My palms are facedown on the mattress and ready to shove off the bed at the right time. To the untrained eye, I probably look like I'm about to do some kind of push-ups. What's strange is I'm normally not timid like this. For some reason with Alex, even though he's become more than familiar with my body over the course of the last twenty-four hours, I feel incredibly self-conscious.

Just like disengaging my nipple from the sheet, I stand up and start strutting over to the bathroom with all the fake confidence in the world. Alex makes a low whistle of appreciation, and I throw him a deadly look over my shoulder, which only serves to make him laugh as I close the door behind me.

I make quick work of turning on the knobs in his shower, and I step back while waiting for the water to get hot. While I'm waiting, I decide to look for toothpaste to take this god-awful taste out of my mouth.

HOLY SHIT! When did I become Dee Snider from Twisted Sister?

I can't even bear to look at myself in the mirror for too long, that's how scary I look. Jesus. And he thinks I look beautiful like this? It might be time for Alex to get his eyes checked. My eyes scan the sink area until I find the tube of toothpaste. I squirt some on my finger and use it to brush my teeth quickly before turning around and stepping into the shower.

It's just what I needed.

Not wanting to take too much time in here, I shampoo and use his bodywash—no conditioner because he's a man and doesn't understand the importance of it—and stand under the streams of hot water hitting me from every angle due to the multiple shower heads for a few more minutes before turning it off. I squeeze out the excess water from my hair before opening the glass door, and then I grab the nearest towel to dry off. After I wrap it around me, I step back into the bedroom to find Alex in the exact position I left him in.

A small smile is playing at the corners of his mouth—just enough for him to look impossibly sexy and irresistible. I can't believe I'm thinking what I'm thinking right now. My freshly scrubbed clean body is wondering the same thing. Even my vagina is in disbelief since I just started to regain feeling down there.

To hell with it. You only live once, right?

I slink over to the foot of the bed, holding up a towel that barely covers me. Alex goes to move, but I raise my hand and wag my finger at him. "Don't move."

He settles back to his previous position of sitting up against the padded headboard. His erection is already straining underneath the sheet, and it brings a rush of warmth between my legs. When my eyes come back to his face, he smiles unabashedly at the fact that he's ready, willing, and able before he drops his vision to my hand holding up the towel.

"You sure you want to get all dirty again?" he asks, his voice thick with desire.

I answer him by dropping the towel, letting it pool around my feet and allowing him to get a good long look at every inch of my body. Placing one knee on the bed, then the other, I start crawling my way to him. When I reach his chest, my tongue starts a trail from the smattering of light hair below his navel all the way up to his right nipple. I take it in my mouth and suck hard before releasing it. The taste of him is so very familiar now as my tongue swirls across it once more and I keep licking my way up to his neck.

I'm straddling him but still perched on my knees when he wraps my wet hair around his hand and pulls back roughly, forcing me to look at him, bringing his mouth to within a breath of mine. We're both breathing heavily; his eyes are a darker shade of blue and full of lust.

"You didn't answer my question," he whispers. "Are you sure you want to get dirty again?"

"Absolutely filthy."

I dart my tongue out to lick his bottom lip, and a low moan escapes him. My God, that moan of his is enough to kill me. Death by ridiculously hot sex with Alex, what a way to go. He kicks the sheets lower and completely off of him. His cock is perched at my entrance, but instead of impaling myself with it, which takes an unbelievable amount of control on my part, I take it in my hand and start rubbing it against my clit.

Alex's hand tightens in my hair as the friction intensifies. "Make yourself come for me," he growls against my mouth.

I'm good at directions too, for all of you keeping score at home.

Using Alex's dick, sliding it up and down and all over the intended target has me on the verge already. What makes it even more intense is watching him watch me while I do it. His eyes burn through me as I use his body to fulfill my need.

"Alex, God, I'm so close."

He takes my bottom lip between his teeth and then sucks on it with the perfect amount of pressure. When he lets go, he swipes his tongue across it slowly. "After you make yourself come, I'm going to fuck the shit out of you."

And that's all it takes. Seriously. He barely gets the words "of you" out of his mouth before I'm shattering into a million pieces and panting his name out loud.

He cups my face in his hand and ravages my mouth with his, our tongues dancing to a rhythm all their own while my body comes down from its high. When we break off the kiss, our foreheads rest against each other's.

"You're so fucking beautiful when you come, Julia."

His whispered words make me feel all warm and gooey inside, but I don't have time to dwell on it. He hugs me to him as he sits up and starts moving us to the side of the bed with my legs wrapped around him until his feet are on the floor. I climb off of him and go to stand, but he stops me.

"Get on your hands and knees on the bed," he instructs me, his voice laced with authority and hunger.

After I arrange myself like he wants me to, I look over my shoulder at him poised behind me, slowly stroking himself. I bite my lip and watch as he settles himself into position and takes hold of my waist before thrusting into me without any mercy. He keeps plowing into me, over and over, setting an unforgiving pace of straight-up, balls-to-the-wall fucking, and God how I love it.

I throw my head back and meet him thrust for thrust. I grip my hands like a vise onto the ice-cream-stained sheets when I feel his hand skim down my spine until he reaches my waist. The next thing I know he smacks my ass with his open palm. Not hard, but hard enough that it stings for a second. At first I'm shocked, but I have to admit, it feels so good that I want more.

"Do it again," I say through clenched teeth and look over my shoulder at him. His brow furrows in concentration, and he draws his hand back and slaps me again, this time a little harder.

He slaps me one more time, not any harder than the last time, but the lingering sting is beyond pleasurable, and mixed with his cock slamming into me, it's the perfect combination. Alex grabs hold of my hair in a tight fist and grips my waist tightly with the other hand. I can't believe it, but I'm going to come again, and hopefully I get to before he does because I know he's close.

He yanks my hair back and drapes his body over my back. His mouth hovers over my ear when he says, "Hold on, baby."

Alex lets loose behind me and turns it up a notch. When he reaches around with his hand to start rubbing my clit, I lose myself in a blinding orgasm, and not a second too soon either, because he follows closely behind me. His movements slow down until he pulls out entirely and wraps his arm around my waist and drops down beside me on the bed. I'm already flat on my stomach when I turn my head to find him staring right back at me with a pleased look on his face.

He leans forward and kisses my temple while his fingers trace my back delicately. So different from the sex-crazed Alex from a moment ago. But I like it, a lot. I could get used to this, whatever *this* is.

"You're dirty again," he points out.

"I know, but it was totally worth it."

He lightly chuckles. "You're not so bad yourself."

I yawn and stretch my limbs before propping myself up on my elbows. "I need to shower again and maybe take a nap. And not for nothing, but you really need to wash these sheets."

"I will," he says and places a kiss on my shoulder. "After we get out of the shower."

"We?" I ask with a raised eyebrow.

"Yes, *we*. I earned it." He sits up and drags my tired body along with him as he pulls us up to standing. "Let's go, sleepyhead."

"I'm not sleepy," I say through another yawn, causing him to laugh. "You should take it as a compliment."

"Trust me, I do," he says proudly. "But I'd like you to stay awake a little longer. You never know what could happen in the shower."

"Fine. I'll stay awake."

When we start walking toward the bathroom, he lightly slaps my ass in the same spot as before, and I rub my cheek to soothe it.

"Hey! What was that for?"

"Just making sure you stay awake," he says, and winks before ducking into the bathroom ahead of me.

I follow closely behind, thinking to myself about how many personalities Alex seems to have. There's at-work Alex, friend Alex, sex-crazed Alex, tender Alex, and now this, this carefree and fun Alex. All of them add up to one hell of a man, and I'm starting to think that maybe I didn't really know him at all before. That this Alex that I'm slowly getting to know is more than I gave him credit for and definitely more than I ever could have hoped for.

Stop it, Julia. Don't get your hopes up. Something always goes wrong.

Huh? Where the hell did that come from? Jesus, I need to get a grip and stop thinking the worst is always around the corner.

"Are you coming in?" Alex asks, breaking me out of my thoughts.

Sweet Jesus.

I can now add soaking wet Alex to the list, and I have to say, it's probably my favorite out of all of them.

CHAPTER EIGHTEEN

I pull into my driveway about an hour later, freshly showered *again*, my legs feeling like jelly, and wearing the same clothes as yesterday. I already texted Sabrina on my way here to let her know that I was alive and well and would be making my weekly Skype call a little later than usual.

The only thing I bet you're wondering about is whether we had shower sex or not. To answer your question: no, we didn't. Instead, he washed my body from head to toe and vice versa. Then the strangest thing happened, which I still can't make heads or tails of; he held me to him under the streams of water for a few minutes. What's even more strange is that I let him. And yet even more odd, neither one of us had a sarcastic, flirty, or biting thing to say to each other. As a matter of fact, we were deathly quiet throughout the whole thing, making it feel far more intimate than all the sex we'd had up until that point.

Ah, the sex.

Hands down, the best sex of my life.

I'm not one to gloat, but I was right. I had a feeling he'd be amazing. What I didn't expect was for it to be so good that I'm craving more from him. A lot more. So much more that it borders on pornographic.

And this is where it gets a bit tricky.

See above where I told you about our Harlequin Romance moment in the shower?

I can't pretend it didn't happen, just like I can't lie about how it made me feel safe, comforted, and . . . cherished. It's not insta-love, by any means. Well, I may be slightly enamored with his dick, but that's beside the point. What I mean is that I've known Alex for a few years. In the last year alone things have definitely been different between us. I don't know specifically when the shift happened from friends/colleagues to flirtatious friends/colleagues, but somewhere along the line it did. It throws a monkey wrench into my vow of staying away from men altogether, but I'm not going to complain. I'm going to try and embrace it and live in the moment instead.

Oh, and did I mention that he wouldn't let me leave his house until I agreed to go out to dinner with him tonight? He was adamant about it and was quite persuasive. Something about how since we were supposed to go out on a date last night, but instead ended up in his bed by midafternoon and didn't leave there until this morning, I still owed him one.

So I agreed. Of course I did; I'm not a complete moron.

He wouldn't tell me where we were going either, only that I should wear something semi-nice. As a woman, that translates into spending an inordinate amount of time in my closet for the rest of the day trying to find the perfect semi-nice outfit before he picks me up at seven thirty later tonight. But before I star in my own episode of *What Not to Wear*, I have to talk to Sabrina.

I immediately take my laptop out and power it up, leaving it on the kitchen table while I make a pot of coffee. As soon as it starts to brew, I cheat a little by putting my mug underneath the stream. Once it's full to the brim, I sit down and make my Skype call to Sabrina.

"Good morning, Scully," she says, pointing out the *X-Files* coffee mug in my hand. "Oh, I'm sorry. I mean good afternoon."

"Is it afternoon already?"

"Are you going to spill, or am I going to have to drag it out of you?"

"Spill what?" I answer coyly.

"Um, let's see. It's after one o'clock in the afternoon on a Saturday, your hair is soaking wet, you have no makeup on, and you're still wearing your work clothes from yesterday."

I glance down at my clothes and chide myself for not changing before starting this session with her.

"How very observant of you, Mulder," I say back, using my old nickname for her since she has the same exact coffee mug as me. "Can we at least get the pleasantries out of the way before I spill?"

"Sure. I'll go first," she says. "I love you, and I miss you like crazy."

"Aw, me too, sweetie."

"Okay, so now that that's out of the way, spill," she demands, leaning back in her chair and waiting for me to fill her in.

I take another sip of my piping hot coffee and then clear my throat dramatically, thinking of the best way to tackle this. I know, I know, it shouldn't be a big deal, but it feels weird.

"Stop stalling, Julia."

"I slept with Alex," I blurt out.

Sabrina doesn't say a word, so I keep going. "I just left his house since I spent the night there."

No reaction from her.

"We had phone sex a couple of nights ago too."

Nothing.

"He's picking me up tonight to take me out to dinner."

She's still quiet as a church mouse.

"And knowing me, I'm probably going to end up sleeping with him again after our date tonight."

Crickets.

Finally, I see the tiniest hint of her shoulders shaking, and a smile creeps up, followed by an explosion of laughter.

"What's so funny?" I ask her defensively.

She wipes away the tears from her eyes from laughing so hard. "You. That's what's so funny."

"Why am I so funny?"

"Because, Julia," she says with another quick swipe underneath her eye, "it was so obvious that there was something going on between you two from the last time we talked. But for whatever reason you didn't want to tell me."

"It's weird," I confess.

"No, it's not. You're only making it seem weird."

"You don't think it's even a little weird?"

She sighs and then leans forward again so her elbows are propped on the desk in front of her. "Nope, not at all. In fact, I think it's great. Alex is—"

"Amazing," I say, finishing the sentence for her.

Sabrina smiles fully then, all teeth and gums. "Yes, he is. But what I was going to say is that I think he's kind of perfect for you and that we're just friends. You of all people should know that better than anyone. So stop saying you feel weird about it, because you shouldn't."

"I know. You're absolutely right, and I'm sorry I kept it from you. Although there wasn't much to keep from you up until recently, to be honest."

"What about that Marisa person you were telling me about?" she asks thoughtfully.

I purse my lips and make a face of distaste at the mere mention of Miss Teen USA before explaining the situation to Sabrina. "They're not dating really. As it turns out, they never were, according to him and his niece."

At the mention of Josie, Sabrina's eyebrows shoot up in curiosity. "Yeah, about that," I say. "Do you remember that deal Alex and I made last year to get your résumé to your now boss?" Sabrina nods in understanding. "Well, he finally decided to cash in on the favor I owe him."

"What does he want you to do?"

"Plan his niece's tenth birthday party at his house."

She lets out a small giggle. "That sounds like fun."

"It is. I'm having the best time planning it."

Right then it occurs to me that with all the crap that went down yesterday, I really was supposed to have a meeting with Alex about the party. Obviously we got sidetracked, so I'll have to remember to bring it up to him at some point tonight.

"So, has he restored your faith in men?" Sabrina asks teasingly.

I bring the mug to my lips with an evasive smile. "Perhaps."

"Oh my God, I just had a great idea!" she yells, making me almost spit my coffee out. "We should all go out to dinner the next time I'm in town."

"Sabrina, settle down. Let's not get ahead of ourselves," I say in between coughs. "We only started dating, or hooking up—whatever you want to call it."

"Well, promise me that you'll at least think about it."

I raise my hand up and twiddle my pinky finger at the screen. "Fine. Pinky swear."

Sabrina does the same thing on her end with her finger before letting me know that she's running late to meet up with Tyler and has to cut the session short.

"That's fine. I have to start looking for something to wear that's 'semi-nice' anyway, and I really would like to take a nap before Alex picks me up later."

"Wore you out, did he?" she guesses with another giggle.

"You have no idea, Sabrina."

We end the session as I finish what coffee is left in my mug. After a quick refill, I head straight into my bedroom. First, I change into a pair of beat-up sweatpants and an old Depeche Mode concert T-shirt that has seen better days before tackling the outfit situation.

An aggravating hour later, I'm staring at possible selections on my bed when my cell phone rings. Holding it in my hand, I roll my eyes and prepare myself for the worst before I answer it.

"Hi, Mom."

"Hello, sweetheart," she replies. "Your father said you'd be coming over today. What time should we be expecting you?"

"Mom, I didn't say that."

"Carter! Pick up the phone!"

Oh dear God, it's one of those calls.

My dad gets on the line in the middle of yelling about a play gone awry in the college football game he's currently watching. "What kind of bullshit call was that, ref? Pass interference, my ass! Let them play the game, for chrissakes!"

"Carter!"

"What?"

"I thought you said Julia was coming over today," my mom says to him.

"No I didn't."

"Yes you did."

"No, I most definitely didn't say that. I told you she'd be calling you today."

"Are you sure?"

"Marilyn, I may be retired, but I'm not senile."

My mom sighs into the phone. "I never said you were going senile, but I could have sworn you told me she was coming over today."

"Are you sure you're not the one going senile?"

I clear my throat loudly to get their attention. "I'm sorry to interrupt you two, but is my presence required within this conversation?"

"Julia?" my dad says, completely puzzled. "When did you get on the phone?"

"I've been here the entire time, Dad."

"Are you watching the Hurricanes game, Julia? The fucking refs are killing us. It's total bullshit."

"No, I'm not watching the game, Dad. I'm kind of busy, actually."

My mom decides to chime in. "Is that why you can't come over?"

"Um, no. I'm trying to find something to wear for a date I have tonight," I confess, and take a seat on the edge of my bed. My dad is momentarily distracted by another god-awful call, so my mom continues with her questions.

"Is this your first date with the lucky guy?" she asks excitedly.

"Yes, kind of."

"It either is or it isn't, Julia," my dad says, popping back into the conversation.

"It's complicated."

"That doesn't sound promising," he adds under his breath.

My mom butts in next. "How can it be your first date and already be complicated?"

I fall back on my bed, exasperated, and onto some of the outfits I'd laid out.

"Well, Carter, obviously there is something Julia isn't telling us."

"You think?" my dad says with a snort. "If he's anything like the other guys she's brought home to meet us, I give it another week."

"Do you remember that one who wouldn't drink anything all night, even with his food? I mean who doesn't want even a little sip of water to clear their palate during a meal?"

"I remember that one," my dad says. "How about the one who kept going to the bathroom every five minutes? He must have had a serious drug habit."

"He didn't have a drug habit, Dad."

"Oh, so he had the shits then? I'm not sure that's any better, Julia."

"Carter," my mom says while laughing, "stop teasing her."

"You started it."

"Julia, maybe this guy is going to sweep you off your feet."

"I wouldn't count on it," my dad says.

"Okay, guys. As much as this conversation has been as enlightening as ever, I've gotta go and start getting ready."

"So you're not coming over?" my mom asks again, like she hasn't heard a word I've said.

"Not today. Maybe next week, okay?"

"Okay, sweetheart. That would be nice. I'll be looking forward to it."

"Julia," my dad says in a cautious voice before I hang up. "Make sure whoever this guy is that he treats you good."

I smile in spite of myself at the warning. Even though my parents might officially be off the reservation, I know in my heart they mean well and care about me, so I put up with their antics.

"I will, Daddy."

We say a collective good-bye, and I toss my phone onto the bed. I'm still smiling while staring up at the ceiling and thinking about last night and this morning. My eyes eventually start to grow heavy, and although I really should decide what I'm wearing later tonight, a nap wins out instead.

I guess Sabrina was right. He wore me out. But in the best way possible.

CHAPTER NINETEEN

It's 7:17 p.m., and as much as the nap did wonders for me and I feel completely rejuvenated, I slept until just after six o'clock, leaving me about an hour to get ready. Thank God I had already taken a shower today, which ended up helping to save me some time. Well, two showers, but who's counting.

I switch off the blow-dryer and put it down amongst the clutter on the counter before performing a thorough final inspection of myself in the mirror.

Word to the wise, ladies: *always* perform the final inspection. The one time I didn't, I ended up with my tits on display because I had an extra button undone on my blouse. Of course it wasn't until my date kept staring at my chest with a lascivious grin that I looked down and noticed it. Needless to say, it was our one and only date.

After a lengthy debate with myself over whether to show too much leg or not, I opted for showing them off tonight. I settled on a simple black shift dress with a plunging split neckline and dolman sleeves that end somewhere along my upper thigh. I paired it with strappy leopard-print high heels. My hair is pulled back in a sleek ponytail, and the only accessory I've added is gold hoop earrings. To the untrained eye it looks like I'm not wearing any makeup, but in fact I'm wearing enough to make it look like I'm not, which takes years of practice to perfect.

Overall I'm extremely pleased with how I turned out, given the fact that I only had an hour to get ready. I turn around and crane my neck over my shoulder to take one last look at my backside in the mirror. Once I've ensured that there is no back fat or panty lines visible, I switch off the bathroom light and head into the living room to wait for Alex.

First, I take to sitting on the couch but quickly decide that it may wrinkle my dress. Next, I try the barstools by the kitchen island and sit comfortably for all of a minute before my leg, kicking back and forth like an impatient child's, drives me crazy and I jump off the seat. I start to pace back and forth behind the couch, but I stop when I realize my pits are starting to perspire again. So I freeze in mid-step and crane my arms up to let them air dry. I probably look like Daniel-san in *The Karate Kid* standing in the middle of my living room when I hear a light knock on the front door.

My heart hammers in my chest, and my stomach does a flip-flop while my adrenaline skyrockets. All because he's on the other side of that door.

It's only Alex. You've known him for years. You've seen him naked now, so calm down and stop being such a spaz.

I snap out of my awkward stance and approach the door. As he starts lightly knocking again, I fling it open, and my mouth drops open in shock.

Because it's not Alex. Nope, it's asshole extraordinaire, Aiden.

Before I can say anything because my head is flying in all sorts of different directions, one of which is that Alex will be here any minute, Aiden steps forward and goes to kiss me hello on the cheek.

When he gets within an inch of me, I take a step back. "What are you doing?"

"I was trying to say hello," he says.

"I get that. I don't necessarily understand it, but I get that's what you were just trying to do." My hands clench into fists at my sides, trying to control the raw anger raging inside of me at the sight of him. "What I meant was what are you doing *here* at my house?"

Instead of answering me, he takes a second to look me over from head to toe. His head tilts to the side before he licks his lips when he's done with his perusal of me. "You look amazing, Julia. Better than ever."

"Answer me, Aiden."

He takes a step forward so that he's now officially standing inside my house. I'm almost surprised the jerk doesn't burst into flames and collapse into a pile of ashes when he crosses the threshold, given the amount of hexes I've put on him over the years. What makes it so much worse is that he looks sinfully good wearing distressed blue jeans that hang low on his hips and a snug white T-shirt that showcases his muscular arms, allowing me a sneak peek at the tribal tattoo around his right bicep.

"You didn't return my phone call," he says, taking yet another step forward.

I answer by taking a step backward.

"So I figured I'd come by to see you instead."

He gives me a cocky look like I should be grateful that he decided to grace me with his presence.

"See and that's where you figured wrong. When someone doesn't return your phone call, it's the polite way of saying they don't want to talk to you. But you're too fucking stupid to realize when I'm trying to be polite, so I'll say it in a way that you can understand." I put my hands on my hips and lean forward until I'm as close as I can afford to be around him without wanting to do bodily harm. "Stay the hell away from me. Don't call me, don't write me, and don't ever show your face here again. If you do, I'll pick up the phone and call your fiancée faster than you can say, 'I'm an asshole.'"

Aiden chuckles and rubs his jaw with his hand. "Now that's the Julia I've missed so much. I knew she was in there somewhere."

"Aiden, just stop it already. You don't know what you're talking about."

"That's not true. I've missed you." He pauses and tries his best
to look sincere. On him it looks more like the devil trying to pass
as an angel. Yes, it's sexy as hell, but I'm not falling for it.

"Seeing you the other day has made me think about things,"
he says.

"Wait a second. Maybe I have wax buildup in my ears or I'm
losing my fucking mind, but did you just say you've missed me?" I
ask incredulously.

He tries to reach for my hand, but I take a couple more steps
away from him. "You know what? Don't even answer that because I
don't give a shit. You left me, and now you're engaged. End of story.
So I'd like for you to leave right now because no one here is buying
the bullshit you're selling today."

"I'm not leaving until you give me a chance to explain," he says.

Through clenched teeth, I say, "Please. Leave. Now."

He doesn't budge. In fact, he crosses his arms and leans against
the wall in the foyer as if he hadn't a care in the world.

And this is when the shit officially hits the fan.

"By my count, the lady has already asked you to leave twice."
Alex's assured and scary calm voice comes from the direction of the
door. Aiden and I both look in that direction to find him with his
hands in his jeans pockets, leaning against the frame. "That's one
more than necessary, don't you think?"

Aiden looks back at me with his lips fighting a grin, and then
he looks back at Alex. "Don't I know you?"

Alex casually starts walking toward me, completely ignoring
Aiden. My heart is in my throat when he comes to stand beside
me and wraps his arm possessively around my waist, pulling me
into his side, blatantly letting Aiden know that he's here for me. He
couldn't have made it more obvious if he would have pissed at my

feet like a dog marking its territory. I'm usually not one for displays of ownership by a man where testosterone starts flying everywhere, but for some crazy reason, what Alex just did makes me so incredibly happy that I find myself moving farther into his warmth.

"Doesn't matter if I know you or not," Alex says tersely. "Julia asked you to leave. Not once, but twice. But you're still standing here. My suggestion is you turn around right now and go home."

Aiden's eyes roam over us in our semi-embrace, and he chuckles as he turns around and starts walking toward the door. Just before he walks outside, he cranes his neck over his shoulder and says, "Julia, I'll be in touch."

Alex's hand tightens on my waist as if he's trying to keep himself in check. Quite honestly, I'm more shocked at Aiden's performance than Alex's. Seriously, what an asshole! But the performance is still not enough that I can't say one more thing before he leaves.

"Don't bother, Aiden."

"Close the door behind you while you're at it," Alex adds with a dimpled smile.

Once the door snaps shut behind him, I exhale a shaky breath in the hopes that it will regulate my sanity and temper. Now I'm left with having to explain the situation to Alex, who did nothing wrong but show up for a date and walked in on a disaster in the making. I turn in his arms and look up at him. He's still smiling from ear to ear.

"Now I have a good reason not to like him," he says. "When I met him at the engagement party the other night, I thought he was a dick, but this just cements it."

"Alex, I had no idea he was going to show up here," I say.

"You don't need to explain. I heard everything."

"Don't you want to know—"

"No, I don't, Julia." Alex's hand comes up and cups my face softly. "As far as I'm concerned, the guy has already taken enough of our time tonight, so let's forget about him and let me take you out to dinner."

I grin with pleasure and relief, not only at what he just said, but at being so close to him again too. And now that I have a moment to appreciate him in all his splendid glory, my eyes make a path from the tiniest hint of tanned flesh visible at his neck and collar, to his black dress shoes, and then back up again where a lazy smile spreads across his face.

"Let's start over, shall we?" he asks. "Hi."

"Hi."

"You look beautiful, Julia."

"So do you."

"Are you ready?" he asks, while taking his turn at looking me over from head to toe.

"I just need to get my keys and purse."

I reach for both things on the foyer side table. When I turn around and try to take one step to start walking toward the door, he grabs my wrist.

"Aren't you forgetting something?"

I scrunch my eyes while I think of what I could have forgotten. "Um, no. I have everything I need."

Alex pulls me to him until I collide with his hard chest, and I put my hands out to brace myself. He cups the back of my neck while his other hand snakes around my waist, vanquishing what little space was left between us. When his lips touch mine, at first it's a flutter of soft and light kisses as if we were becoming reacquainted. But it switches gears, and when I feel his tongue graze across my bottom lip, I lose myself to the kiss and to him. I grip onto the lapels of his jacket, and a soft moan escapes my throat, which encourages him further. He deepens the kiss but never once lets his hands wander.

I don't know how long we stand there kissing, but when we break it off, we are both gasping for breath and our foreheads are resting on each other's.

"Much better," he says, his voice softer now as he caresses my cheek. "I've been thinking about doing that since you left me this morning."

"You mean when I left you this *afternoon*."

He tries to hide the smirk on his face, but the dimples give him away. "I stand corrected. I've been thinking of doing that since you left me this afternoon."

Cupping my face with his hands, he presses a silky kiss to my already swollen lips that has me wanting so much more and has me quickly forgetting about dinner if we stay here any longer.

"Alex?"

"Julia?"

I keep my eyes closed as his mouth moves meticulously over to my neck, where he lavishes it with more kisses. "If you keep doing that, I'm not going to want dinner at all."

I feel his smile against my skin, and then he stops and picks his head up to look at me. "I did promise you dinner, didn't I?"

"You did."

He answers by dropping his hands from my face and taking one of mine in his. After I lock the door, we walk to his car parked in my driveway, the whole time feeling oddly at ease and relaxed given the altercation with Aiden. But I'm not going to let him ruin my night at all. As of this moment tonight, I will not waste one more thought on him.

Alex opens my door for me and helps me in, then strides around the front of the car to his side. He gracefully slides in next to me before starting the car.

I turn in my seat to look at him as the dashboard illuminates his strong jaw and makes the blue of his eyes have an almost ethereal quality to them. Oh dear . . . I'm waxing poetic to myself about his eyes. Can you believe this? My thoughts sound as if they are straight out of a fucking script for *General Hospital*. But I can't help myself. He really is breathtakingly gorgeous, and I'm at a loss for words around him sometimes. And that's how I know I'm elbow-deep in some shit I have no idea how to navigate through.

I always have something to say. Always. I basically can't keep my mouth shut, ever. Men don't make me stumble to find my words. Men don't make me anxious. And men certainly don't leave me wanting more.

"Where are we going?" I ask him.

"It's a surprise."

"I hate surprises, Alex."

"No you don't. Everyone says they hate surprises, but they secretly love them."

"Well, not this girl," I say defiantly.

With a smile in his voice he says, "Is this what it's going to be like all the time with us?"

"And what exactly does that mean?" I ask, crossing my arms and trying not to analyze his use of the word "us" in that question.

"I mean," he says, then pauses to steal a glance in my direction, "are you going to fight me every step of the way?"

Ever so smoothly, he puts his hand on the exposed skin of my thigh. The contact immediately garners a zing-like jolt from every nerve ending in my body. He starts to rub small circles against the skin with his thumb, and he adds almost as an afterthought, "Because I love proving you wrong."

"I don't fight you every step of the way. Am I not sitting in your car right now on my way to dinner with you?"

"Yes, you are. But if it was up to me, you would have been sitting in that seat a long time ago."

See, *that* right there—when he says stuff like that to me, I'm left feeling like a complete idiot. How long has he been interested in me? Besides the flirting, there really was no indication that he had been waiting to make a move on me. Or was there? And I like to think of myself as having a modicum of intelligence, but now I'm starting to question if I'm as clueless as Sarah.

"Why didn't you do something about it sooner?"

He doesn't even hesitate with his answer. "You weren't ready."

"I wasn't ready?" I say back to him in disbelief. "You're a cocky bastard, you know that?"

Alex suddenly turns right onto a side street and parks the car.

"What the hell are you doing?"

He doesn't answer. Instead, he unlatches his seat belt, leans over the center console, and grabs my face in his hands. His mouth is on mine before I can utter a single sound or protest. At first I'm in shock, but I quickly get over it. That might be due to the precise forcefulness of his lips and tongue, which makes me want to surrender myself to him every goddamn time. I'm like putty in his hands, and he knows it. And not for nothing, but that kind of turns me on.

He slows things down, and all I can do is follow suit, because at this point, I literally feel like I'm just along for the ride. When I open my eyes, his are staring right back at me, full of lust and something else that I don't want to acknowledge . . . yet.

"Now that I have your attention," he whispers, "I'll say it again. You weren't ready. Does that make me a cocky bastard? Maybe. Do you think I give a shit that you think that? No. The truth is that you wouldn't have believed me if I told you. You would have thought I was just looking for a piece of ass and blown me off."

"But—"

"I wasn't finished," he says, cutting me off. "I have wanted to be more than . . . whatever we are for a while. And before your mind goes off the deep end, no I do not mean just fuck buddies."

"You make me nervous," I blurt out of nowhere.

Alex's lips curve upward with a small grin at my admission. "Why?"

"Because I never know what's going to come out of your mouth, that's why. Perfect example, what you just finished telling me. Who says that kind of shit? No one, that's who. But you, you . . ."

"Me, what?" he asks, now with a full smile on his face.

"You say something like that and it throws me off my game. It's infuriating."

"I like throwing you off your game," he admits quietly. "But what you don't get, Julia, is that you have the same exact effect on me."

"I do?"

He pulls my chin up and presses a light kiss to my lips. "You have no idea."

Oh, I like that. I like that a lot.

And like any red-blooded female out there who finds out this kind of information, I try to use it to my advantage. First though, I have to sweeten the pot, so I lean forward and loosely wrap my arms around his neck. I run my nose along his, secretly hoping that I don't get any snot on it before ducking my lips to his ear.

"Alex?" I say, barely above a whisper.

"Hmmm?"

"Where are we going to dinner?"

He chuckles as he pulls away and latches his seat belt again. "I told you, it's a surprise. Nice try though."

"I hate surprises," I mumble under my breath when he starts to drive again.

I have to look out the passenger window to hide the grin on my face while he's still laughing. It has a lot to do with everything he's admitted to me a few moments before. But if you promise to keep a secret, I'll tell you the real reason for it.

The cocky bastard was right. I love surprises.

185

CHAPTER TWENTY

When he starts to drive on the Dolphin Expressway and the landscape outside my window changes to the vastness of the Atlantic Ocean, I know we are heading toward South Beach. Alex still won't tell me where we are going when I ask again though. And I do ask again. I think I might ask another five times the whole way, until we pull up to a driveway that is nestled amongst tons of palm trees and I see a long, tan, tarp-covered walkway that leads to the restaurant's front door.

Barton G.

Oh. My. God.

For those of you who do not live in Miami, this restaurant is as upscale as they come. There are only two of them, the other being in Los Angeles. It's known for its eclectic presentation of dishes and romantic ambiance. And I guess for being super pricey. I've only been here one time before, and that was for a private party hosted by a longtime client of mine. Ever since then, I've been dying to come back and have a sit-down dinner. But given the long list of losers I've had the pleasure of dealing with, a romantic dinner here was never in the cards for me.

Dear Lord, I was not prepared for this. I was thinking something along the lines of a swanky place on Washington Avenue or something like that. Never did I imagine he would opt for cozy and intimate. This puts the "not just fuck buddies" comment he made in perspective for me. And I know we have crazy chemistry; that's not it. My problem is I've had such bad luck with men that it's hard for me to discern at which point I can let go and be on the receiving end of real affection and love—the whole package. On top of all that, men have a hard time in general dealing with my . . . ahem, rough edges. But I make no apologies for who I am. You either like it or you don't.

"Stay right there," Alex instructs as he gets out of the car to hand the valet his keys.

He opens the door for me, and I swing my legs out to carefully balance my feet on the concrete. He holds his hand out and helps me up, but not before I notice how he looks at my legs in appreciation for a second.

The valet whisks Alex's car away, and we walk up, hands entwined, to the front door. I lean in to say something to him privately. "You know, you didn't have to go all out."

"I know I didn't," he answers, then quickly adds, "I wanted to."

We reach the door, and he goes to open it for me, but I can't let what he said go unnoticed. So I reach up on my toes and softly press my lips to his. "Thank you," I whisper, then duck into the restaurant ahead of him.

The hostess spots us coming toward her, and she focuses all of her attention on Alex, eyeing him up and down as if I'm not even here. Can't say that I blame her—I mean look at him, for chrissakes! But at least try and be a little discreet about it.

"Hello there!" the hostess says, addressing only Alex as if I don't exist. She leans forward and purposely displays her cleavage for him.

Bitch, please. Find your own man.

That's right, I'm officially staking my claim on his ass.

Alex puts his arm around my waist and pulls me to him, ignoring the hostess's feeble attempt at distracting him, and gives her his name to look up the reservation.

She shoots me a look of surprise. "Aren't you the lucky one?" she says under her breath, but not enough that I don't hear her perfectly clear.

Normally I would say something just as biting back to her, but you know what? She isn't even worth it because nobody is going to ruin this evening for me. Not Aiden and certainly not this woman.

She darts out from behind her stand and leads us toward a small flight of stairs. When we get to the top, she walks us through a maze of tables that are partially filled with people enjoying their meals. We keep following her to a set of French doors covered with sheer curtains on the far side of the room. She opens the door to unveil a solitary table illuminated by outdoor lights, hidden from everyone else in the restaurant.

Holy shit!

Mind officially blown.

"Do you like it?" Alex asks in my ear, placing his hand on the small of my back and gently nudging me forward.

I more than like it because it confirms that he really put some thought into this. And that alone is what makes it even more special. I can't remember the last time a man has gone so far out of his way to impress me. It's been so long that I'm temporarily at a loss for words until Alex asks me again if I like it.

"I love it," I finally say when I find my voice.

He smiles while leading me to my seat and pulls it out for me. I sit down, and he immediately bends down to kiss my neck, sending shivers up my spine. My God, I'm like a puddle of goo over here with all this attention from him, and I love it. The hostess looks on with her mouth agape.

Alex lifts his head and looks at the hostess. "Thank you, and for the record, I'm the lucky one."

I think I'm in love.

No, no, no, I'm not *in* love. But damn, if he keeps this up, I won't be far from it.

The hostess leaves after bumbling through letting us know that our server will be with us shortly, and Alex goes to sit across from me. Once she's gone, we're alone and hidden away from prying eyes. But not for long. Our server arrives with a bottle of champagne, proceeds to open it, pours us each a glass, and then leaves us alone again.

Alex picks up his glass and with a dashing smile says, "To new beginnings."

I take a small sip after we clink our glasses together, and then I say the first thing that comes to mind. "You are *soooo* getting laid tonight."

He chokes on his champagne before laughing out loud. He really does have the sexiest laugh; it lights up his whole face and makes him look so relaxed. I meant what I said though, even if it sounded crass. But it's the truth. He's getting laid for pulling out all the stops. Probably a blow job too; that's how impressed I am right now.

"Sorry, my mouth sometimes has a mind of its own," I say with a giggle while he's still clearing his throat.

"Don't apologize. I love your mouth."

"Is that so?" I lean forward and put my elbows on the table. "Then you're really in for a treat later."

He leans forward, and since the table is for two, he's much closer to my face. "If you keep saying things like that, we'll be taking this meal to go."

"Saying things like what?"

"Saying things that make me want to do things to you."

"What kind of things?" I coyly ask.

"Things that I've been imagining for quite some time. Things that will have you screaming my name out loud again and again."

The sound of someone clearing his throat turns both of our heads. Our poor server has been standing there for who knows how long listening to us. I want to die of embarrassment. If the ground could open up and swallow me whole, I'd be totally fine with it right now.

The server sounds flustered when he speaks. "If you're ready, I'll be bringing out the appetizer now."

Alex answers in an assured voice. "We're ready."

When the waiter walks away, I ask Alex, "Don't I get a chance to look at the menu?"

"I already ordered for you. For both of us."

"Um, how do you know I'll like what you picked? Aren't you afraid that I'll hate it?"

"Don't you trust me?" he says with that dimpled grin of his that does things to me.

That's not only a good question but a loaded one too. One that I can't answer yet because unfortunately I've been burned so many times before by other men. I know it's not fair to hold Alex accountable for the assholes who came before him. And I know I'm making it sound like there was a goddamn army of men, but there were enough who wasted my time and made me feel like garbage that I have a hard time letting down my guard.

"Hmm, I better like this food you picked out for me. If not, then I may have to take the blow job offer off the table."

Alex's eyebrows fly up toward his hairline, and when he opens his mouth to make a witty comeback, the waiter appears at our table with our first dish. His face is somewhere between shocked and uncomfortable. I'm wondering how I can slip a packet of Tic Tacs in the guy's pocket so I can hear him coming next time. He places a silver circa 1950s vintage style toaster on our table with two flaky pastry pouches sticking out of it and tells us to enjoy before trotting off to wherever he came from.

Curiously, I ask, "What are those?"

Alex reaches over and takes one of the pastry pouches out of the toaster and puts it on my plate for me and then takes the other one for him. "Lobster Pop-Tarts."

I dig in, and when the first forkful hits my taste buds, it's like I've bitten into a slice of heaven. My eyes shoot up to find him clearly enjoying himself watching me eat.

"Good?"

"Oh my God, it's delicious."

"You have no idea how glad I am to hear that," he teases, and takes a bite for himself.

"Ha! I'm pretty sure I have a very good idea of how glad you are that I like it. But we still have the rest of the meal to go, so I reserve the right to withhold my opinion until that time. Deal?"

He wipes his mouth with his napkin and takes a sip of his champagne. "Just to be clear, we're still discussing what I think we're discussing?"

I give him a look that confirms his assumptions and take another forkful of food.

"Well then, how could I possibly pass up a deal like that? You're on."

When the main course is presented a little while later, which consists of "Mouse Trap Mac 'n' Cheese" and "Eat the Beef Ribs," which are equally delicious, we get on the subject of his niece.

"I saw Josie again the other day. Vanessa brought her by my office to go over some party stuff."

"I know," he says. "I talked to her earlier today."

"She's awesome."

He smiles warmly and then says, "I couldn't agree more."

"So if what I'm about to ask is too personal, don't hesitate to tell me, okay?"

He nods and takes a bite of his food.

"Is her dad in the picture? Because I noticed that Vanessa doesn't have a wedding band, and Josie has never mentioned anything about him."

"No, he's not," he replies in a clipped tone.

"I'm sorry, I didn't mean to pry. It's just that she's so amazing, and I was curious."

He puts down his fork and gives me an apologetic look. "No, I'm sorry. I didn't mean to sound so put off. It's a bit of a sore subject. He skipped out on my sister when she found out she was pregnant with Josie. She's never had the pleasure of meeting her father."

"Never?" I ask.

He shakes his head. "Not one single damn time."

"Wow, I'm really sorry to hear that. Not only for Josie but Vanessa too. That's just awful." I lean forward and rest my elbows on the table. "But that's why you're so close to her, right?"

Alex smiles faintly and nods again. "From day one."

"So Vanessa was right about how you spoil her rotten."

He tilts his head to the side as he goes to grab his glass of champagne. "Maybe just a little."

"More like a lot, I bet. Case in point, this party you have me planning for her."

"Well," he says with a boyish grin.

"Well what?"

"There's something I should explain about that. It has to do with you."

What could his niece's birthday party have to do with me, other than the obvious? My eyebrows knit together in confusion, waiting for him to explain further.

"I may or may not have used my own niece in this little plot to get your attention. I'm not particularly proud of that, but a man's got to do what a man's got to do."

"Is there anything else I should know?"

"That deal we made? You know the one that started all of this party stuff for Josie to begin with?"

I nod.

"I made that deal with you so that you'd owe me at some point. Although I will say that it's been a pain in the ass trying to figure out a way for you to repay me."

I take a second to wrap my head around what he's trying to say. "Hang on a second. *I'm* the reason you took the deal in the first place?"

"Yes."

"Is that why you gave me all the business from the gallery for the last year too?" I ask.

"Yes again," he says.

"But that deal was like a year ago. You waited all this time, and may I remind you that in that time besides Marisa"—I pause while I roll my eyes at the mention of her name, and he chuckles—"I'm sure you weren't sitting around alone at home pining for me."

"And?"

"And I'm just wondering why you waited so long."

"I told you in the car, you weren't ready," he says. "So I waited for the right opportunity to present itself."

I tilt my head to the side and give him a look that suggests I'm not satisfied with his answer this time any more than I was when he told me about it in the car.

"Are you fishing?" he asks with a light chuckle.

"Maybe," I say with a shrug of my shoulders.

"Do you remember the day that I drove Sabrina home and Tyler was there waiting for her?"

"Of course I do. How can I forget? I wanted to murder him for having the balls to show up unannounced."

When I don't say anything for a moment, he goes on to explain. "You were wearing a pair of Cat in the Hat pajama bottoms with a tank top, and your hair was up in the messiest knot I've ever seen. You went after him, and you didn't back down because you were protecting your best friend. You looked gorgeous, and I was so impressed with your attitude and the passion in your eyes while you were arguing with him. You really did a number on me that night, Julia, because that was it for me."

"I was so close to kicking his ass," I interrupt, and his mouth twitches to keep himself from laughing.

"I'm sure you were," he says, still fighting off laughing. "Anyway, if I would have told you that I was interested that night that you looked sexy as hell tearing Tyler a new asshole in those adorable pajamas, you would have laughed in my face, and more than likely, you would have kicked my ass instead of his."

I chew on my lip, thinking that he's totally right. I would have laughed in his face. I don't think I would have kicked his ass, but given that I was pretty high-strung that night, it's a strong possibility.

"Ever since that night I knew that I had to try and I would do anything to make this happen between us. Even if it meant waiting a whole year for the perfect chance to present itself. So when the idea of Josie's party came up, I must confess I was getting a bit desperate."

My hand covers my mouth from laughing out loud. I can't help it. It's so damn adorable.

"Desperate, huh?" I ask while still giggling.

"Desperate times call for desperate measures," he says with a sexy grin. "And she's getting a party out of it, so I'd say she's making out on the deal."

"And what do I get?"

"We'll just have to wait and see, won't we?"

"What if I don't want to wait?" I shoot back at him.

He puts down his glass of champagne and leans forward. His voice is low and restrained when he says, "Would you like a reminder that it's worth the wait?"

"It depends. What kind of reminder?"

"The kind that's going to have to wait until after dessert so I can properly refresh your memory."

Alex is really surpassing my expectations, and not just in the sex department, because that goes without saying. It's refreshing since men can't usually keep up or deal with me. He doesn't seem put off by my personality. He doesn't hesitate to go toe-to-toe with me on anything. In fact, he seems to enjoy it immensely, as evident by him revealing that it's my attitude and personality that attracted him to begin with.

After the "Cotton Candy" dessert a little while later, which is absolute perfection and delicious, he makes quick work of paying the bill and ushering me out of the restaurant. It's as if he's in as much of a hurry as I am at this point to get on with refreshing my memory. Tack on to that a few glasses of champagne and this girl is anxious to move on to the next phase of the evening.

The drive home is full of desperate kisses at every red light, hands roaming over clothes, and promises of pleasure that have me weak at the knees and dying to get him in my bed.

And oh, how I'll be having my way with him, because now it's my turn to surprise him.

CHAPTER TWENTY-ONE

As soon as we walk in the door, I ask him to get us a couple of glasses of wine while I freshen up. Once he's out of sight, I dart into my bedroom and head straight for the lingerie drawer. I have stuff in here I've never worn that has been dying to see the light of day. Mind you, I also have stuff in here I've worn before that I'm not about to put on ever again. I don't even know why I keep it, to be honest. It's pretty much soiled once you break up with someone, and it reminds you of that time you ate bad clams, and you say to yourself, *Never again,* when you look at it.

I'm rifling through until I hit pay dirt. A matching fire-engine red lace push-up bra and barely there panties. Immediately, I unzip my dress and take everything off. I'm pulling up the barely there panties when Alex calls out to me from the kitchen.

"Julia, where are the wineglasses?"

I yell back, "The cabinet closest to the refrigerator."

I hear him close a cabinet door a second later and then call out, "Red or white?"

"Doesn't matter. Surprise me."

I'm adjusting "the boys" in the push-up bra when he shouts back, "I thought you hate surprises?"

Fucker has the memory of an elephant.

"Smart-ass."

I hear him laughing in the background while I stand before my closet mirror doing a final inspection. Hmm, I'm missing something. I mean, I look good as is, but it's lacking something, and I can't quite put my finger on . . .

Aha!

I run back to my lingerie drawer and pull out a pair of thigh-high black sheer stockings and then run right back to my closet for a pair of the best fuck-me pumps I can find. Plopping my ass on the edge of the bed, I carefully, but lightning fast, roll up the stockings and then slip on the shoes. I walk over to the mirror again and . . .

Oh, hell yes! Amy Winehouse knew what she was talking about when she sang about those "Fuck Me Pumps," because that's exactly what was missing.

"I can do this, I can do this. I'm good enough. I'm smart enough. And doggone it, people like me," I chant out loud to myself in the mirror, and then I hear the pop of the cork from the wine bottle that he's opening.

Perfect timing.

I open the door to my bedroom, but not before lifting my arms to smell myself because with all the running around and my previously mentioned issue with sweating, you never know. Peering my head around the door, I look down the hallway to see his back is to me. So I walk fast on my tippy toes until I reach the end of the hallway and position myself while his back is still turned. I'm leaning against the wall with one hand on my hip, my feet crossed at the ankles and patting myself on the back because I seriously could not have timed this better if I tried.

"Did you pick red or white finally?"

Alex turns around while pouring what I can now tell is a glass of red wine and says with a grin, "You said to surprise you."

He looks up at that point to find me standing there in my sex-kitten outfit, and his grin vanishes. It's replaced with his jaw clenching and a hiss of breath from his nose that I can hear from over here.

"Surprise," I singsong.

The wine overflows in the glass and spills onto the kitchen floor, causing him to break out of his spell and curse out loud. I'm rather enjoying watching him fumble around looking for a towel to wipe up the mess when I calmly say, "Leave it."

I don't have to tell him twice.

Alex drops everything and elegantly strides toward me as his eyes canvass every piece of my body. When he's about a foot away, I shove off the wall and start walking backward toward my bedroom, matching him step for step. It's really a fucking miracle I don't fall and bust my ass in these heels, but I finally make it inside the confines of my room with him still following me.

"Stand right here and don't move," I say, pointing to a spot right in front of the foot of my bed.

One corner of his mouth twists up in a sinful grin as he follows my directions. I walk behind him and press my breasts to his back as I reach around him to grab the lapels of his blazer and slowly ease it off. I toss it on the floor and walk back around to face him. He reaches for me, but I take a step back out of his grasp.

"Uh-uh. No touching," I say, shaking my head.

Alex reluctantly drops his arms and tilts his head to the side, his eyes in silent protest at my instructions. I'm having entirely too much fun as I start to unbutton his shirt. Once it's off, I run my hands up from his defined abdominal muscles to his upper chest before fanning out to his shoulders and down his arms. His skin is hot to the touch, and he's taking shallow breaths. I look up at him at the same time my lips press against his chest to leave a lingering kiss there.

"Payback is a bitch," he whispers playfully.

I giggle because little does he know this little game is driving me crazy too. It's taking every ounce of willpower I have not to scrap the seduction act and jump his bones.

"Promises, promises," I say coolly while running a finger down to his belt buckle. "Take off your shoes."

He kicks them off, and I go right into unbuckling his belt while keeping my eyes on his baby blues, which are tracking my every move. Next, I trace my hand lightly over his rigid length, and he sucks in a breath.

My voice is quiet and steady while I stroke him over his pants and ask, "Do you like that?"

He licks his lips and just as quietly answers me. "Baby, it feels amazing, but please let me touch you. I'm dying here."

"Soon enough. Don't you know that good things come to those who wait, Alex?"

"And better things come to those who make it happen, Julia."

"Oh," I say in appreciation. "I like that one even better."

I stop stroking him only to unbutton his pants and push them down his hips until they fall with a soft whoosh to the ground. Alex steps out of them and is now standing before me in black boxer briefs that hug every inch of his male perfection to the nth degree. I feel like grabbing my phone so I can take some pictures to capture the moment for future reference, but I figure he'll probably think I'm nuts.

My eyes fixed on his, I remove the boxer briefs and then duck my head to look down. God, I've become fairly acquainted with his dick already, but dammit if I still stare at it like it was a mirage in the desert.

"I'm so glad that you enjoy staring at my cock, but if you don't do something about it sooner rather than later, I'll be forced to take over," he warns in a gravelly voice.

I push him backward until the backs of his knees hit the bed. "Sit down, and remember . . . no touching."

I drop to my knees in front of him, and he opens his legs to make room for me. Without wasting any more time, I cup one hand around the base of his dick and give a light squeeze. I steal a furtive glance upward and keep my eyes on his as my tongue darts out and starts to lick from the base all the way up to the tip-top of the head like an ice cream cone. "Fuuuuck," Alex groans.

His dick gets even harder when both my hands grip the shaft, and I leave my mouth on the head, moving up and down while massaging it with my tongue. Alex's head falls back on his shoulders, and the sight of him getting off on me sucking on his cock gets me in a frenzy of my own. I need some sort of relief, so I keep the pace as is and then let him take over and do the thrusting for a minute or so. He's watching me with the most lustful look in his eyes as he fucks my mouth while my hands start to roam down my body.

First, I pinch my nipples through the lace fabric, the sensation like a bullet straight to the junction at my thighs, and I moan with my mouth still around him.

"Jesus Christ, Julia," he hisses under his breath.

It's not enough. I trail one hand down the front of my body and rub my hand over the already swollen nub. That's *soooo* much better.

"Are you kidding me?" Alex says in disbelief. He looks on for a moment while I keep rubbing myself until he reaches his breaking point and mutters, "To hell with this."

His hands are under my arms and scooping me up from the floor so fast that I don't even have time to blink. The next thing I know, I'm tossed onto the bed like a feather, landing on my back. He's hovering over me in a split second, pulling down the cups of my bra and sucking on one nipple, his hand massaging the other.

I moan out loud, and he chuckles against my breast. He lifts his head at the same time one hand skims down to the edge of my panties, and he says, "It's not so fun to be tortured and played with, is it?"

"I'm sorry. I'll make it up to you, I swear."

With that, he sits up on his haunches between my legs. His hands grip one side of my panties, and with brute strength, he tears it apart.

"Alex!"

He's in the process of snaking them down the one leg they are still together on and doesn't answer me. Don't get me wrong, it's hot as hell, but damn these things were stupid expensive.

"Do you have any idea how much those cost me?"

"Do you really think I give a shit right now? I'll buy you a hundred more pairs, and I'll tear every goddamn one of them off of you if you ever pull that shit again, do you understand?"

I don't answer because his hands are spreading my thighs apart. His fingers start to slide inside of me slowly, and my eyes close as my back arches off the bed.

"Do you understand me, Julia?" His voice is thick with desire.

"I understand, Alex. Now please, fuck me."

He blankets my body with his, bracing his weight on one forearm and lifting one of my knees to his shoulder before ramming into me with no hesitation.

Perfect. Brilliant. Sensory overload.

"Don't stop," I plead in between moans.

Alex keeps pumping in and out of me, my body meeting his every thrust, and on the verge of bursting from the inside out.

He drops my knee from his shoulder and burrows his hands behind my back. Sitting back on his haunches, he takes me with him so that I can be in complete control. I find the perfect rhythm, and at this angle, the friction against my clit quickly becomes too much for me. Alex roughly grips my waist and takes back control of my movements as my head falls backward.

"Look at me, Julia," he says between clenched teeth. "I want to see your eyes when you come."

My head lolls forward, and I pull his lips to mine. His tongue grazes my bottom lip, but he doesn't kiss me yet. He pumps me hard up and down on his cock a few times and then hits the sweet spot, and I splinter in two, my inner walls gripping him tighter and pulling his orgasm out of him while I'm still riding mine out.

We slow down our movements until I'm fully seated on his semi-hard length, both of us slick with sweat and gasping for breath. I run my hands through his hair and gently pull back so that his lips are level with mine and I can finally kiss him. Our mouths open, and the feel of our tongues gliding against each other's melts me. It's slow, deliberate, and exquisite—the perfect description for Alex.

Then like a bullet to the brain, a fleeting thought runs through my head: if I'm not careful with him, there will be no *if* I fall in love with him, it will be more like *when* I fall in love with him. I try to shoo it away, but that's hard to do with the way his fingers are soothingly running up and down my spine. Mix that with him still being inside me and his searing kiss, and I know I'm in big trouble. And this is technically our first date.

Who am I kidding?

I'm already falling for him.

CHAPTER TWENTY-TWO

The next week is kind of surreal for me. I can't tell you how many times within the first week of dating someone they had me running for the hills. But with Alex, it's been nothing but smooth sailing. I'm sure most people will say that it's only been a week and every relationship in the beginning is like that. My ass every relationship is like that in the beginning. That's the biggest crock of shit. Pure propaganda bullshit spouted out by, yet again, books and movies.

Does any of this sound familiar? There is a fair young maiden—a virgin, of course, because she's never had sex in all her twenty-one years of living. And before you go off the deep end and start hollering about how there's nothing wrong with being a virgin, I agree there is absolutely nothing wrong with it. But in these stories the chick is always a virgin with a magic vagina who apparently has a beacon in said vagina that *only* attracts tattooed bad boys or roguish millionaires who are without one flaw and sweep her off her feet so they can live happily ever after.

Not one fucking flaw.

Like I said, propaganda bullshit.

You know why?

Because *no one* is perfect. Not even the virgin with the magic vagina. Everyone has skeletons in their closet. Actually, some people have a whole goddamn graveyard in there. So the sooner you get all that shit out in the open, the better.

Unfortunately for me, I've usually had the pleasure of finding out about those skeletons within days of dating someone. Don't get me wrong, there are some who have slipped through the cracks, and I've let down my guard long enough to get zapped in the ass. And I mean that literally. Ladies and gentleman of the jury, I present to you exhibit A: Jake Ryan.

No, not *the* Jake Ryan from *Sixteen Candles*. That was just a coincidence, but that was his real name. We met, of all places, in the checkout lane of a grocery store. I'm rolling my eyes just thinking about it. Anyway, we dated for a few weeks, and everything was going great. Really great. He *seemed* perfect.

One night post-coital, I dozed off. Next thing I knew, a pair of teeth bit down really hard on my ass, which made me shoot straight up in bed and yell so loud that the paint may have chipped from the walls. In total shock, I rubbed the spot and asked him what possessed him to chew on my ass like he was Hannibal Lecter. He said he was trying to get me back into the mood and thought I'd enjoy it. I don't know when I gave off the vibe that I'd be into having my ass chomped like it was a cheeseburger. I spent the rest of the night with one eye open until I could make a clean getaway in the morning, and Jake was never to be heard from again. I had teeth marks and a welt on my ass for a good week afterward, making sitting down a chore because I could only sit on one ass cheek comfortably.

I have plenty of stories like this one. Too many. So when I say that so far this week has been surreal, I mean it.

Alex and I have spent the last week together in a blissful bubble of happiness. With every layer that is peeled back and revealed to me about him, I find myself wanting more, needing more from him. And that is saying a lot because I may be a lot of things, but needy is not one of them. So for me to admit that to myself is pretty huge. No, I'm not in love with him, but I'm definitely more in like with him than before.

And what's not to like?

He's attentive, thoughtful, caring, affectionate, sexy, gorgeous, suave, insatiable, interesting, funny . . . I could probably go on.

Every night has been spent either sleeping at his house or at my house. He's even come to my office a couple of times this week and brought me lunch because he thought I was working too hard. Add *sweet* to the list. So can you blame me for thinking somewhere in the back of my mind that there has got to be something wrong with him? Like maybe he saves his toenail clippings in a ziplock bag. Or maybe he has to repeatedly wax his back because if not he'd look like Sasquatch. I'm actually right in the middle of trying to block out a few of these crazy theories while sitting in my office—one of which involves Alex potentially being the Zodiac Killer—when my office phone rings.

"Julia," the receptionist says cheerily. "Your one o'clock appointment is here."

I swipe my mouse and open my desktop to see that I do in fact have an appointment at one o'clock that I had completely forgotten about. Probably because I've been spending the better part of my morning trying to find out if Alex's personality fits with a serial killer's profile.

"Thank you," I tell her. "You can send them in."

As I hang up, I take another look at the calendar on the computer and note the name of the appointment: *A. Locke.*

It can't be him. He wouldn't come here to see me in the guise of an appointment after I told him not to ever contact me again. He couldn't possibly be that dense. My head pops up at the sound of the door to my office opening to find Aiden walking in. Yes, apparently he can be that dense.

"Are you serious?" I ask. "You made an appointment to see me?"

He confidently strides to the chair in front of my desk and then unbuttons his suit jacket before sitting down. "Completely serious," he says, grinning from ear to ear.

"Aiden, you have two seconds to get up and get out."

He leans forward and rests his elbows on his knees. "All I'm asking for is a few minutes of your time, Julia. You owe me that much."

I give him an incredulous look because he must be insane for even saying that. "I owe *you* that much," I repeat and then point to myself. "You're saying I, as in me, the person who got screwed royally by *you*, owe you? Did I get that right?"

"Okay, okay," he says. "You don't owe me, but ever since I saw you at the engagement party—"

"*Your* engagement party."

"Yes, *my* engagement party," he concedes with a chuckle. "It made me really stop and think about you, about what happened, and how I should have made things right between us a long time ago."

Gone is the air of confidence that had accompanied him when he walked in my office. In its place is a sincere and soft expression that helps to placate some of the tension between us. Not completely. I'm still wary of him, but I'd be a liar if I say that there isn't a small part of me that isn't curious to hear what he has to say.

"Fine," I say after a long pause. "You've got five minutes."

He flashes a crooked smile before running a hand through his hair in relief. "Thank you."

"Don't thank me yet." I glance at my watch. "And you're down to four minutes and thirty seconds."

"I don't even know where to start. I didn't think you'd ever let me explain. I thought I'd have to keep annoying you like a bad cold or—"

"Genital warts," I finish for him, and after a long sigh, I go on. "Why don't you start by explaining why you left?"

"It's not that easy. There were so many things going through my mind back then."

"Like what?" I ask.

"For one thing, I kept worrying that I wasn't successful enough for you," he says. "You had your career all mapped out, and you hit the ground running right after college, while I was stuck trying to figure out what the hell to even do with my degree."

"So you're saying that because I had a career, that's how your dick ended up in another woman's vagina?" I ask. "Aiden, if that's your excuse, I don't want to hear any more."

"No, there's more to it than that." He takes a moment to collect his thoughts and steeples his fingers together underneath his chin. "I couldn't wrap my head around the fact that you were more successful than me. I couldn't stand knowing that there was no way in hell that I could provide for you, even on my best day. Every day I was digging myself deeper and deeper into a trench that I had no idea how to get out of.

"Julia, I was stupid. So fucking stupid. In my stupidity, I started chatting online in a group for people who felt the same way about their lives. And in yet more of my stupidity, I started chatting privately with a woman from that group. I had never met her in person, but somehow I could relate to her on so many levels because she was going through the same thing as me."

He smiles sadly as if he's remembering something and then continues. "The great thing about the Internet is that you can let your guard down and be yourself. I'm not going to lie and tell you that I didn't have a connection with her. I did. Obviously, since I went all the way to California to be with her. But I also can't lie and tell you that I didn't know it was a mistake the moment I did it, and I've regretted it every day since."

I don't know what I expected to hear. If it would come close to providing me with some sort of closure that I never thought I would have. Maybe I was hoping that he would say something that would validate all my years of hatred toward him. But his words don't do that at all. He's just made me more confused and hurt. Because all he's really saying is that he was weak. There was no big bad reason or clandestine planning that was done behind my back. He knew what he was doing as he was doing it. So should I forgive him? Is that what his repeated attempts to contact me come down to? His absolution? Because I have to be honest, I'm not very good at forgiving. If that makes me a bitch, so be it. It's the truth. After somebody does me wrong, I tend to write them right out of my life for good. The way I see it, that's one less Christmas card I have to send out.

As if he were reading my mind, Aiden says, "I'm not looking for your forgiveness, Julia. I know that I don't deserve it after what I did to you."

"Then what do you want? Why bother coming to see me after all this time?"

He smiles again and sits back in the chair. "When I came back home to Miami, I wanted to seek you out. I really did. But every time I thought I had worked up the courage, I would find an excuse not to come see you. Before I knew it, too much time had gone by, and I tried to move on with my life. And then I met Sophia. I knew she had hired you to plan the engagement party. That's why I never came to one meeting with her since it would have been awkward, to say the least. I couldn't very well tell her how I knew you either. But I knew that I would have to see you eventually."

"You think?" I ask sarcastically.

A small chuckle escapes him before he says, "After seeing you at the engagement party, it brought up all those old feelings again."

"Feelings?"

"Not like that," he says. "I mean the feelings of guilt over what I did to you."

"Oh," I say in a small voice.

"I don't expect you to accept my apology, but I need to say it." Aiden takes a quick breath and then finally says those magic words. "I'm sorry."

It's so quiet you can hear a pin drop. I take the opportunity of silence to gather my thoughts on those two little words. Everything hinges on them. At least for me they do. Do I believe him? Or is it that I am all of a sudden so desperate to want to believe him that I'm willing to accept his apology and finally let it all go? Dammit. The scorned bitch in me doesn't want to so fast. It's like she's hanging on for dear life. But there is another part of me that rarely shows itself to the outside world, that *needs* to let it all go. That logical and very sensible part of me knows that I need to accept his apology and move the hell on with my life once and for all. That part of me knows that there is a certain amount of freedom in forgiveness and is ultimately why I choose to tolerate his words.

"I accept your apology, Aiden. Even though it's five years late, I'll take it," I say with a hint of hesitation that makes him chuckle again.

"I know it's not easy for you, Julia, but thank you. I needed to say it, whether you believed me or not."

"Don't get too excited. I still don't like you very much."

"I wouldn't expect anything less from you," he says with a wide grin.

In spite of myself, a matching grin fights its way onto my face.

"Who knows, maybe we can be actual friends one day," he says.

"Slow your roll there, big guy," I reply with a laugh. "How about I agree not to spit in your general direction the next time we see each other and work ourselves up from there."

"Fair enough." He nods and then tilts his head to the side while looking me over thoughtfully. "So how are things going with Alex? You know, the guy I saw you with the other night. His name is Alex, right?"

"It is, and I don't see how that's any of your business."

An awkward silence ensues, and I take a moment to glance at my watch. "Listen, Aiden, I think it's best if we just end this conversation right here and call it a day."

"You're right, it's none of my business. I'm sorry, it's just that . . . never mind." He seems indecisive for a second and then stands up. "It was great to finally get a chance to talk to you, Julia. Thank you again."

Aiden turns and starts walking toward my door, but dammit all to hell if that little bit of "never mind" doesn't already start chewing away at my curiosity.

"Aiden, wait," I say and stand up.

He stops at the door and turns around to face me.

I reach him in a few short strides and ask, "What were you going to say about Alex?"

"Julia, I'm sure it's nothing, and you're right, it's really none of my business."

I roll my eyes because when someone says something like that to you, they have to be crazy to think that you wouldn't want to hear whatever it is they know.

"Fine," he says in a sigh. "It's just that Sophia seemed to think they're quite serious. She's friends with her, I'm sorry I don't remember her name but—"

"It's Marisa."

His lips turn up in a half smile. "Yes, that's the one. I guess Sophia knows her pretty well, and Marisa told her that they are very happy together."

"Well that was before we started dating," I say a tad too defensively.

Aiden leans forward and puts his hand lightly on my arm. "Julia, she also told Sophia that they've started talking about marriage."

Have you ever had the wind knocked out of you? Well that's exactly what it feels like when Aiden drops this little nugget of information on my lap. Actually, it feels worse. More like someone punched me in the gut and then kicked me in the heart for good measure.

"Look," he says in a soft voice, "I just thought you should know. I don't want to see you get hurt."

"Again," I say through clenched teeth.

He lets go of my arm and nods his head in silent agreement.

"I'm sorry, Julia," he says quietly and opens the door to my office, leaving me standing at the threshold in absolute shock.

I walk back to my desk and plop my ass down in the chair in a daze. *Think, Julia, think.* Shit, I *can't* think, at least not clearly after what I just found out. There is a part of me that doesn't want to believe Aiden. When I replay his visit in my mind, it's almost a bit too contrite. Like he was really playing up the apology angle and I just fell for it hook, line, and sinker. But . . . what does he have to gain from telling me any of it, apology included? Nothing.

On the other side of the fence is Alex, who has told me very little about Marisa but enough that I was convinced there was nothing going on there. Am I simply blind to what has been right in front of me all along? Or is he really telling me all there is to know about his relationship with her?

Okay, I need to get a grip and figure this all out later. I take a few calming breaths before I lose my mind and start throwing shit from my desk. Next, I pick up the stress ball and start going to town on it, hoping that it does exactly what it's supposed to do. A short while later, I'm still massaging it while I'm reviewing the guest list for Josie's party that Alex e-mailed me this morning when what do my wandering eyes stumble upon?

Marisa's name, clear as day on the guest list.

What the hell?

Okay, I'm not going to panic. At least that's what I try and tell myself while I'm having a full-on freak-out. The massage ball bursts

in my hands, and the granulated sand within it goes flying everywhere. I mean everywhere. Down my blouse and in my bra, in my
hair, and worst of all, in my eyes.

"Shit!" I yell because of the burning sensation in my eyes. "I'm
blind!"

I hear my office door swing open, and Lisette's familiar voice
shouts in alarm, "What happened?"

"I can't see anything because this thing just exploded in my
face!" I shout back at her.

The sound of her footsteps rushing over to the right side of my
desk makes me turn my head in that direction and try to open my
eyes again.

"Lisette, can you help me walk to the bathroom so I can wash
my eyes out?"

"Of course. Come on."

She grabs hold of my wrist and takes the destroyed stress reliever
ball out of my hand before helping me stand up. While my eyes feel
like they are being stabbed by a million tiny razor blades and I'm
cursing up a storm, I let Lisette lead me to the ladies' restroom.

Once inside, she turns on the faucet and helps me duck my
head underneath the running cool water so I can rinse out each eye
thoroughly. It takes a while, but finally I'm able to open my eyes
and see again, albeit with some discomfort.

I pick my head up and look at myself in the mirror to find a
rabid raccoon with red, half-closed eyes and mascara running down
its cheeks staring back at me. My eyes are still sore when Lisette
hands me a few damp hand towels and instructs me to keep them
on my eyes to relieve the puffiness.

"Do you mind telling me what happened?" she asks soothingly.

"I told you, that stupid stress ball thing busted open and
exploded everywhere."

"Obviously," Lisette says, "but that's not what I'm asking you."

"I just got upset at something and didn't realize I was squeezing it as hard as I was," I answer quickly. Too quickly because it's apparent to me that I sound like I'm trying not to be affected by everything I've found out today.

"And what got you so upset?"

"It's not important."

"Julia, I've known you for a long time. You can't pull the wool over my eyes, so you better start talking," she warns in a light tone.

"Fine," I say, my voice low and uneasy. "Do you remember that Marisa chick?" She nods. "Well, her name is on the guest list for Josie's party, and I kind of freaked because I didn't expect to see her name. Like at all."

"Why don't you just ask Alex about it?"

I bring down the damp hand towels from my eyes and sigh out loud. "I don't know about that."

"Do you think he's seeing her on the side or something?" she says curiously.

Thinking back to what intel I've found out about Marisa from Josie, Alex, and now Aiden, I have to assume that there is definitely something rotten in Denmark, but I'm not going to go into too much detail with Lisette about it. Especially the Aiden part because if she finds out he has a part to play in this, I'll never hear the end of it.

"I can't say for sure," I say, my eyes still stinging. "It's only been a week that we've been together, so I really shouldn't assume anything, and at the same time I don't want to come across as a jealous bitch, you know?"

Her ruby-red lips, which I can make out semi-clearly through my pain-filled eyes, quirk upward as if she's trying not to laugh. Then her shoulders start to shake. Then she's full-on laughing as if this is all funny.

"Do you mind telling me what's so goddamn funny?" I ask her impatiently.

"Julia, it's too late. You're already a jealous bitch," she says through her laughter.

Um, she might be right that I'm a tad jealous of Marisa. It's a knee-jerk, territorial reaction kind of thing. But that doesn't mean I want Alex to see this side of me.

"Shut it, Lisette," I say under my breath. "You're not helping."

She clears her throat and puts both her hands on her hips in a defiant stance. "Julia, I've known you for a very long time, and I can honestly say that in all that time, I have never, *ever*, seen you all worked up over a guy."

"And what's your point?"

"*¡Dios mío,* Julia! Seriously?" she says, throwing her hands up in the air. "You are so into him that it scares the living crap out of you. And I get it, I really do, but you need to let that go, live for today and stop being so afraid. From everything I've seen, Alex feels the same way, so cut the bitch act and talk to him about it. There's probably a damn good reason for Marisa to be invited, but you'll never know what that reason is unless you ask him."

I start to dab my eyes again in an effort to absorb what Lisette said in all its glory. God, I hate it when she's right. Actually, I hate being wrong period, but admitting it out loud is even more painful. Worse than that is that I don't know if I can take one more crushing disappointment at this point in my life. And I know it will crush me, so that's why I'm being extra cautious.

"Say something," Lisette says in a rush. "Tell me to go to hell or to mind my own business, but at least say something, because you're kind of freaking me out now."

"You're right."

She tilts her head, and then her eyebrows knit together in confusion. "What did you just say?"

I clear my throat and mumble under my breath, "I said, you're right."

"Is it the apocalypse?" Lisette asks and then crosses herself before plucking the cross charm attached to her necklace out of her cleavage and giving it a kiss. "Did you actually agree with me on this?"

"Yup."

I drop the damp towels from my eyes again and peer at her as she quietly looks on with a beaming smile on her face. "Don't gloat, it's not attractive."

"Oh, I'm going to gloat, so get over yourself." She clasps her hands behind her back while staring at me with a pleased look on her face for a few seconds and then exhales loudly and says, "Okay, I'm done gloating. Go ahead, start talking."

"It's only been a week, Lisette. A week full of a lot of hot and crazy sex and pillow talk. And I'm not complaining because, well, you know." She winks in understanding. "Anyway, we're in this nice and cozy little bubble that I don't want to burst yet."

"Burst how?"

"I mean everything is perfect right now as is. I don't want to rock the boat and start digging up shit that could potentially ruin everything." As an afterthought I add, "Plus, who's to say there isn't anything more to us than sex?"

I know Alex has told me we are more than fuck buddies, but still . . . there's a possibility that that's all there is. One that I've had in the back of my mind regardless of his repeated attempts to pacify my concerns.

See what years of craptastic dating can do to your psyche?

"It's definitely more than sex, Julia," Lisette calmly says. "The way that man looks at you . . . trust me, it's more than that, so you need to get that thought right out of your head."

"That's easier said than done."

"Stop doing that," she says, her voice going flat.

"What?"

"That. Where you compare every guy to Aiden. It's not fair to Alex. You need to give him a chance to explain this *and* give him a chance period."

"I hate it when you're right, you know that?"

Her mouth curls into a delighted grin. "I know you do. But don't worry, your secret is safe with me."

She gives me her elbow so I can loop my arm through, and she guides me back to my office, where she helps me clean up the mess left from the stress ball explosion. After she leaves me alone, and after another reminder that I need to give Alex a chance to explain, I shoot off a quick text to him.

Dinner at my place tonight?

He answers back right away.

Absolutely. What time?

7:00 p.m.

He agrees with a return text, and it literally takes all of me from responding with a litany of questions, the first of which would be something like: *"What the fuck is going on with you and Marisa?"* But cooler heads prevail, and I decide to wait until later tonight to dig into Alex's past so I can decide what the truth really is.

CHAPTER TWENTY-THREE

As soon as I get home, I change into my comfy clothes, which consist of distressed fitted jeans with a black tank top, and start to work on dinner. I have to stop myself from taking off my bra, since that's usually the very first thing I do when I walk through the door. What woman doesn't after a full day of having those suckers strapped in? But I figure we're not that comfortable in our relationship where I can walk around braless in a T-shirt yet. Here's to hoping though.

I'm in the midst of popping the tilapia filets in the oven when the doorbell rings. I turn down the volume on the iPod that is currently blaring Elvis Costello's "Everyday I Write the Book," before opening the door. If it wasn't for me holding the door handle and it effectively helping me to keep my balance, I may have literally swooned at what I see before me: Alex, wearing a backward baseball hat, a white V-neck T-shirt, black athletic shorts, and sneakers.

Now, you all should remember how I mentioned that I have two weaknesses when it comes to men. One being a man's forearms. But the other and far more potent form of kryptonite is a good-looking man wearing a backward baseball hat. I can't even fully explain or rationalize the how and why of it. It just is. So when I see Alex standing before me wearing a red one with the tips of his mussed-up hair poking out of it, I temporarily forget that

I'm supposed to be having a serious conversation with him tonight about Miss Teen USA because all I can do is stare.

"Can I come in?" he asks with a good-natured chuckle after a few seconds of me staring without saying a word.

"Why do you look like that?"

"I went for a run right after work and then came straight here." He steps into the foyer while I'm still standing in the same exact spot. "Is it okay if I use your shower to wash up before dinner? I promise I'll be really fast."

He presses a light kiss to my lips and drops his overnight bag on the floor. "Sure, go ahead. Dinner should be ready in about ten, fifteen minutes tops."

His dimpled smile is the last thing I need to tack on to the visual ambrosia I'm still feasting on as he starts to walk toward my bathroom.

"Alex," I call out to him. And yes, I'm still holding the freaking door open and letting a crapload of mosquitoes in the house. I can't help it; I'm a goner right now. I point at the hat on his head and ask, "Do you normally wear those?"

Shrugging his shoulders while still smiling, he answers, "I usually do when I'm working out. Why?"

"No reason. Just curious is all," I say, trying to sound dismissive.

He's about to start heading down the hallway when he stops and looks back at me with a confused look on his face. "Julia, are you okay?"

"Yeah, why?"

"Because you're still holding the door wide open and looking at me like I grew two heads, that's why."

"Oh shit," I mumble under my breath and close it finally. I hear his laugh floating down the hallway until it disappears behind the bathroom door.

The smell of the food in the kitchen that I still need to tend to breaks me out of my trance. Just barely though. I get my bearings long enough to traipse back in there and get back to work, all the while envisioning Alex wearing that hat. Lord help me, it may be my undoing, which sucks because I need to focus and be able to have this conversation with him. I promised Lisette I'd do it, and knowing her, she'll be in my office first thing in the morning to make sure I did.

Okay, I need to cut the shit. I start prepping the plates and silverware on the kitchen table. When I turn back around to open the oven, I hear the shower being turned off, signaling to me that Alex will be back out here momentarily.

"That smells delicious," I hear him say behind me a minute later. "What did you make?" I pivot my torso while talking. "Baked tilapia in garlic butter sauce with . . ."

My mouth is probably still moving, but I have no clue as to what is coming out of it since I'm staring at a very scrumptious Alex still a little wet from the shower with a towel wrapped around his waist. His arms are crossed over his chest, and he's leaning against the wall. Were it not for the fact that I know this is Alex, I would have thought Sawyer from *Lost* was standing right in front of me. As a matter of fact, there is an episode of *Lost*—season one, episode twelve, called "Whatever the Case May Be," and yes, I'm an über *Lost* geek—where Sawyer goes swimming, and when he comes out of the quarry he looks so incredibly delicious. That is *exactly* what Alex looks like right now.

I'm watching a rivulet of water roll down his chest when I hear Alex say my name, which breaks me out of my fantasy of skinny-dipping in a quarry with Sawyer. Oops, I mean Alex.

"Dude, you have got to be shitting me right now."

"Did you just call me *dude*?"

I motion my hand toward him up and down as I say, "I did, because have you seen yourself? First the hat and now this?"

Alex bites his bottom lip to keep from laughing. "I had to come out here to get my bag that I left by the door."

"Well go and get it before I start calling you Sawyer and make you call me Freckles."

"Who are those people?" he asks in an amused voice.

"It's not important right now," I answer quickly. "Just please, for the love of everything that is holy, *please* put some clothes on."

Now he's stalking toward me with a devilish smirk on his face. When he closes the distance between us, he pulls the oven mitts off of my hands and places them on the counter. Next he hooks his hands loosely around my neck while his thumbs are softly rubbing up and down against my pulse, which is probably beating errati-cally right now.

"You have a thing for hats, huh?" Alex asks while still grinning.

"You could say that."

Using his thumbs for leverage, he tilts my face up and brushes his lips against mine, so feather-soft that it barely registers, but it's enough that I know if it keeps up we'll be forgetting about dinner.

"Alex?"

"Julia?"

I smile against his mouth and open my eyes to find his blue ones sweetly staring back at me.

His voice full of concern, he asks, "Why are your eyes so red? Did something upset you?"

With a small sigh, I grab hold of his wrists. "No, nothing like that. It's really stupid, actually, and you're going to laugh when I tell you about it during dinner." I inch up on my toes and kiss him lightly again before I add, "Speaking of which, go on and get dressed so I can finish up in here and we can finally eat."

"That's right, before you call me . . . what was the name again?" he playfully asks.

"Sawyer," I mumble under my breath.

"Right. I guess I have some competition."

"Um, he's a character on my favorite TV show, so you're pretty safe."

His eyebrows knit together as he asks, "Which show?"

"*Lost.*"

"I never watched it," he admits.

"Well that's something we'll have to remedy if you're going to be sticking around."

Alex's eyes light up, and I'm sure it has nothing to do with the fact he'll be watching the greatest TV show of all time—which it is, and that is the beginning and end of any debate, thank you very much—but more with the fact that I've alluded to him, to us, in the future, kind of.

"You've got yourself a deal," he replies with a sexy grin.

He kisses me one last time before heading into the foyer to pick up his overnight bag. All the while I'm craning my neck and gawking at his muscular back until he catches me and shakes his head in mocking disapproval. Once he's completely out of sight, I pick up the oven mitts he tossed onto the counter and quickly fan myself. I swear, he's going to be the death of me.

By the time he comes back into the kitchen fully dressed in jeans and a plain old black T-shirt, I'm already setting the last dish of roasted vegetables on the table. Alex sits down and starts to fill my wineglass from the chilled bottle of pinot grigio I have on the table and then looks up at me as I go to sit across from him.

"This really does smell delicious, Julia. I had no idea you could cook," he says while now pouring his own glass of wine.

A perfect segue. Really, I couldn't have planned it better if I tried.

I smile, genuinely happy that I could surprise him, and as I'm serving him his food I reply, "Well, I'm sure there are a lot of things we don't know about each other yet." He looks on curiously as I keep on talking. "But to answer your question, I'm not that much of a cook. I know how to make some dishes and can probably cook the shit out of a steak, but that's about it."

He takes his first forkful, and I wait to see his reaction. "I beg to differ." He stops and wipes his mouth with the napkin. "This is absolutely delicious, but I'm going to have to take you up on that steak sometime too." He sets his fork down to grab his wineglass and takes a sip before talking again. "So what's this about us not knowing a lot about each other? Are you referring again to outside-of-work Alex?"

"Kind of," I say matter-of-factly. "I mean, we know each other in the physical sense pretty damn well, but I think it's time we got to know each other a little more in other ways, don't you think?"

"I agree," he answers with a forkful of food perched in front of his mouth. "You can start by telling me why your eyes are so red."

"Funny you should mention that, because my eyes being so red has to do with you sort of." Alex's eyebrows shoot up in response before I tack on the rest of it, leaving out Aiden's visit. "See, I was in my office massaging my stress ball while looking over the guest list you sent me for Josie's party."

"And?"

"Well, I came across one name that kind of surprised me. Marisa."

"And how does her name have anything to do with your eyes being red?" he asks in a low voice.

"I must have been squeezing the ball too hard when I came across her name, so it exploded all over me and some of the sand got in my eyes."

"I'm sorry." His eyes are apologetic and concerned. "I should have told you about it sooner."

I remember what Lisette told me earlier today—give him a chance to explain and not jump to any conclusions. That is exactly what I intend to do when I say to him, "No better time than the present."

"It's complicated."

Ugh, I don't like the sound of that, and I'm already wondering if Aiden was right. I half smile, and in between sips of my wine I say, "Just start at the beginning."

"Our parents have been friends for a long time and are very close. So growing up, Vanessa and I were around Marisa and her big sister quite often." He smiles then, but it doesn't reach his eyes. "Marisa is about eight years younger than the rest of us, and as we got older it was Vanessa, myself, and Marisa's sister, Katerina, who were *always* together. We were inseparable."

I'm not sure where this is heading, but I can tell that wherever it ends up I'm not going to like it one way or the other. Regardless of that, I smile and nod to let him know he can keep talking.

"Vanessa eventually went away to college, leaving Katerina and me behind. We became even closer, and things started to change between us." Alex looks up at me then, his expression hesitant. "By the time we started high school together, we were officially a couple and started to make plans for our future. When we decided to go to different colleges, it was difficult, but we made it work. I would visit her as often as I could and vice versa, but it put a slight strain on our relationship that neither of us really wanted to admit to."

"You loved her," I say to him softly.

"I did," he admits with an exhale of breath. "Looking back on it now, the fact that we had been together so long and shared so much at such a young age bonded us, and we didn't want to let each other go."

"You were both afraid to move on. I get it."

I can tell he's reliving a terrible memory. All I want is to crawl up in his lap and comfort him. And I can honestly say that I have never felt the need to want to do that with any man before him. It's a terrifying feeling for me, but instead of acting on it, I sit still and steeple my fingers underneath my chin so that I'm not tempted.

"During my final year of college, she came to visit me. Things were rocky then, to say the least, and we argued off and on that last day. It got to the point that things were said that couldn't be taken back or unheard . . . and so she left."

"I'm sorry, Alex."

I can tell he's struggling to say the next words by the way his fingers clench together into tight fists. "I'm sorry too, because if I had gone after her instead of waiting for her to come back to me, she would still be alive today."

I gasp out loud because that is the very last thing I expect to hear. "Oh my God, how did she—"

"I don't know all the details other than she lost control of her car and slammed into a guardrail over an embankment. The only thing I do know is that she didn't suffer and died instantly."

My eyes tear up because of the pain I see in his, and more than anything, the obvious guilt he still feels over losing Katerina. I can't even begin to imagine what that must be like, and it makes my so-called sob story of being jilted by Aiden all those years ago seem like a cakewalk.

He smiles in an effort to lighten the heavy mood in the air, but it's forced. Both of us have long forgotten about eating at this point. Alex unclenches his fist and then reaches for his wineglass and takes a sip. When he sets it back down on the table, he clears his throat before filling in the rest of the gaps, namely Marisa's place in all of this.

"That was eleven years ago, and it took a while for me to move on, but I did. Marisa, on the other hand, as well as her parents, never has." His index finger starts to trace the rim of the wineglass before leaning back in his chair. "Marisa was fourteen years old when Katerina died, which is a very difficult age to lose someone you care so much about. But I think what has made it worse for her over the years is the fact that their parents idolized Katerina and put her on a pedestal as if she could do no wrong. As a result, Marisa has been living the last few years of her life in a shadow."

"I don't understand," I say to him, genuinely confused. "But what does that have to do with you all these years later?"

"Guilt is a funny thing, Julia," he replies with a forced grin. "As I said, my parents are still very close to Marisa's parents, and I guess in their minds they think me taking Marisa out every so often is helping the situation. But it's not, it just makes everything more . . ."

"Complicated."

"Yes," he confirms in a rush of breath. "Very complicated."

"So that explains the invitation to the party and why she's so interested in you. If I'm being too nosy with my next question, by all means tell me." Alex nods as an eyebrow cocks upward in curiosity. "Should I be worried about her?"

He runs a hand through his hair and then starts to rub the back of his neck, and that alone makes me nervous of his answer. "Not really."

Before I can ask him to clarify that answer, he says, "We kissed one time a few years ago, but I swear that is as far as it went. I had a few drinks, and in a moment of complete stupidity I let it happen."

I want to believe him when he tells me there is essentially nothing going on between the two of them other than the one kiss and him escorting her out sometimes. I'm certain he's doing it more out of guilt than anything else. Is it weird and creepy? A little bit, but I get it. However, that doesn't explain why Marisa would be telling Aiden's fiancée that there is more between them. But I make a conscious decision not to dig deeper. The way I see it, I have to believe Alex's explanation versus Aiden's because . . . well, Aiden's track record speaks for itself.

"What are you thinking?" he asks, his voice quiet and unsure. "You're awfully quiet."

"Honestly? A bunch of things."

"Care to pinpoint?"

"Well, I never thought I'd say this, but I feel sorry for Marisa, and even worse that I was kind of a bitch to her," I say sheepishly. And it's the truth. I can't even begin to imagine what she's gone through.

"So you're okay with all of this?"

"As far as understanding it and why you've continued to take her out, yes, I am. But I have to be totally honest with you," I say. "I'm not really okay with you continuing to do so if we're going to be together." I pause and take note of his expression softening, as if he was holding a breath until I answered. "I don't share, Alex."

"I haven't been anywhere with her since that opening at the gallery a couple of weeks ago," he clarifies. Then he adds with an impish grin, "And I'm glad to hear you don't share, Julia, because I don't either."

My lips twitch to keep my smile in check. We sit there for a few seconds not saying a word. The pull I felt a little while ago of wanting to comfort him is still battling within me. It's such an odd feeling to want to comfort a man I'm in a relationship with, and I would normally brush it off, but I don't want to with Alex. Before I can chicken out, I stand up, his eyes tracking my movements as I walk around the small table to him. He pivots in his seat and makes room for me in between his legs. I take his face in my hands and tilt his chin up as I bend down and place a light kiss on his forehead. Alex closes his eyes at the contact, so I keep planting soft kisses down the bridge of his nose, eyelids, cheeks, chin, and finally his mouth. For some reason, this moment feels far more intimate to me than the ones we've shared in the bedroom, and I like it. A lot.

His arms encircle my waist, pulling me closer to him, and I weave my fingers into his hair until I'm cradling his head against my stomach. "I'm sorry I ruined this amazing dinner you made just for me with all of this, and that your stress ball exploded. I really should have told you sooner, and I feel terrible about it," he says, his voice slightly muffled against my body. "Let me make it up to you."

"The dinner can be nuked, so that's easily fixed. As for the stress ball, it was about time I got rid of that thing anyway. So you see"—I stop and pull his face back to look into his questioning eyes—"you didn't ruin a thing, and there is no need to apologize. But . . ."

"But what?" he asks with a smirk on his face.

"But I do know how you can make it up to me."

"Even though you just said I have no reason to apologize," he shoots back with a hint of sarcasm.

"Yup." I bite my lip to keep from laughing.

"Go ahead, name it."

Ah, this . . . this banter that I can do with my arms tied behind my back is definitely more my speed. I don't regret the intimate moment, but I need to use baby steps with him because I know that I'm letting my guard down, and there won't be any turning back.

"It involves the baseball hat and other things."

Alex brings his hand up to hook his arm around my neck and pulls me down so my lips are level with his. His breath is warm when he speaks, causing all my nerve endings to prickle with delight. "Start heating up the food so I can show you other things."

I whisper back to him, "With the baseball hat?"

"Most definitely with the baseball hat."

I reheat our food, we eat, and move the evening along to other things that may or may not include him calling me Freckles in bed once.

Okay, okay, maybe twice.

CHAPTER TWENTY-FOUR

I wake up in Alex's bed, and we make love in a semi-sleep state that feels as if I'm suspended in a dream.

This isn't out of the ordinary for me, seeing as how I've been having sex with him on a daily basis for the last month. But the fact that I set his alarm to go off at the ass crack of dawn for Josie's birthday party today and the alarm hasn't gone off yet has me wondering what the hell is going on. Not complaining or anything, just slightly disoriented, but in the best way possible.

Afterward, when we're both coming down from our high, he nuzzles his nose along mine and starts to press featherlight kisses across my cheek until he reaches my ear. "Good morning."

"Good morning to you too," I answer on a contented sigh. "I know it's a lot to ask, but do you think you can wake me up like that every day? I'd be forever grateful."

He rolls over onto his back and takes me with him. Smiling as his hand trails up and down my spine while he's still inside of me, he replies, "I'll see what I can do."

I tilt my head over to peek at the clock and notice the time. Ugh. It's five forty-five a.m. Seriously, if it wasn't for Josie's party today, I could easily stay in this bed all day with him after taking a nice long nap.

We kiss and I start to move off of him, but he wraps his arms around me and pulls me back down. "Alex," I say through a giggle, "I have to start getting ready. Some of the deliveries are going to be here in about fifteen minutes."

"Two more minutes," he says, sounding muffled against my neck. "Then you can get out of this bed."

I'm a sucker for his two-minute request, so I stay right where I am and let him hold me in his strong arms. My hair blankets each side of his face when I pick my head up to look at him. I cup his face in my hands as a lazy smile sweeps across his lips along with the dimples.

My finger traces the outline of one before I kiss it. "I really need to get moving here, Alex."

He tilts my head and kisses me softly on the lips before letting me go. I nearly tumble out of bed in a dead sprint to the shower and hear him laughing behind me. So much for trying to be graceful, but I literally have just a few minutes to get myself in gear before the delivery trucks start arriving.

When I finish with my half-ass shower and go back into the bedroom, he's making the bed while wearing a pair of dark pajama bottoms and looking as yummy as ever. I swear to Christ on a cracker, watching his lean and muscular body move around the side of the bed is a sight to behold, and I don't think I could ever get sick of it.

"If you keep staring at me like that, you'll only have yourself to blame for being late this time," he says over his shoulder, catching me red-handed.

I scrunch my nose at him, making him chuckle, before I go to my overnight bag to grab my clothes and get dressed as quickly as possible. Since I'm setting up the party, I don't have to go all out yet with the nice outfit, makeup, and hair. Which translates to I'll probably have to shower again after I finish and before the guest of honor arrives.

I turn on my heel and head into his kitchen to turn on the coffee machine. While waiting for it to start brewing, I rummage through my purse and pull out my iPad. I'm checking off the items I can easily take care of when Alex comes strolling into the kitchen and wraps his arms around me from behind.

His stubble tickles my neck as he says, "I think you're more excited for this party than my niece is."

"I don't know about that." My eyes stay focused on the list in front of me. "Last time I talked to her she was busting at the seams."

"What time is she supposed to be here?"

"I told Vanessa to bring her over at noon, and no sooner, because the guests will start arriving about a half hour after that. By then everything will be set up, and I want to be able to give her a private tour of everything."

My head pops up like a dog hearing a faraway whistle at the sound of the first truck pulling into Alex's driveway. I tilt my head to the side and give him a quick peck on the lips. "Trucks are starting to pull up. I've gotta go."

"I'll be in my office if you need anything. Something tells me you won't, but it makes me feel better saying it anyway." He drops his arms and spins around to grab a mug of coffee for himself. "Go ahead, I'll bring you a cup once it's done."

With my iPad in one hand and phone in the other, and smiling like an idiot because he's right—I may very well be just as excited as Josie and want to get on with decorating the shit out of his house—I lean forward and kiss his cheek again before saying thank you and heading toward the door.

While I'm overseeing the delivery trucks, I'm thinking how much my life has changed in the last month. How this relationship with Alex has grown into something more than I thought it could ever be. I smile thinking about how much I've grown to care about him and how much I miss him when we're not together. Sometimes it feels like we can't get enough of each other.

And I love that.

I never thought I'd feel that way about someone ever again, but miracles do happen.

I feel it in his touch, his eyes, his words, and most importantly his actions. Because a guy can say just about anything, but it's what he actually does that proves he means those words. Trust me on this one, I've heard and seen it all before.

"Here you go," he says, sneaking up on me and handing me my cup of coffee. Just like he promised he would.

I say a quick thanks, and he kisses my forehead before retreating into the house.

A huge grin on my face, my eyes stay focused on the closed door long after he's gone.

Yeah, Alex definitely isn't just some guy.

Not by a long shot.

CHAPTER TWENTY-FIVE

I've spent the last six hours knee-deep in Muggles, Squibs, wizards, and witches. But it paid off because Alex's house and backyard looks like Harry Potter took a dump all over it and then some. In other words, it looks so freaking awesome that it might even give Universal in Orlando a run for its money.

From the makeshift brick wall in his foyer emulating platform nine and three-quarters and the broomstick parking spot affixed to it—since the children invited were told to bring a broom of their own for a Quidditch match later in the day—to the Sorting Hat area and a replica of Professor Trelawney's and Professor Snape's classrooms just to name a few, everything looks amazing, and I couldn't be more pleased.

All of this might have propelled me to super-duper geekdom status, but I'll gladly wear the moniker because when Josie arrives in a few minutes she is going to flip her lid.

I leave Lisette running around outside directing the caterers while I duck inside to take another shower and get dressed again. This time though I put on something a little nicer in the form of a strapless black maxi dress with embellished sandals, and I work a French braid into the front of my hair that ends in a side ponytail. I am racing around Alex's bedroom looking for my earrings when he steps inside and leans against one of the bedposts, watching me run around like a chicken with its head cut off.

"My parents just called me and said they'll be here any minute," he says casually.

Um, yeah, I kind of completely blanked out on his parents being here too and that I would be meeting them for the first time today.

I freeze in mid-step and throw him an *oh shit* look because now I'm all kinds of nervous. Granted, I've met his sister and obviously his niece, but *this* is pretty huge. Especially for me, since I never get far enough with a guy I'm seeing to meet his parents, and He-Who-Must-Not-Be-Named doesn't count. In fact, let's just forget about him, shall we? Sounds like a plan.

"What's wrong?" Alex asks, concerned and coming over to where I'm standing.

I mumble something unintelligible under my breath, trying to play it off like everything is cool when it's totally not.

He rubs my arms up and down as a small smile plays on his lips. "Are you nervous that you're going to meet my parents?"

"Maybe a little," I admit.

Truth be told, I'm scared shitless.

"Julia Boyd, the toughest woman I know, is afraid of my parents. Well, this just got all kinds of interesting."

I roll my eyes and smack him lightly on the arm. "Alex, it's not funny. This is kind of a big deal, and I'd like to make a good impression."

With his thumb and index finger, he lifts my chin and brushes his lips against mine while still smiling. "You have nothing to be nervous about. I promise you that they're going to love you."

"That's easy for you to say."

He cocks his eyebrow in response. It takes me a second, but I realize that I somewhat intimated that he loves me with my answer, and yeah, that would be a little presumptuous seeing as how we haven't gone there with each other yet.

I hastily backpedal my response. "What I mean to say is *you* know me, truck-driver mouth and all. They don't, so . . . yeah, that's about all I got right now, and . . ."

Alex bites his bottom lip to keep from laughing while I ramble on. He pulls me into his arms, his lips poised over mine, and he quietly says, "Shut up, Julia."

"Don't tell me to shut up."

"I just did."

"Yeah, well, don't do it again."

"Are you going to keep talking, or are you going to let me kiss you?"

"Not if you tell me to shut up again."

"Are you done talking now?"

"Are you really asking me that?"

"Are you answering my question with a question?"

I open my mouth to say something back to him that is not in the form of a question, but he starts to kiss me, and quite frankly, I don't give a rat's ass anymore because he can shut me up like this anytime he likes.

The doorbell rings, and we reluctantly break off the kiss.

"Remind me to pick this up later right where we just left off," he says in a low voice that makes my insides squirm.

"You've got yourself a deal."

The doorbell sounds off again. I grab the backs of my earrings and put them on as I'm walking toward the front door to answer it, Alex following behind me.

I peek through the side glass panels and see that it's Josie and Vanessa on the other side. Without a minute to waste, I swing the door open to find Josie smiling so wide all I see is her braces. God, she is so freaking cute.

"Julia!" she squeals and throws her arms around my waist.

"Hey, girlie!"

Vanessa pushes her sunglasses up on her head and sighs. "She's been awake and fully dressed since seven o'clock this morning, asking me every ten minutes if it's time to go yet."

"Seriously?" I ask her, but Josie answers instead with a resounding yes.

Alex appears beside me and bends his head down to Josie's level. "You're not even going to say hello to me, are you?"

"Don't be silly, Uncle Alex," she says in a matter-of-fact voice and releases me.

It gives me a chance to properly say hello to Vanessa while Alex scoops Josie up in his arms. Her feet dangle at least two feet off the ground, her blond curls bouncing down her back.

When he puts her down, Alex gives his sister a big hug and kiss on the cheek as Josie looks on impatiently.

"Okay, girlie, are you ready to enter Hogwarts?"

She clasps her hands underneath her chin and nods.

"Give me your hand and close your eyes," I instruct her.

I walk a couple of feet to the end of the foyer where the platform nine and three-quarters wall is waiting to be pulled back.

"Open your eyes, Josie."

She complies and bounces from foot to foot, staring in awe at the sign painted to look exactly like the one from the movie. If she's this excited by a fake wall, wait until she sees the rest of the place!

"Can I open it?" she asks in wonderment.

"Yup."

Josie's hand inches up and snatches the end of the fabric, pulling it back slowly and peeking her head through to take a look at the other side. She drops the curtain, and it falls back in place, her face in a stoic expression.

I bend my knees until I'm at eye level with her. With my hand I brush back a loose curl from her forehead. "Is everything okay?"

She nods but doesn't say a word. I look up at Vanessa and Alex, who are just as confused as I am. "Josie," I say quietly, "why aren't you saying anything?"

She wraps her arms around my neck and hugs me to the point of choking. Through choked-up tears, she whispers in my ear. "It's amazing."

I'm sure the PMS hormones have something to do with it because I start to get teary-eyed and all emotional by her display of gratitude.

Jesus Christ, what the fuck is happening to me? I'm turning into a mushy person, and I actually like it.

I peek up at Alex, who gives me a sweet smile with a wink, and I swear I have to avert my gaze to the floor before I start to really bawl like a baby. I quickly pull myself together and thank God I do before the waterworks really start for me. It's one thing to see a child cry but quite another for a grown woman. And really nobody should have to see me cry. It's downright frightening. I do the whole bottom lip quivering thing, and my nose gets as red as Rudolph's. Seriously, it's not pretty.

"But you haven't seen everything yet," I say, patting her back softly. "Come on, let me show you the rest."

"Okay."

She lets me go so I can stand up, and I grab her hand in mine again. I pull back the curtain and step over the threshold into party central, which has been separated into three specific quadrants. A Sorting Hat section that has a walkie-talkie attached to the back of the chair so that whenever a guest sits in the chair with the hat on, an actor I hired stationed in another room is signaled to speak. Once a guest has been assigned to his or her respective house, there's a rack of rented authentic robes that have one of the four crests on it. The second quadrant is a potions section that has a giant witch's cauldron filled to the brim with dry ice bubbling over and bottles lined up in front of it with the following ingredients: dragon's blood, mandrake root, salamander blood, pickled slugs, eel eye, and goosegrass, to name a few.

To the left what was once Alex's living room is now a large white fabric tent that has a small opening at the bottom left corner. I nudge Josie forward with my hand and crouch down, lifting the corner of the tent up so she can look inside.

"It's Professor Trelawney's Divination class!" she yells back to her mom, who is trailing behind us with a huge smile on her face.

Inside the tent is an array of eclectic pillows surrounding a table with a big crystal ball on it. The actor I hired looks so much like the real Professor Trelawney that it even freaks me out, so I can only imagine how Josie is feeling.

We step back out, standing up, and I walk us toward the set of French doors that leads to Alex's backyard. The pool has several ivory candles floating around it, mirroring the look of the floating candles in the Great Hall. Past the pool and taking up the large open space of the yard is a Quidditch field with hoops on each end.

"Oh my God!" Josie yells. "It's a freaking Quidditch field!"

"Hey," Vanessa warns with a laugh. "Watch your mouth, kid."

Through a laugh of my own, I say, "I can't say as I blame you, girlie. It's pretty freaking awesome, if I do say so myself."

"Alex?" a woman's voice calls out from inside the house.

We all turn around to see what I assume must be Alex's parents walking toward us in amazement. Jesus Christ, no wonder their children are so good-looking. These two look like they just stepped out of the pages of a Calvin Klein advertisement. No, not the Kate Moss, emaciated heroin-chic kind either. I'm talking the elegant and perfectly put together kind of models—if they were in their fifties—which they aren't usually, but whatever, you get the picture.

His mother is dressed in a white blouse tucked into a pair of black checkered capri pants, and her blond hair is cut in a smart bob that falls around her jawline. From where I'm standing, I can see where Alex gets his bright blue eyes as hers sparkle in the sunlight when she gives her son a hug and kiss on his cheek. His dad, for lack of a better way of putting it, is one smooth and handsome-looking man, and I can tell that's where Alex gets his suave and sexy swagger.

"Grandma, Grandpop, did you see everything Julia did to make Uncle Alex's house look like Harry Potter's world?" Josie says in a rush, running over to them.

"I did," Alex's mom answers and looks up at me.

I take it as a signal that I should introduce myself, so I bite the bullet and pray to the deodorant gods that my pits aren't sweating and walk over to her with my hand extended.

Before I reach them, Alex wraps his arm around my waist and says, "Mom, Dad, this is Julia, my girlfriend and the person responsible for all of this." He tops it off by kissing my temple as I look down at Josie, who has both her thumbs up and a joker-like grin on her face.

Okay, up until this point I'd been thinking that he was kind of sort of my boyfriend, but I never publicly said that to anyone or even addressed him as such during any of our conversations. To hear him say it out loud is surprising, but in a really good way.

"Hi, it's very nice to meet you, Mr. and Mrs. Holt," I say, my voice sounding way more calm than I thought it would.

Alex's mom takes my hand in hers. "Oh dear, please don't call me that. It reminds me of my mother-in-law. Call me Allison. I insist."

I nod as she lets go of my hand, and his dad steps up and takes it in his for a firm shake. "Don't listen to her or whatever she has to say about my mother. She's still upset that she didn't approve of our wedding color choices over thirty years ago." I laugh in spite of myself as he goes on. "But she's right, please call me Alex."

My head turns to my right to look up at *my* Alex. "You never said you were a junior."

"Because I never tell people that," he answers under his breath.

Josie steps in then and commands the attention of her grandparents, taking their hands in hers and dragging them along back toward the house.

Over her shoulder as we watch them walk away, his mom says, "It was very nice to meet you, and we'll catch up more later."

Vanessa smacks my butt as she brushes past me, making me jump in surprise. "See, you had nothing to be nervous about, Julia."

She laughs as she walks away, trying to catch up to Josie and her parents, and leaving Alex and me outside.

"That wasn't so bad, was it?"

"You told her I was nervous?" I ask him in disbelief.

"I did."

"Why would you do that?"

"Because I thought it was cute."

"Listen up, Junior." His eyes squint in jest, and he smiles. "Don't be telling people things I say to you in private."

"Even if I think it's adorable and cute as hell?"

He turns me around and wraps both arms around me while waiting for me to answer.

"If I answer you with a question, will you keep asking me questions again?"

"Too late, you just asked me a question, so I'll take that to mean it's okay for me to tell people when I think my girlfriend is being cute as hell."

"Yeah about that," I coyly say.

"Here we go." His voice drops to a low murmur. "I was waiting for you to freak out about that."

"Actually, all I was going to say was . . . I like it."

His eyes light up, and he grazes his lips against mine. In the background I hear Josie squealing again, signaling the arrival of her first guests. Which means she's also probably just finding out that each guest received a personalized Hogwarts acceptance letter. I really outdid myself with those, and it might be my favorite thing out of all this stuff.

I let go of him, and we walk back toward the house. He goes off on his own while I catch up with Lisette, who is overseeing the catering staff in the kitchen. After getting the lowdown from her for a while and confirming she's got everything under control as usual, I start to walk around and get a lay of the land.

After about a half hour of making sure everything is running smoothly, which thank God it is, I make my way back outside where the kids are all gathering for the first round of Quidditch. Approaching the small crowd of spectators on the edge of the field, I'm trying to squeeze through the last grouping of bodies when I hear a familiar woman's voice mention my name.

So what do I do?

Yup, I eavesdrop like you know you would too.

"I can't believe she's here," Marisa says, clear as a bell and loudly enough that I can hear, along with anyone else within a five-foot radius.

I shimmy over to her left and around a couple who are cheering for their child so that I'm standing right at the front, keeping Marisa in my peripheral to make sure she doesn't notice me so she'll keep talking. And she does.

"Seriously, she's like white trash, and he's way too good for her," she rattles off to the person she's talking to.

"So why is he with her then?" an unknown woman's voice asks.

"He's not . . . or at least he won't be for too long," Marisa answers.

I'm going to freeze right here and remind you all how I had a feeling about her when I first met her—the whole women's intuition thingy. Yeah, about that. Well, after Alex told me the history behind Marisa, I felt terrible about how I had labeled her a whiny bitch and treated her awfully.

Now is about the time that I say *aha!* in my head because I was so right about her from the very beginning. Really? I'm trash? Who the fuck does she think *she* is? And that nonsense about me not being good enough for Alex? Bitch, please.

Yes, I admit it, I'm in love with him, but that's not important right now. What's important is getting Miss Teen USA to shut the fuck up in the most reasonable way possible in front of all these people without making a scene.

At this point I'm craning my neck sideways to look over to where she's standing so I can get her attention, but her back's turned my way. The next thing I know, I get pelted in the face hard by something. I don't know what it is, but it's hard enough that it knocks me on my ass until I'm lying flat on the ground.

Well it worked—she shut up.

That might be because everyone is crowding around me to see if I'm okay. My hand is covering the left side of my face, which feels like it's already black and blue, and I can only see out of one eye when Vanessa crouches alongside of me.

"Are you okay?"

"I think so." I go to sit up, and she helps me. "What hit me?"

She smirks and says, "A Quaffle ball."

"Awesome."

"Come on, let's get you up and inside to check out your eye."

Vanessa gets me to stand up and leads me toward the house, but not before I catch a glance from Marisa, who is smiling like the conniving bitch that she is from ear to ear.

"Bitch," I say under my breath.

"Who's a bitch?"

"Nobody, never mind."

"Uh-huh, right," she says quietly and then turns around to the crowd still standing around staring. "She's fine. Go back to enjoying the party; we'll be right back."

She leads me straight to the bathroom in Alex's bedroom. Sitting me down on the closed toilet seat, Vanessa proceeds to turn on the water in the sink. She grabs a hand towel, running it under the stream to get it wet. She wrings it free of excess water and then comes over to me.

"Okay, let's see it."

I shake my head, afraid of what my face must look like by now.

Growing exasperated at my childish behavior, she starts to pry my fingers away from my face.

She blows a long whistle after the big reveal and says, "Nice welt, sweetie."

"That bad?"

"Honestly?" She takes a breath and blows on the area for a second or two. "It's pretty bad."

I stand up and go to the mirror to see for myself. The left side of my face just below my eye is swollen and already has a purplish hue to it. You have got to be shitting me.

"Here." She hands me the wet towel. "Put this on it for a little bit to help with the swelling and sit down."

Feeling defeated because I look like I've gone a full twelve rounds in the ring with Mike Tyson, I sit back down on the toilet seat. After a few moments of silence, Vanessa finally speaks up.

"So this has to do with Marisa, huh?"

"What makes you say that?"

"Women's intuition." She leans against the wall casually and crosses her arms.

I can't help but laugh a little at that, but it starts to hurt my face. Plus, now I have a pounding headache, so yeah, it sucks.

"Julia, don't worry about her. She's been trying to get her claws into Alex for a while, but he wants nothing to do with her. Trust me when I tell you that I have not seen my brother this happy in a very long time, and that's all because of you."

"Really?"

"Scout's honor."

And speak of the devil, Alex appears in the doorway of his bathroom looking concerned and worried.

"What the hell happened?"

He bends down and kneels in front of me while Vanessa tells him I got nailed in the face by a fucking prop.

He kisses my forehead and tries to gently tug my hand away. "Let me see."

"Nope, it looks ugly as all hell, and I don't care if that makes me a vain person, but you definitely don't need to see this."

Vanessa chuckles and starts to walk out of the bathroom. "You two lovebirds can figure this out while I go find Julia some aspirin." She gives me a wink over her shoulder and closes the door behind her.

Alex tries again to pry my hand away, but I don't budge. "Baby, no matter what it looks like, you'll still be gorgeous to me."

I breathe in through my mouth and blow it out through my nose. Closing my eyes and on the count of three, I drop the towel from my face.

He doesn't say a word, so I open my eyes. "It's awful, isn't it?"

Alex leans forward and ever so gently places a kiss over the welt on my face. He pulls back an inch until he is all I can see with the one eye because the left one is squinty at this point.

"Gorgeous. Perfect," he whispers.

I smile. "You're just saying that because you're my boyfriend and you know I'd kick your ass if you didn't."

He chuckles and brushes the ponytail off my shoulder. "You would, wouldn't you?"

"Not right now, but definitely in the foreseeable future." I bring my hand up to lightly touch my face and add, "I'm going to have to wear a goddamn eye patch or something and look like a freaking pirate, aren't I?"

"You'd be the sexiest pirate I know."

"I'd be the *only* pirate you know."

He brings the towel back up to my face and gets me to stand up. When he opens the bathroom door, he makes sure that his bedroom door is closed before leading me to his bed.

"Alex, what are you doing? We can't be fooling around while the party is going on. Plus, I have to go and keep an eye on everything."

"Shhh, stop talking," he says and sits me down on the bed.

He arranges the pillows behind me on the headboard and pulls my feet off the floor and onto the mattress.

"Okay, before the *stop talking* thing was really cute, but now . . . not so much."

He ignores my commentary but grins anyway as he arranges me until I'm propped up with the pillows on his bed. He sits down beside me on my right side and throws his arm around my shoulders.

"Stop worrying about the party. I'm sure Lisette can handle it for a bit by herself while you rest."

"You have a house full of people. You really don't need to stay with me. I'll just rest for a while, and I'll meet up with you later," I say.

"Vanessa will take care of the guests."

"But—"

"But nothing," he insists. "Lean into me and relax for a little while."

Well this certainly isn't how I thought the day would go, I think, resting my head on his shoulder. On top of that, I feel terrible that I'm taking him away from his family on such a big day.

"Alex, this sucks, and I'm sorry that you're stuck in here with me when you have a house full of people over for your niece's birthday party."

He tilts my face up carefully. "I'd rather be here with you right now than with anyone else at this party."

"Don't let Josie hear you say that," I say through a chuckle.

"You know what I mean," he says, his voice growing sincere.

I do know what he means, and it makes me feel incredibly happy. I'm sure I'm grinning like a one-eyed pirate at him right now because of it.

He ducks his head to press a feather-soft kiss on the top of my head before letting me adjust myself on his shoulder again. "Get some rest, baby. I'll be here when you wake up."

My heart may have just skipped a beat or two. It definitely does a few seconds later when his hand starts to rub small circles on my back. Melting farther into his warmth, I let him lull me into a state of complete relaxation. My eyes grow heavy, and I have no choice but to give in to sleep, where I dream about Marisa getting pelted with Quaffle ball after Quaffle ball until she's covered in huge, ugly welts. Best dream ever.

CHAPTER TWENTY-SIX

It's been a week since Josie's party.

The welt is still visible but not swollen anymore. The purplish hue has grown to a lovely shade of yellow *and* purple. I think because it's so close to Halloween most people think I'm wearing zombie makeup or something, so it's all good in the end.

Anyway, I'm on my way to meet my brother Darren for a couple of drinks in Coconut Grove. I was supposed to have dinner with Alex, but he had to cancel because of a last-minute meeting he scheduled with an artist at a studio that he's trying to book for the gallery. He did say he'd be coming over afterward, so that gave me enough time to play catch-up with my little brother.

After circling all of Coconut Grove twice while cursing up a storm in my car, I finally find a parking spot close enough to the bar where I'm meeting Darren for drinks. As soon as I walk in, I spot him. It's not hard since he's flanked by two busty brunettes who are both vying for his attention like he's some prize cattle or something.

Seriously, ladies. Ugh. I can't even.

He sees me heading toward him as he tips his beer bottle to his mouth and takes a swig. He puts the bottle back down on the bar and grins like a kid who was caught with his hand in a cookie jar. When I finally reach him, he picks me up in his usual bear hug while I hear one of the girls he was talking to say to the other one, "Who is that?"

"I don't know," the other brunette answers.

Darren puts me back down and then turns around to grab his beer off the bar. "Ladies, it's been a pleasure."

He leads me to the far side of the bar while mumbling under his breath, "Thank God you showed up when you did. I couldn't take another minute with those two."

"Sure looked like you were enjoying yourself, Maverick."

"Please, give me some credit. I do have some standards."

"And what would those be?" I ask him with a laugh. "A pulse?"

The bartender comes over at that point, and Darren asks for two more beers. "God, you're hysterical, and by the way, what the fuck happened to your face?" he asks.

"I got hit by a ball."

"That's what she said," he adds quickly.

I put my hand on my hip and give him the evil eye. "Shut it. I really did get hit in the face by a ball, and believe it or not, this looks a hundred times better than it did a few days ago."

The bartender puts our beers in front of us, and Darren shells out the money to pay for them while I promise to pick up the next round. At that moment, a bevy of women comes strolling in the door. There's about five or six of them, all young and each more gorgeous than the next. Darren of course is mesmerized. What else is new?

The last girl, a leggy blonde, has her head buried in her purse but pops her head up at the last second, and wouldn't you know it? It's Sarah.

"Julia!" she yells like she hasn't seen me in years.

"Sarah!" I mimic.

She comes over to us and waves her friends away, letting them know she'll catch up to them. "Oh my gosh, what the hell happened to your face?"

Darren almost chokes on his beer.

"Long story," I deadpan.

"Isn't it always?"

Whatever the hell that's supposed to mean . . . your guess is as good as mine.

Sarah looks over and notices Darren for the first time. Her eyes scan him from head to toe, openly and without any shame. "Julia, aren't you going to introduce us?"

"Sarah, this is my brother Darren. Darren, this is Sarah, a friend of mine who works for Alex at the gallery."

My little brother, the player that he is—insert eye roll—takes the hand that Sarah extends for him to shake and turns its palm face-down so he can kiss the back of it. "A pleasure to meet you, Sarah."

"Oh my," she says, and starts to fan herself with her free hand.

Darren, of course, loves the effect he has on Sarah and moves in closer.

"Okay, you two," I announce and push Darren back a step. "Break it up."

He puts on his best innocent face while grinning at me. "What did I do?"

"Whatever, just put it back in your pants, for chrissakes." I look over at Sarah, who's still practically drooling over him, and sigh out loud. "Sarah, you can put it back in your pants now too."

She giggles and flips her hair off her shoulder, giving it one last shot before turning her attention back to me. "So what are you doing here anyway?"

"What does it look like I'm doing? I'm having a couple of drinks with my brother and then going home."

"Well, aren't you late for dinner with Alex at Lu Lu's?"

"Um, no."

"Oh," she simply says.

"Oh, what?"

"I'm just confused is all." She pulls her phone out of her purse, and after a few quick swipes, looks back up at me with a weird face. "He asked me to make a reservation for two for dinner at Lu Lu's kind of last-minute today. I figured it was for the both of you, but I guess not."

"No, I guess not." My spidey senses kick into high gear.

"Anyway, I have to catch up to my girlfriends. I'll call you next week so we can get together." She extends her hand out to my brother again. "Darren, it was *soooo* nice to meet you."

His voice lowers to a ridiculous level as he takes her hand in his and says, "The pleasure was all mine, Sarah."

She bounces away giggling while I'm trying to figure out why Alex would tell me he was going to meet an artist at a studio when he's half a block away having dinner with someone who isn't me.

Darren notices me getting agitated and asks, "Julia, are you okay?"

"Nope. Let's go."

I chug back the rest of my beer and slam the bottle down on the bar. I'm already walking toward the door when Darren yanks my arm to stop me. "Hey, what are you doing?"

"We're going to go across the street and see who the fuck Alex is having dinner with."

"So, we're going to spy."

"You're damn right I'm going to spy on him."

"Julia," he says, while running a hand through his hair nervously. "There's a guy code. I can't do that kind of shit."

I pivot my body around to face him and look him dead in the eye. Through clenched teeth I say, "Are you serious with your guy code bullshit? I'm your sister, which supersedes any stupid-ass guy code."

"Dude, I'm just saying—"

"You're just saying what?"

"I'm just saying that this has *bad idea* written all over it, Julia."

"You know what, Darren? I'll gladly tell Sarah you have elephantitus of the nuts the next time I see her if you don't let me go so I can see what the hell is going on across the street."

He lets go of my arm instantly and puts his beer down on the nearest surface. "Let's go."

We leave Taurus and turn to the left, heading toward Lu Lu's with my heart in my throat and my stomach in knots. In the back of my mind I'm thinking that it's nothing, or at least I'm hoping it's nothing, but something tells me I'm not going to like what I find when I get there.

Lu Lu's has a ton of outdoor seating, so I have to be careful not to be seen right away. Plus, it's on a corner, so from one side you wouldn't be able to get a look at the other and vice versa. Darren picks up on this immediately and tugs my arm so that we're hidden behind a bush. He holds up two fingers, points at his eyes, and then taps his arm before pointing to his eyes again and then finally pointing toward the restaurant.

"What the fuck does that mean, Helen Keller? And why can't you just tell me what you're trying to say via Navy SEAL sign language? It's not like anyone can hear us behind this bush."

He leans over and whispers, "I'm trying to be unnoticeable."

"Well, it isn't working, so tell me what you were trying to say."

Still in a hushed voice, Darren proceeds to map out his plan. "You should go across the main street so that you're behind those parked cars so you can scope out that side of the restaurant."

I sneak a peek over his shoulder while he's still giving instructions and see the one person I didn't want to see.

Marisa.

She's facing me. And sitting across from her with his back to me is . . . you guessed it, Alex.

"I'm going in," I say, cutting off Darren's plans.

"You can't just go in there. That defeats the entire purpose of spying."

"Hell yes I can. Watch me."

"Julia," he says, "sometimes things aren't as they appear. Stop and think for a second before you do something stupid."

I walk around the bush before Darren can stop me. With each step that brings me closer to their table, I feel more empowered. Finally, with only a couple of steps left, Marisa lifts her head and sees me coming. And I watch as she takes the opportunity to reach across the table and take Alex's hand in hers while smiling.

"Well, well, well." My voice is surprisingly steady given the circumstances. "What do we have here?"

I stand in between them, looking right at Alex, who lets go of Marisa's hand and shoots me a confused look.

"Julia," he says, genuinely surprised. "What are you doing here?"

I bring my hand up and point to myself. "What am I doing here? Funny you should ask that question since I'm wondering the same thing about you. You know, seeing as you're not supposed to be here."

"I can explain."

"Explain? I simply figured that this is one of your surprises since you know how much I love your surprises. Isn't that right, Alex?"

"It's not what you think, Julia."

Marisa speaks up then. "It's none of your business."

I lean forward, bracing my hands on the table, afraid I may slap the grin right off of her face. "Little girl, no one is talking to you, so do yourself a favor and shut the fuck up."

I turn my head to face Alex, who is rubbing the back of his neck and not saying a word. And honestly, there isn't anything he can say at this point that I would even want to hear, that's how pissed off I am.

I stand up straight and start walking quickly to my car. I totally forget about Darren in my anger-fueled haze until I see him coming toward me.

"Julia," he calls out to me, trying to get me to stop walking.

But I don't stop until I'm safely tucked away in my car, where I sit for a few seconds without starting it.

His fingers gently tap on the driver's side window. "Julia, come on. Talk to me."

Here's the thing. I don't cry much. With the exception of getting choked up at Josie's party, which technically doesn't qualify, I can probably count on one hand the number of times I've cried in the last ten years. But when I do, you should leave me be because it's going to be freaking epic. And that is exactly how I feel. The dam is about to break, and I know if I turn my head to look at Darren, I'm going to bust out with the hysterical crying right here in my car, parked on the street where I just found my boyfriend out to dinner with another woman.

"I'm going home, Darren," I choke out to him and start my car. "I'll be fine."

"No you're not. Please don't leave like this."

"I'll call you, okay?" I say, my voice starting to crack.

After a few beats, he relents. "Okay. Take care of yourself. And Jules?"

"Yeah?"

"Love you."

"Love you too, Darren."

I watch him step aside and move to stand on the curb so I can pull into traffic. The whole drive home I'm thinking that I shouldn't have anyone to blame for this but myself. I knew it was too good to be true. He was probably just better at hiding it, and I was only too eager and willing not to see it. I really pulled the wool over my own damn eyes, and it was right there in front of me all along. Aiden was actually right, and I chose not to believe him.

What kind of world is this when that asshole ends up being the good guy?

Because that right there might be the very first sign of the apocalypse.

CHAPTER TWENTY-SEVEN

I lock the front door behind me and slide down until my ass hits the hardwood floor. And that, ladies and gentlemen, is when I officially lose it. I wrap my arms around my knees and cry myself into a stupor. I curse myself for giving him a chance, for giving us and even love a chance. It always comes back to bite me in the ass, and I don't know why I even bother anymore.

This pity party of one goes on for a solid ten to fifteen minutes. It's interrupted by the sound of a car door slamming outside and way too close to think anything other than it being in my driveway.

Dammit, Darren is checking up on me even after I told him I'd be fine. Which I totally am not, but he doesn't need to know that.

His light knocking on my door gets me to stand up off the floor and peek through the peephole. To my surprise and absolute non-delight, it's Alex.

This guy cannot be serious right now.

"Go home, Alex," I shout through the door.

"Open the door, Julia," he calmly says. "We need to talk."

I rest my forehead against the cool wood and answer him. "There's nothing to talk about. Please, just go home."

"I'm not leaving."

"Fine, have it your way," I say, my voice cracking slightly. "Have fun sleeping in your car."

I peek through again to see him link his fingers behind his head and pace back and forth a few times. He stops suddenly and puts his hand on the door. I mirror him on my side as if we were having a prison visit.

I know, super cheesy. But when your heart is breaking, you tend to do shit that you would never do. Not in a million years.

"Julia, please . . . open the door."

The soft tone of his voice somehow breaks through to me even though I vowed to myself while crying on the floor a few minutes ago that I didn't want to see or talk to him again. So I undo the chain and turn the locks but don't open the door. I scurry off to sit on the couch with my arms wrapped around my knees.

"It's open," I yell out to him.

I watch as the knob turns and Alex appears in my foyer, closing the door behind him. He silently walks over to where I am and sits beside me. Leaning forward, he puts his elbows on his knees and rests his head in his hands.

"I'm sorry. I shouldn't have lied to you."

"Why did you then?" Then I quickly add, "Not that it matters anymore."

He turns his cheek to face me. "Because I knew you wouldn't understand."

"Wouldn't understand what exactly? That you were going on another date with that . . . that girl? You're right, I don't understand."

"It's not what you think." He quietly breathes out. "It wasn't a date."

"Alex, I'm not fucking stupid. I saw you holding hands with her, remember?"

"No you didn't."

"Are you calling me a liar?" My voice is almost screeching. "I saw you with my own eyes."

"No, you saw her reach over and grab *my* hand. What you didn't see was my expression or hear what I was telling her as a result, which is what I'm trying to explain to you."

"By all means, go ahead."

"She did come on to me, but I told her I had a girlfriend and I would appreciate if she respected that."

I laugh out loud. I can't help it, it's that goddamn funny. "You're joking, right?"

"Not at all."

"Okay, let's assume for a moment that you're telling me the truth about that."

"I am."

I shoot him a look, letting him know that he really need not interrupt me because it only pisses me off more than I already am. "Fine, whatever. Why were you out with her to begin with?"

He runs his hands through his hair again, some of it falling onto his forehead. With a long sigh he leans back and rests his head on the back of the couch. "She's been calling and calling me since Josie's party, and I was ignoring it until today when I decided enough was enough. So I called her to let her know we needed to talk. I swear I was telling her about us—that we're together and that she needs to move on with her life already."

He inches over to me then, placing his hand on my back, and I close my eyes at the contact. "Julia, I'm telling you the truth. Please believe me."

"Alex, what happens when she calls again? Because you and I both know that she will."

"She won't."

"You don't know that."

"Neither do you."

"Ugh, seriously, are you blind? She's in love with you or infatuated with you, and she won't stop until she's *with* you." He's quiet, so I keep going. "Do you have any idea what it was like for me to see the man I love having dinner with the girl who called me trash and said I wasn't good enough for you?"

Alex's eyes widen in shock because I guess it never got back to him what happened at Josie's party and how I ended up with this lovely reminder on my face.

"What did you just say?"

I point to my face. "This right here was caused by not paying attention because I was too busy eavesdropping on Marisa telling someone at the party how I was trash and not good enough for you." And then as an afterthought I add, "Oh, and that she couldn't believe we were dating at all and that it was basically only a matter of time before you're with her."

"I know. Vanessa told me all of that already. That's not what I was asking about."

"You knew about that and yet you still lied to me and went out with her?" My eyes roll up to the heavens in disbelief. "This shit just gets better and better."

"I spoke to her about that and told her she needed to apologize."

"Alex, if I ever see her again, I cannot be held accountable for what I do. So she can save the apology, and you can tell her in person because I have no doubt that you'll be seeing *her* again."

He grabs my chin then and tilts it toward him in a swift movement. "Enough, Julia. Go back and tell me what you said before."

"When? What are you even talking about?"

"When you were telling me about what it was like for you tonight to see me with her."

My hand shoots up and latches on to his wrist to pull him off of me, but he's too strong for me. "You know what, Alex? I think it's time for you to go because I'm done with this conversation."

He grins at me before letting go of my chin and casually kicking back on my couch. "I'm not leaving."

"You're not leaving?"

"Nope."

Fucking men! Jesus H. Christ, do they ever listen?

I stand up, so infuriated by him, and start to pace in front of the coffee table. Through my clenched teeth and in the quietest, calmest voice I can muster, I say to him again, "Please leave."

"Like I said, I'm not leaving until you tell me what it was like for you to see me with her."

Have you ever seen a cartoon where one of the characters has smoke blowing out of their ears? Or when they blow off the top of their head from anger or rage? That is exactly what I feel like when I start to shout at him. "Fine! You want to know what it was like? It was like a fucking knife to the heart! I hated it and wanted to scratch her eyes out *after* I kicked your ass up and down Coconut Grove!"

He stands up and starts coming toward me when my tears make an appearance again. I put my hands up and walk backward until my back comes in contact with the nearest wall. Alex braces an arm by my head and the other by my hip, trapping me in place like a caged animal. And considering what my face probably looks like right now from all the waterproof mascara that is never really waterproof, it's not a far stretch.

"That's not what you said before, so how about I help you remember?" he coolly says. "You asked me if I could imagine what it was like to see the man I love with another woman."

Dammit. I did say that out loud, didn't I?

I wipe my eyes and don't say a word. His eyes search my face until settling back on mine. "You love me."

"So?"

I know, childish and immature, but I'm grasping at straws here.

"So, when were you going to tell me?"

"How about never?"

"Guess what, it's half past never because you just did not five fucking minutes ago."

I try to dart out from under his arm, but he pulls me back against the wall and presses his body against mine. My hands shoot up and brace themselves against his chest, where I can feel his heart pounding away like a bass drum. His hands cup my face, and before I can think, feel, say, or do anything, his lips devour mine.

At first, my mind is blank and my body is a completely willing participant. It's a rough, hair-pulling, and clothes-being-tugged kind of kiss, leaving no doubt in my mind that if it keeps up we'll be fucking against this wall in about ten seconds.

Then a flood of memories of the last man who broke my heart, Aiden, seeps into my thoughts. And that's when I realize I need to stop this. I need to put distance between us. I cannot and will not let another man break me, especially when I'm so close to my breaking point already.

I pull his lips off of me and drop my hands, which were gripping his shirt for dear life. "You need to go now, Alex."

His confused expression matches the tone of his voice. "Why?"

"Because I can't do this anymore. I'm done . . . we're done."

"Are you kidding me, Julia?" Alex rubs the heels of his hands against his eyes before looking at me again. "You just told me you love me, and now you're going to turn around and tell me to get lost?"

"You don't get it, Alex," I say. "I can't trust you. You can explain until you're blue in the face. But the fact remains that I saw you with her. I heard her, and I know other things that have made me see the light and call this for what it was—a mistake."

"What other things?" he asks.

"It doesn't matter."

"Fuck if it doesn't," he says.

"I'm sure you won't be lonely too long," I say to him quietly. "Marisa is just a phone call away, isn't she?"

"Can you please stop talking about her?"

"I bet she looks just like Katerina." His eyebrows knit together in confusion as I keep on riding the runaway train that is bitchy Julia. "When you finally do fuck her, I bet it will be like fucking your dead fiancée. So it's kind of a win-win situation for the both of you."

As soon as the words are spoken, I immediately regret them. In my mind, I'm already trying to formulate excuses for myself, but I know without a doubt that there aren't any. I willingly crossed the line, and there is no going back.

His face is stoic and his voice is calm when he says, "You mean like it was a win-win situation for me when I couldn't fuck Sabrina but fucked you instead?"

Pow! Straight to the heart and the gut and the kisser.

But I deserve it and then some.

"Jesus Christ," he says, his voice matching the expression of shock on his face. "Why the fuck are you doing this?"

The tears start to flow, and he follows one stream down my cheek until it falls to the floor. He takes a few steps back and digs through his pockets for his keys. Once in his hand, he stares at me in quiet disbelief for a few seconds before heading toward the door.

"I came over here after you left me at the restaurant because I wanted to explain what happened. But I also came over here to tell you that I love you and that I would never do anything to hurt you again." My stomach bottoms out to hear him say this to me, but he's not done yet. "I hope you're happy with what just happened here, Julia. Because you fucking blew it for yourself."

He slams the door behind him, and I hear his car pull out of my driveway shortly thereafter.

It's then that I slide down the wall and collapse into a heap of tears and choking sobs. I tell myself I deserve it, that I did it all to myself, but it doesn't ease the pain whatsoever. And adding to the pain is the knowledge that he loves me, and he's right . . . I so blew it.

CHAPTER TWENTY-EIGHT

Note to self: you are no longer in college and too old to be sleeping on a hardwood floor all night.

My eyes are burning as the first flicker of light filters through my windows and hits my face like a spotlight. I wake up in the same exact spot on the floor from last night, and as much as my body is in pain from being in this position, I can't quite motivate myself to get up. I'm sure my eyes are all kinds of puffy and red from the off-and-on crying I did after Alex left last night.

God, what the hell did I do?

After he left, I went over and over everything in my head, trying to figure out what would possess me to say those things. Every time I came up with the same answer: self-preservation. I realize it's a cop-out—a huge one at that—but it's the only thing I have.

I have spent most of my adult life preventing men from breaking my heart by keeping them at arm's length. Whether it's by trying to find the littlest of things that would drive any sane person crazy or simply by hanging on to a past heartache and reminding myself of that whenever someone got too close. The latter is the category Alex falls into, and through no fault of his own because he never knew that he was going up against so much baggage. And you're right, it isn't fair. I wasn't fair to him, to myself . . . to us.

So even as I spoke those awful and hurtful words to him last night, I knew in my heart of hearts that I shouldn't be saying them. But the part of me that wants to keep my heart safe from any potential pain reared her ugly head and said, *"Fuck it, better now than later when he chews you up and spits you out."*

Trust me, I am fully aware how that logic is the stupidest and most idiotic thing I could imagine in my screwed-up head, but it's hard breaking yourself of a habit that you've been implementing for years.

Don't you think I want to?

I do. I *sooo* do.

I'm sick and tired of being so bitter, of pushing away my one shot at a happy ending that's full of unicorns with rainbows flying out of their asses. I want that for myself just as much as the next person. But like a carousel ride, I spin round and round, not knowing where the hell I'm supposed to start fixing this because I undoubtedly end up right at the very beginning of the ride—alone and mounting a mechanical machine.

I will admit to wanting to pick up my phone a bunch of times last night and call or text Alex. Hell, I even considered jumping into my car and heading over to his house to beg for forgiveness, but pride kept me planted on this floor in a writhing ball of tears and stubbornness.

Taking a deep breath through my lungs, I blow it out on a long sigh and roll onto my back to stare up at the ceiling, counting all the imperfections as if they were sheep. My eyes grow heavy again, and I succumb to sleep, not caring at all that I'm still on the goddamn floor.

A knock on the door—actually more like a pounding—wakes me up. I have no idea how long I've been asleep this time, so I glance over at the clock on the cable box by the television to see that it's a little after eleven o'clock in the morning. The pounding on the door starts up again, so I slowly peel myself up off the floor and go to see who it is.

Before I peek through the peephole, there is a second where I hope it's Alex waiting for me on the other side. But it's not.

I open the door to find Lisette and Sarah standing in front of me, both in their work attire since it's a Friday morning and they should be at work. Come to think of it, *I* should be at work. Ugh, whatever, this is my official notification to myself that I'm taking a mental day.

My voice sounding hoarse, I ask both of them, "What are you doing here?"

They barrel in, not speaking a word, and both sit down on my couch, staring up at me as I'm still holding the door open.

I close the door and lean against it while rubbing my eyes. "Seriously, guys, aren't you supposed to be at work?"

"Aren't *you* supposed to be at work?" Lisette asks in a quiet voice.

"I'm taking the day off."

"It would have been nice if you would have let me know or at least answered one of my calls or texts this morning when I was trying to figure out where the hell you were," she says, her voice growing more agitated by the second.

"Looks like you found me," I mutter, then direct my attention to Sarah. "I understand why she's here, but how did *you* get here?"

"Darren."

My head pops up at that. "Excuse me? What the hell does my brother have to do with you being here?"

"He called me at the gallery to ask me out. While we were talking, he told me what happened last night after I left you guys at Taurus," she explains in a rush. "So I called Lisette to see if she'd heard from you, and I told her what happened last night. Then she kept trying to get in touch with you, and then . . . well that's it. We came here."

My brain just exploded.

"Okay, let's try this again. Slowly this time so I can understand." I rub the heels of my hands against my eyes and move to sit on the coffee table to face them. "You're telling me that my brother Darren called you to ask you out on a date?"

"Yup!" she chirps happily. "First thing this morning at the gallery. I guess I made quite an impression on him last night!"

She raises her hand to high-five me, but I don't reciprocate, which causes her to frown. So she turns her hand toward Lisette, who indulges her and gets her to smile again.

"Sarah," I say in a hesitant voice. "My brother told you what happened last night? All of it?"

"He did, and I'm so sorry, Julia." Sarah's hand shoots out and pats my knee like I was a small child. "And by the way, he's all kinds of worried about you, so you might want to call him."

I dart my eyes to Lisette, who's watching me like a hawk. I point to Sarah when I ask Lisette, "She told you everything?"

"She did. I'm so sorry."

Obviously, they don't know the worst of it.

I start to chew on my bottom lip, and then Sarah chimes in. "Yeah, Alex hasn't shown up for work and isn't answering any calls or texts either."

"How did you get out of work then?"

"I told the office manager I had to buy tampons."

I can't help it. I start to laugh my ass off because this is now the second time in a month that she's used that excuse. "You do realize that you can't keep using that excuse."

She waves me off and rolls her eyes at me. "*Pfft!* Anytime you mention your period to a man, he clams right up. Works like a charm every time."

Once my laughter dies down my mood changes drastically, and I go right into crying, covering my face as the both of them sit there not knowing what to do since they've never seen me like this. Hell, I've never seen me like this!

"I'm a terrible person," I admit out loud and through my tears.

Lisette speaks up first. "No, you're not. How were you supposed to know about that woman?"

"Yeah," Sarah agrees softly. "That's kind of messed up."

I shake my head and drop my hands. "You guys don't get it. I really fucked up."

Both of them look confused, as well they should be. So I proceed to tell them exactly what happened last night. Every last gory detail up until I passed out on the hardwood floor.

After a long silence once I'm done retelling the night's events, Lisette looks me dead in the eye and says, "Julia, I love you with all my heart, but what you did last night, even for you, is really messed up. What the hell were you thinking?"

I open my mouth to explain, but she cuts me off. "You know what? Save it! Because I know what you're going to say."

"Lisette, I—"

"Don't 'Lisette' me, Julia! I told you to give him a chance, and you're sitting there telling me that he basically did nothing wrong and you still sent him packing?"

She goes to stand, but Sarah grabs a hold of her arm and pulls her back down.

"No puedo creer que hayas hecho esto. ¡Es increíble!"

"I don't know what Lisette just said," Sarah says quietly, "but I have to agree."

"But you just said you have no idea what she said," I answer back defensively.

"I mean everything she said before that." Sarah leans forward and takes my hands in hers. "Julia, you did a terrible thing, but it does not make you a terrible person."

"Ha! Didn't you hear what I said to him last night? I swear, I'm going straight to hell in a handbag."

"No you're not," she says with a small smile. "This can all be fixed."

I go to say something back, but Lisette speaks up again. "She's right."

My eyebrows shoot up at her agreeing with what Sarah said.

"He loves you, and you love him," Lisette says simply and crosses herself. "This can definitely be fixed."

My head tilts to the side as I wipe the tears from my eyes. "Sometimes love isn't enough."

Sarah and Lisette both look at each other and then back at me. They both start to shake with laughter, biting their lips to keep it in until they both explode.

"What's so funny?"

"You," they answer in unison.

"What did I say that was so funny?"

"When did you become a Hallmark card?" Lisette asks through the last of her laughing fit.

Sarah adds, "Yeah, this is most definitely fixable."

"I'm so glad that I can be the source of your entertainment today, but I'm not finding this funny at all. *Sooo*, if you don't mind, I'd like to get back to feeling sorry for myself and maybe eat a fuckton of white chocolate chip and macadamia nut ice cream."

I stand up and go to the door to open it for them. They follow me and whisper amongst themselves when they get outside.

"Go on and eat your ice cream," Lisette says over her shoulder at me while walking to her car. "We'll take it from here, don't you worry."

They climb into their cars and drive off, finally leaving me alone to try to make sense of what just happened. I plop down onto the couch still wearing my clothes from last night and expel a long-ass sigh.

Seriously, could my life get any more confusing or dramatic? I've turned into my own worst nightmare—a telenovela on one of those cheesy Spanish stations that I sometimes watch, even though I don't understand most of what's being said.

As a matter of fact, that might be what would go perfectly with a pint of ice cream.

I walk over to the kitchen and pull the emergency pint out of the freezer and then turn on the TV. Searching through my stored episodes on the DVR, I find *Corazón Indomable* and start the first of many episodes while I eat ice cream using a giant spoon. It won't make the pain go away, but it will at least make me forget for a little while, and that's all I need right now.

CHAPTER TWENTY-NINE

You tend to do really stupid things when you're down in the dumps. Not showering would probably be high on that list. It is for me at least. Eating lots of ice cream is another. Inventing a drinking game while watching *The Real Housewives of New Jersey* is yet another. This one was surprisingly easy, with the majority of tequila shots happening when any of the housewives looked at jewelry, talked about jewelry, or tried jewelry on. I had to stop playing since I was getting hammered twenty minutes into the second episode.

Another really stupid thing I've done is ignore Sabrina's calls and texts all weekend. I cannot bring myself to talk to her yet. I know she'll be full of sage advice and soothing words of comfort and all the other good stuff that comes along with being my best friend. But for right now, I want to wallow in my despair just a little while longer.

Alex still hasn't called or texted me. Not that I expected him to.

There was a very small part of me that was hanging on to the crazy idea that he'd show up here as if nothing had ever happened. Well here it is, Sunday night, and nothing, not a peep. Just me and my jar of peanut butter, which I've been eating with my fingers while watching the *700 Club* for the last hour because I'm too lazy to change the channel.

I'm in the midst of trying to figure out what is going on with Pat Robertson's hair when my house phone rings again. I glance over at it thinking that it's Sabrina again, but it's not. It's Aiden.

I can't explain why I reach over and answer. You might as well ask me why the sky is blue. I would probably have a more logical answer for that one. Because I know that I shouldn't be talking to him at all. Even though what he told me about Alex and Marisa was partially true, I think, I do realize that any further discussion with him has *bad* written all over it. But being the complete jackass that I am and a glutton for punishment, I pick up the phone.

"Hey," he says.

"Hey."

"I didn't think you'd answer the phone."

"That makes two of us," I answer.

After a brief silence he says, "Listen, I heard what happened."

"How did—"

"Sophia."

"Oh, that's right," I reply with a sarcastic laugh. "Your fiancée."

"I'm really sorry, Julia."

"Please don't. It's worse coming from you of all people. No offense."

"None taken," he says. "How are you doing?"

"Let's see . . . I've definitely had better days, and if the remote doesn't magically come to me, I'm going to be forced to watch the *700 Club* for the rest of my life. So yeah, on a scale of one to ten on the suckage scale, I'd say I'm about a solid nine right about now."

"I was thinking maybe I'd come by and keep you company for a little while," he says.

I almost choke on the dollop of peanut butter I've just eaten clean off my finger.

"Are you okay?" he asks.

"Um," I sputter while still trying to clear my throat. "Yeah, I'm fine. Listen, Aiden, I don't think that would be a good idea right now."

"Have you eaten dinner?" he asks out of left field.

"No, not really, but I don't see how—"

"I'll swing by and bring you something to eat," he says, interrupting me.

"Aiden, I really—"

"Julia, please let me do this. I feel awful and would really like to make it up to you."

"I am hungry, but—"

"Great, I'll be there in about half an hour," he says and then hangs up after saying a quick good-bye.

I stare at the phone still in my hand, wondering what just happened. The only rational explanation that I can come up with is that I've crossed over into the Twilight Zone. It's either that or coming to terms with the fact that I've somehow agreed to eat a meal in my house with my engaged ex-boyfriend while I'm feeling sorry for myself about Alex. And that sounds absolutely insane, so I'm going to go with the Rod Serling explanation on this one.

This also means that I'll have to cut short my pursuit of how many days I can go without a shower. My personal best is four days, and that stretch was due to the one and only Aiden. Not that I'm particularly proud of it, but it's an accomplishment nonetheless.

I drag my ass to the bathroom and take a brisk shower and then get dressed and don't even blow-dry my hair. Before I make it back to my home base on the couch, I unlock the door so I won't have to be bothered to stand up again when he gets here.

Dammit all to hell.

I forgot to pick up the remote control before I sat back down, so it looks like I'll be stuck watching this crap until Aiden shows up. Instead of trying to make sense of the ramblings coming from my television, I try to figure out why he's even coming. He said something about wanting to make it up to me. Again with the absolution bullshit. Or am I that much of a bitch that I can't wrap

269

my head around the fact that he's really trying to be sincere and genuinely feels bad about the current state of affairs? I massage my temples as the light throbbing in my head gets worse with each minute that I sit here trying to analyze Aiden's motives. I give up. Maybe he truly does want to make amends, and hey, I'm getting a meal out of his repentance, so there's that.

A few moments later a knock on the door breaks me out of my thoughts. I shout to let him know that the door is unlocked, and it slowly swings open. Aiden pokes his head inside, and as soon as he spots me on the couch, his smile widens.

"Can I come in?"

"Enter at your own risk."

He chuckles as he closes the door behind him. In his hand is a white nondescript bag with visible grease stains. My stomach grumbles in response.

Aiden glances at the television as he comes closer. "Shit, you weren't kidding with the whole *700 Club* thing, huh?"

My eyes are still focused on the bag of food when I answer him. "Nope, and if you don't mind, can you please hand me that remote control over there?"

I point toward the far corner of the ottoman where the god-damn thing has been taunting me for the last couple of hours. He picks it up and then hands it to me, and I immediately start browsing the channel guide until I settle on a *Friends* rerun.

It's then that I get a whiff of the food in the bag. And if my olfactory senses are still attuned to anything and everything that comes from Sergio's, then he's brought me one of my favorite things to eat in the entire world.

"Is that what I think it is?" I ask.

"What?" he asks, then lifts the bag up to his eye level. "You mean this?"

I nod just as my stomach starts to growl again. "Did you bring me a frita?"

"I did," he says, handing me the bag with a huge grin on his face. "I remembered how much you used to love them. I was hoping you still do."

He sits down next to me as I dig in and take my first bite. "Oh. My. God."

"Good?"

I answer him by taking another bite.

While I'm devouring my food, we sit side by side in silence with the occasional chuckle brought on by something funny on the television. Him being here does feel all kinds of weird, but I don't want to say anything about it yet. At least not until I'm done eating. At that point, I can politely say thanks for the grub and call it a night. After my last bite and during the next commercial break, I get up to get rid of my garbage and start thinking of the best way I can do exactly that. As I open up the refrigerator door to grab a Diet Dr. Pepper, Aiden sneaks up on me though and scares the living shit out of me.

He puts his hands up and then goes to lean against the kitchen counter. "Sorry, I didn't mean to scare you."

"It's okay," I say. "And thank you for bringing me something to eat."

"You're welcome, Julia. I meant what I said about wanting to make it up to you, so it was the least I can do."

"Yeah, about that, Aiden, I appreciate the gesture, but you really don't have to keep doing that."

"But I want to," he says.

I hesitate to find the right words so that I don't sound like an unappreciative bitch. "That's just it, Aiden. You shouldn't want to do anything. It's been five years since we were together. We didn't leave off on very good terms, and granted, you did apologize recently, and I really do appreciate that as well, but you're engaged, and it's just . . ."

"Just what?" he asks and takes a step toward me.

"It's just really strange." I wave my hands around me and then say, "All of this is."

"It doesn't have to be strange, Julia."

"But it is," I say in a huff and then catch my breath. As calmly as possible, I add, "Aiden, I'm sorry, but there is no other way to put this than we simply can't be friends. It's not healthy for me or you. And I'll bet you a million dollars that if I don't get it, then Sophia won't either."

He takes another step closer to me. Now he's within arm's reach and looking at me with an amused expression in his eyes. "What she doesn't know won't hurt her."

"Oh my God, Aiden," I gasp. "She doesn't know that you're here, does she?"

He shakes his head slightly, and then to my complete shock, his hand comes up to softly cup my cheek. "You're right, she wouldn't get it."

I stiffen as he comes even closer to me. So close that our bodies are brushing against each other. "What are you doing?" I whisper.

Aiden doesn't answer me with actual words. He does however answer me by bending his head and pressing his lips to mine. It all happens so fast but in slow motion. It's as if I'm having an out-of-body experience where I'm hovering above us in my kitchen and watching myself be kissed by him. And as strange and foreign as it all looks and feels to me at first, I let him.

I lose myself for a few moments, reveling in the sensation of having him this close again, so desperate for affection from someone that I willingly follow Aiden's lead. When his hand slowly wraps around my waist to bring us closer together, my hands inch up his chest and grab fistfuls of his T-shirt. He takes this as a sign of encouragement. Aiden groans into my mouth and then spins me around so that my lower back presses against the kitchen counter. It's when he attempts to lift me onto the countertop a second later that I break off the kiss.

I get a glimpse of his eyes, which are clouded with lust, before he ducks his head and starts raining kisses across my neck and collarbone. I close my eyes and see nothing but Alex. I see the pain I caused him and the pain I'm inevitably creating for myself and others by what's happening. That's when reality comes crashing down around me and common sense finally decides to make an appearance.

My hands push against his chest as I say in a quiet voice, "Aiden, please stop."

"Why?" he asks, slightly breathless against my neck.

"Because I don't want this."

He does stop then and lifts his head. Slowly, he grins as if he knows a secret or something. "I know what you want, Julia. I saw it in your face that night at the engagement party. I can see it in your eyes every time you look at me."

"I don't know what the fuck you're talking about, Aiden."

"Yes you do," he says with a light chuckle before attempting to kiss me again.

I push back on his chest a little harder this time, and he takes a step back.

"This was nothing more than temporary insanity. I'm sitting here depressed and heartbroken, and you come in with your food and white knight shit, and I fell for it. *That's* what this is and nothing more."

"Is that what you think?" he asks. "Because your body is saying something completely different."

I snap my fingers in front of his face. "Aiden, you're engaged, remember?"

"I remember just fine, and I have no intention of ever forgetting that. In fact," he says while closing the distance between us again, "this will stay just between us. You know, for old time's sake."

"Are you mental? Did you lose IQ points when the blood flooded to your dick a few minutes ago? Because there is no way in hell that I end up with you in my bed tonight. Or ever, for that matter. I love Alex."

"I did you a favor. That guy's an asshole," he says. "Looked at me as if I'm beneath him or some shit when I met him at the engagement party."

As his lips touch my skin and his hands grab my waist, it all clicks into place like pieces to a puzzle. "Aiden, what did you do?"

"I told you, I did you a favor. Now stop talking so we can get back to what we were doing a few minutes ago." He lifts his head and looks me dead in the eyes. "I promise you that you won't be faking it this time."

"Are you fucking serious?" I ask in disbelief. "Am I understanding this correctly? You said all that shit about Alex and Marisa and it wasn't true? All of it because I said I faked every orgasm?"

He chuckles against my skin. "It worked, didn't it?"

I am officially the stupidest person on the face of the planet. I should have gone with my gut instinct where Aiden was concerned. But instead, here I am, trapped between a rock and a hard place, literally, and I've royally fucked everything up with Alex when he had been telling me the truth the entire time.

I seethe with rage, and my voice almost cracks when I say, "You have three seconds before I go Bernadine on your ass."

"Who's Bernadine?" he asks, but keeps right on pressing kisses against my neck.

"Three, two, one. I warned you."

I bring my leg up and knee him in the balls, silently thanking Billy Blanks for that one month of Tae Bo that I did religiously during the summer.

He stumbles backward a step or two while cupping himself and writhing in pain, and he has the nerve to look genuinely surprised. "What the fuck, Julia?"

"Get out of my house right now, Aiden. I'm warning you. Don't make me angry—you won't like me when I'm angry."

Barely standing up, he slowly walks toward the front door while cursing under his breath. I follow closely behind. When he reaches it, he turns around to say, "You're not going to tell Sophia, are you?"

"Good-bye, Aiden."

He asks one more time.

I put my hands on my hips and swing the door wide open to spell it out for him. "Three, two—"

"Okay, okay, I get the hint," he says and finally leaves.

I slam the door shut behind his sorry ass and then let out a scream of frustration and anger for falling for his bullshit from the very beginning. How could I have been so easily manipulated? And of all the people to believe over Alex, who has been nothing short of perfect, I chose Aiden? What is wrong with me?

After a few minutes of letting it all sink in, I go into the kitchen to grab my good friend Grey Goose from the freezer. It's then that I see the list that I was so gung ho about a couple of months ago staring back at me. I stop and tear it out from underneath the magnet that's keeping it in place, staring at the final entry.

4. Forget about dickhead and have fun with Alex.

I read it another few times before crumpling it in my hands and throwing it in the garbage can in disgust. Forgetting about the vodka, I end up on the couch again instead. I curl up into a tight ball, mentally cursing myself for not taking my own advice, for not seeing what was right in front of me all along. And trying to figure out how the hell I can possibly get myself out of this mess.

CHAPTER THIRTY

Did you tell Sophia?" Sabrina asks.
"Of course I did," I say. "I'd want to know if it was me. Wouldn't you?"

She thinks about it for a second and then says, "Yes, I would. I guess we'll have to wait and see what she does with the information."

"Ah, that's the million-dollar question, isn't it? But at this point it's out of my hands. If she chooses to stay with him, so be it."

It's been a few days since the whole Aiden debacle. I finally came to my senses and realized I needed my best friend's advice sooner rather than later. So I texted her earlier today to let her know that I would Skype her tonight after I got out of work. To say she was shocked to hear about the developments with Alex and me would be putting it mildly. But she was more shocked to hear about Aiden's part in all of it. Quite frankly, I still am too.

"So what are you going to do?" she asks in a soft voice.

I sigh out loud and rub my eyes with the heels of my hands in frustration.

"Uh-oh, you're sighing—that can't be good," she says.

"Sabrina, I'm scared."

"Alex obviously loves you. What's there to be scared about?"

This time my sigh is tinged with a small chuckle.

"Seriously, I love you to death, Julia, but if you sigh one more time, I'm going to stab you in the eye."

"I really fucked up, Sabrina. Like huge, gargantuan fuckup. The kind of fuckup that if I was him, I don't know if I have it in me to forgive so easily."

She raises one eyebrow and grins. "And who said it was going to be easy?"

"Nobody, that's the point," I say with another sigh.

"What did I tell you about sighing?"

"Duly noted," I reply.

"Look, Julia, there's no doubt that you messed up. What you said to him about Katerina was so harsh, even for you. But sometimes we say and do things that we don't mean. We don't think about the repercussions while it's happening because all we *can* think about is protecting ourselves. And that's exactly what you were doing."

"Do you mind explaining that to Alex for me?" I ask. "It sounds so much more logical coming from you."

"Very funny," she says.

"I have feelings for Alex that I honestly thought I would never have for anyone after—"

"Don't you dare say his name," Sabrina says, cutting me off. "He forever shall be known once again as He-Who-Must-Not-Be-Named."

"Right. Sorry, I forgot. Anyway, as I was saying, I never thought I'd feel this way again. But it's different."

She tilts her head to the side and asks, "Different how?"

"Well with Alex . . . shit, I don't even know how to explain it to you. He just is. He's . . ."

"He's what?" she asks and then leans forward so that her face is consuming my screen and not in a cute way.

"Dude, back up, you're freaking me out."

She does and immediately asks the same question.

"He's amazing, Sabrina," I admit with a sad smile. "I don't know if it's because we were friends for a while before we started dating or what, but whatever it was between us was pretty goddamn perfect."

Her mouth drops open in shock, so I lightly tap the screen with my finger. "Close your mouth; you don't want flies going in there."

The initial shock wears off, and Sabrina is all smiles now.

"Why are you smiling like that?" I ask her even though I can already imagine what the hell is going through her head.

"You're so head over heels in love with him."

I all of a sudden become interested in a small string hanging from the hem of my T-shirt. Here's the thing—up until this point, I've been telling myself that maybe I'm in love with him, maybe I'm not, back and forth like I'm on a seesaw. However, in the deepest recesses of my mind and heart I know the truth. I *am* in love with him—head over heels, dedicating songs to each other, in love with him.

"Hey," she says, trying to get my attention again, "stop trying to ignore me."

"I'm not ignoring you."

Then Sabrina's lips morph into a sneaky smile. "Julia, I'm going to ask you a couple of questions, and you must answer them honestly with the very first thing that comes to mind, okay?"

Rolling my eyes at her attempt to play psychiatrist, I wave my hand at her and tell her to go on. Can you guess what she asks me? Yeah, pretty predictable.

"Are you in love with Alex?"

"Oh, Sabrina, aren't you the clever one?"

"I learn from the best," she says sarcastically. "And answer the question."

I take a quick breath and then exhale, and in a rush of words I say, "Yes. I'm truly, madly, deeply in love with him."

"Yes!" she exclaims with a fist pump. "I knew it!"

"Shhh, keep your voice down. I don't want Tyler to come and—"
Too late.

Tyler comes in behind her dressed all in black from head to toe, leaving no room for interpretation of what his favorite color is still. He's smiling his signature "I'm hot as hell and I totally know it" smile at us. Well, he probably doesn't call it that, but to me that smile should be branded and is all kinds of trouble.

I wave to the screen halfheartedly. "Hey there, Tyler, I see that you're still trying to bring sexy back."

"Julia," he tries to say with a straight face, "I see that you're still as blunt as ever."

Sabrina rolls her eyes and laughs. "Don't encourage her."

He bends down and kisses the top of her head. "I only came in because I heard you yell. Is everything all right?"

"It's far from all right, Tyler," I say. "In fact, I'd say it couldn't get much worse."

He knits his eyebrows together and looks at Sabrina. She shakes her head in a dismissive fashion and then says, "Don't listen to her. She's being dramatic because she's heartbroken, but she won't be for long."

"Would you stop with that?" I say to her. "You're embarrassing me in front of your man."

"You have got to be kidding me. You're telling me to stop after the countless times you've embarrassed me in public? Oh, hell to the no!"

Tyler looks between us and shakes his head. "Okay then, I can see that I'm not needed here."

He turns on his heel and leaves the room as quickly as he appeared.

I start to laugh because she's totally right. Me, Ms. Big Mouth herself, telling her to stop embarrassing me is definitely a sign that things are changing in my life. So what do I do? I let her bask in the glory that for once she has the upper hand on me.

She stops her gloating as I come down from my laughing fit. "Seriously, Julia, you need to talk to him. Be honest and don't hold back. Tell him what you told me, and I guarantee you everything will be fine."

"You really think so, Sabrina?"

"I know so," she says. "I pinky swear."

She raises her hand to the screen and wiggles her pinky finger at me. I smile in spite of myself and do the same thing back at her, hoping that she's right.

After we disconnect the session, I pick up my cell phone. Alex's name is the first one that shows up on my contact list, but I'm probably the last person he wants to hear from right now. Even after Sabrina's pep talk, I'm still too much of a coward to reach out to him. Then again, something like this should be done face-to-face.

Yes, that's it. That's the excuse that I'm going to go with for yet again tucking my tail and running away from the very best thing that's ever happened to me.

I'll do it tomorrow. Isn't that what Sabrina's always saying anyway? Everything looks better tomorrow, or some shit like that. God, you would think that I would have that memorized by now. I catch myself sighing again and stop. Tomorrow it is.

CHAPTER THIRTY-ONE

I stare blankly at the calendar on the desk in my office, counting off the days since I screwed myself over with Alex with the nub of an eraser on my chewed-up pencil.

Ten days have gone by since I spoke to Sabrina about it and told myself that I'd be contacting him the next day. Not because I don't want to either. But I figure if he hasn't tried once at this point, why bother?

Does that make me a chickenshit?

Most definitely.

The *only* good thing to come from this is that I've lost about five pounds, so my ass can fit more comfortably in my jeans. Not that I have anyone to impress, but it's a start.

I've barely gotten any work accomplished this week. This makes me feel more like an asshole because that means that Lisette has had to really pick up the slack for my being a basket case. All I've been doing is drinking coffee and waiting until it's five o'clock when I can get back home and crawl into my hole to hide until the next day.

Ugh, I know. It's pathetic.

So here I am, staring at the calendar, when Lisette pops her head into my office at quarter to five with a funny look on her face.

"We need to get going," she says dryly.

I keep my eyes on the calendar. "Get going where?"

"Did you even look at your calendar?" she asks with a sigh.

"You're joking, right? What does it look like I'm doing right now?"

"I mean the one in that machine to your right that lights up when you actually turn it on."

I point my thumb to the computer sitting on my desk. "This thing? Nope, haven't gotten a chance to."

"Because you're so busy," she mumbles.

"Whatever."

She comes to stand right in front of my desk and crosses her arms. Her toe tapping on the carpet starts a second later. I look up at her and roll my eyes, pushing my chair away from the desk at the same time.

"Fine, where are we going?" I ask while grabbing my purse.

"The gallery."

My ass falls back down on the chair. "Um, no, I don't think so."

"He's not going to be there, Julia."

"How do you know?"

"Oh my God," she says, walking around the desk and grabbing my arm. "Because we have a meeting with the new gallery assistant that he hired, not with Alex, so let's go. If you'd checked your calendar, you would have known this already."

Pulling me up to standing—although, let the record show I let her—she starts to drag me like a child. I yank my arm out of her grasp and smooth down my skirt. "There's no need to get physical, thank you very much. I can walk all by myself."

"Good, I'm so glad to hear it. Now, let's go."

"Okay, jeez!"

The ride over in Lisette's car takes all of ten minutes, and before I know it she's parking the car in front of the building. We walk to the door and open it, and I'm expecting to see Sarah perched at her desk, but she's nowhere to be found. As a matter of fact, there isn't a single soul or sound in the entire place.

"Where is everybody?" I whisper to Lisette.

She shrugs her shoulders. "I don't know."

She walks ahead of me toward the back offices but makes a quick left toward the actual gallery portion and then a quick right into the alcove.

What I see in front of me makes me take a couple of steps backward. Lisette turns around and grabs my arm again to get me to stop, dragging me back into the room to face the music, so to speak. Because sitting at a candlelit table for two is Alex with Sarah behind him, her hands planted on his shoulders as if to keep him right where he is.

"Sit down," Lisette commands.

I shake my head.

She gets all up in my grill right then, and in a deathly quiet voice she says, "If you don't sit down and do this, I will never speak to you again. I swear on Santa Bárbara that I will quit working for you if you don't do this for me right now."

I scrunch my eyes together at her threat, which for all intents and purposes sounds as serious as a heart attack. So I relent and plant my ass down on the chair opposite Alex, who looks as thrilled as I am to be here.

"Yay!" Sarah says from behind Alex. She lets go of his shoulders and claps her hands together softly. "Now, the two of you are going to have a civilized dinner, which we've already taken care of, and talk this thing out." She leans her head down to Alex's ear, but we can all hear her when she says, "Because you know I'm kind of tired of seeing you so grumpy."

Before they both walk out of the alcove, Lisette lifts the covers off our plates to reveal a juicy steak with mashed potatoes and mixed vegetables on the side. Meanwhile, Sarah pours us each a glass of red wine with a huge smile on her face. My stomach starts yelling at me to dig in, but on principle alone I cross my arms and decide not to. Alex, on the other hand, picks up his fork and knife and gets right to it. I decide to grab my wineglass and start drinking instead.

He sets his fork and knife down and wipes his mouth with the napkin. As he picks up his wineglass, he shoots me a curious look over the candles. "Aren't you going to eat?"

"No, thank you. I'm not hungry."

My stomach picks this moment to growl loudly because I'm sure it's sick of peanut butter, Doritos, and ice cream and wants nothing more than to eat a real meal for a change.

"Are you sure about that?" Alex asks with a grin. "Or are you simply fighting me on this like you do everything else?"

"I might be just a little hungry," I mumble under my breath.

So I start eating. Well, we're both eating, but in complete silence. It's strange because I really want to drop this tough exterior act, apologize, and tell him how much I wish I'd never said those things to him. But I don't.

It's killing me to the point that I lose my appetite after three or four bites of food and put the fork down on my plate with a loud clank. I can't even sneak a glance at him across the table for fear I may lose my shit again. And by *lose my shit* I mean cry a river, and I've had enough of that to fill my days and nights for the rest of my existence.

"Julia," Alex says in a tender tone that breaks my heart.

I dart my eyes up at him to find his eyes soft and as blue as ever. It gives me a fleeting sense of hope, but I don't say anything back to him.

"Come here."

I hesitate for a moment, then answer him by standing up slowly and walking over to him, his eyes following me every step of the way. When I reach him, he pushes his chair out and grabs both my arms, pulling me to sit down on his lap. And I don't know why, but the tenderness that he shows while he arranges me makes me teary-eyed.

He uses his thumb to wipe away a tear on my face with a small smile playing across his lips. I clasp my hand onto his wrist to keep him close. Alex responds by cupping the side of my cheek as I burrow into the warmth of his skin and close my eyes at the feeling.

God, I've missed him. Every little thing about him. And I know in the back of my mind I don't deserve him after what I did, which makes this moment even more bittersweet for me.

"Alex, I'm so sorry."

"Julia, before you say anything, let—"

"No, you let me talk for a minute, even though I'll probably stick my foot down my throat again somehow."

He nods, so I pour my heart out and give it my best shot.

"I'm so unbelievably sorry for saying all those awful things to you. You didn't deserve it, and I didn't mean it, really I didn't." I take a quick breath and blow it out, trying to focus on his gorgeous eyes, which are staring intently at every word coming out of my mouth. "I was burned once—badly—by someone who I thought loved me, and I've been hiding and pushing people away ever since. So when I saw you with Marisa at an innocent dinner, I took it as my out to save me from the potential heartache down the road. And for that I'm truly sorry because I never gave us a chance."

Alex tries to interrupt, but I place my finger on his mouth to stop him. "I also want to tell you that I've missed you like crazy. I've been a fucking mess every day since you walked out my door. I would have come crawling back to you sooner and begged for your forgiveness, but the way you left . . . it scared me, and I didn't think you'd ever want to see me again after the things I said that night."

Again, he tries to speak, but I press my finger against his mouth with more force. "And I'd like to say one more thing." This time I close my eyes because I haven't said this to any man in what feels like an eternity. So just above a whisper I confess it to him. "I love you, Alex. So much. And you don't have to say it back to me, but I at least wanted to be honest with you for once."

I open my eyes and watch as he smiles against my finger until all I see are his dimples. He pulls my finger down, and his hand that is cupping the side of my face slides to the nape of my neck.

"Are you done?"

I nod and wipe away a stray tear. His hand on the back of my neck tightens, and it brings a flurry of butterflies to my stomach. He pulls me closer until his forehead rests against mine. I close my eyes again, wanting to memorize this moment forever, and then he opens his mouth to speak.

"I spoke to Sabrina."

My eyes fly open. "You what?"

"She told me everything," he says.

"Oh my God, I'm going to kill her," I say under my breath.

"No you're not. She's a good friend and loves you very much and was only looking after you. Something about a pinky swear."

I smile. "We did pinky swear."

"I was only giving you until the weekend to get your shit together before I came pounding on your door." He goes on. "I'm so sorry that I didn't come sooner, because I love you too, Julia, and I missed you like crazy."

I want to kiss him so badly, but I'm afraid, so I lick my lips to keep myself from making the first move. Yup, still a chickenshit.

"Alex?"

"Julia?"

I grin because I've missed this too.

"Will you please kiss me?"

"Not until you tell me you love me again."

I loop my arms around his neck and poise my lips over his. "I love you, Alex."

"Again."

"I love you."

"One more time, please," he whispers against my mouth.

"I. Love. You. Now, please kis—"

He angles his mouth over mine and starts to do as I ask. It's soft, tender, and oh so perfect. Before long it escalates. And sweet Lord how I've *definitely* missed this.

Our breathing is becoming labored as each of us is grabbing and pulling at the other. He adjusts me on his lap in one swift movement until my skirt is hiked up to my waist and I'm straddling him. My hands start to make quick work of his belt buckle to release his—

You know what?

I'd like for once to make love to my man without all of you getting a free show. This one is just for me and my man. "My man," has a nice ring to it, don't you think?

Yup, I couldn't agree more.

EPILOGUE

About eight months later . . .

I'm not a man of many words.

I say what I want, when I want, with as little fuss as possible. This is particularly effective when it comes to the woman in my life.

She, on the other hand, can talk my ear off and question every little thing to the point of distraction. I especially enjoy when she gets that look on her face as she's about to go off on me. Because all I have to do usually to get her to calm down is wrap her up in my arms and kiss her senseless until she shuts up. Then she's back to her normal self, spouting off pop culture references that I sometimes can keep up with, but for the most part I have no goddamn clue what she's talking about.

As of late, this has been happening more often.

No, no, no. It's not what you think. She's just . . . how can I put this delicately?

I'd say she's a bit stressed what with the move and all.

Julia and I now live together. It was a natural progression in our relationship, seeing as how we essentially were living together but not sharing a closet. At least that's how her father nicely put it the last few times we had dinner with them. Actually what he really said was, "When the fuck are you two going to move on to the next step already? Inquiring minds want to know."

So now we share a closet and everything else that comes with it. Today will be the third day since she's moved all of her stuff into my house. Sorry, I mean *our* house. I have to try and catch myself with that because if she hears me say it wrong one more time, she's threatened to pack her stuff up and move back to her old house.

There's still boxes scattered everywhere as we try to decide what will go where and piles of clothes in the bedroom that scare the living crap out of me. I've never seen that much clothing in one place before without it being a mall, but she swears she needs all of it.

I glance up at the clock on the wall in my home office and notice that she should be home soon. I've been checking off and on for the past ten minutes since we have reservations for dinner in about an hour, and I don't want to be late.

And like clockwork, I hear the front door open not a minute later.

And not even a second after that I hear her voice floating down the hall. "Motherfucker! Are you fucking kidding me with this shit? Jesus Christ! No fucking way!"

I cringe before calling out to her as calmly as possible. "Julia?"

"Hang on a second, I'll be right there."

More cursing ensues for a few more seconds, and her voice gets closer until she's standing in the doorway of my office holding a letter in her hand and looking as beautiful as ever. No joke, she takes my fucking breath away every time I see her. Especially now.

I beckon her with my finger, and she walks over to me with a worried look on her face. She comes around my desk, and I swivel my seat to make room for her to stand in between my legs. I grab her hips and kiss her stomach before looking up at her.

"What's wrong?"

"I just got Sabrina and Tyler's wedding invitation in the mail."

I smile as she shows me the invitation in her hand so I can read it for myself. "Baby, we already knew about this. I don't understand why this is getting you so upset that you have to curse like that. We had a deal, remember?"

"I know, I know, I owe the curse jar like a hundred bucks, but I don't give a shit."

I have to bite my lip to keep from laughing because I love it when she gets so worked up. She looks beyond adorable when she's angry. "That's another ten bucks. Keep it up and you'll be able to pay your rent here for the next year in advance."

"Very funny," she says with a smile creeping up on her face.

"Tell me what's the problem without cursing, and I'll take you out to dinner."

"You're taking me out to dinner anyway."

"I know, but watching you try not to curse is fun."

She drops the invitation on my desk and plants her hands on my shoulders. I rest my chin on her stomach as she goes on about the date of the wedding, getting more worked up with every passing word until she drops the f-bomb again.

"Don't say it," she warns playfully.

"I still don't understand what the problem with the date of the wedding is."

"Alex, do the math." Her eyes go wide as if hinting at something when it finally clicks.

My fingers lift up the hem of her T-shirt so that I can kiss the skin underneath her belly button. I shoot my eyes up to find her watching me as I press more kisses softly against her stomach, and my hands grip her hips to keep her in place.

"Alex?"

"Julia?"

She smiles then and weaves her fingers through my hair, holding me close to her.

"My tits are going to be fucking huge after this kid is born in November. Have you ever seen a woman after she gives birth?

Seriously ginormous fucking tits. And the wedding is supposed to be in December on a fucking beach on some island. What the hell am I supposed to even wear to cover those puppies up?"

"Cover your ears, kid," I say against her stomach.

"Stop calling our baby *kid*. She's going to come out thinking that's her name."

"You think it's a girl?"

She gnaws on her bottom lip for a second, thinking it over before she answers. "I'd be a liar if I didn't want you to have your own little girl after seeing you with Josie, but I really don't care what it is because it's ours."

I kiss her stomach once more, and all the cursing is forgotten because when she says things like that my whole body reacts to her. And for the record, I really don't care about the cursing. It's just a way for her to practice curbing it before our baby is born in about five months.

I change positions and pull her down on my lap so she can straddle me. "Uh-uh, this is how we got ourselves in this mess to begin with."

"Aren't you the one who forgot her birth control pills and told me not to pull out?"

"Yeahhhhhh," she says, drawling out the word and tilting her head to the side. "But you were the one who decided to whisk me away to a remote island where there were no pharmacies around to buy condoms."

She grins at me as I curl my hand around the side of her neck, pulling her to me so I can taste her. As soon as my lips meet hers, she melts into me. Her tongue, silky soft, darts out and reaches for mine, and I more than willingly oblige, angling my mouth to give her better access. I gently tug at her hair to break off the kiss before it spirals out of control, and she pouts, making me chuckle.

"Don't you worry." I press another kiss to her lips. "We'll pick this up later."

I help her stand up, and as she's backing out of my office she says, "You've got yourself a deal."

She disappears toward the bedroom but shouts out a second later to me. "How much time do I have before we have to leave for dinner?"

"Half an hour," I shout back.

I start to read the wedding invitation she left on my desk, focusing on the date, and I grin to myself because she fell for it. This invitation is really for *our* wedding in Bermuda. Sabrina and Tyler are getting married in December as well, but in Philadelphia and after us. Julia won't know until the day it happens. And yes, I'm prepared for the wrath of my beloved. But I'm sure she'll get over it.

Because you all know how much Julia loves my surprises . . .

ACKNOWLEDGMENTS

Christian, thank you for being my sweet little boy and warming my heart with every hug and smile you grace me with. I love you, little man.

Belinda, thank you for showing me how to be a mom and a best friend all rolled into one. You constantly amaze me, and I learn something new every day because of you. I love you, mini me.

Kyle, I would not be here were it not for you. Thank you for your unending support, encouragement, and love. Sorry, but this book doesn't have a hot dog cart scene in it either. Maybe next time . . .

Dionne Simmons, woman . . . thank you for being there whenever I need it and for being the bestest friend a girl could ever ask for. Love you so much!

Lisa Chamberlin, thank you for being such a great friend in every sense of the word and for making me laugh whenever I need it. Your loyalty goes beyond the normal bounds of friendship, and I love you for it.

Claribel Contreras, thank you for always being so supportive and for simply being there for me when I need it. Oh, and for sharing your love of serial killers with me too . . . it makes me feel so much better about myself. Love you!

Sara Queen, you are amazing! You have continued to be a great friend, and your support continues to amaze me. I am forever grateful to have found you in this crazy book world. Love you, SAQ!

Mimi Abraham, thank you for believing in me. Your encouraging words have helped me more than you will ever know. Love you! Vicky Carballo, thank you for just being you, Void. Your Null loves you no matter the amount of time between talks and visits. Xoxo!

Jessica Carnes, thank you again for taking the time to look at my work and always finding the little things that I would have missed along the way. Without your eyes AND you, I would be completely lost.

To everyone at Montlake Romance who has been so welcoming from the very beginning, especially Jessica Poore in Author Relations and my editor, Maria Gomez, you both have made me feel like I was part of the team and have made all of this so much more worth it.

Melody Guy, thank you for taking the time to go through my story with such a fine-tooth comb. Working with you has been a complete joy.

Kara Malinczak, thank you for all of your time, comments, and suggestions. Your input has been so helpful in getting me closer to the finish line.

Thank you to EVERY SINGLE BLOGGER, big and small, who has helped to get my name out there, supporting me in every sense of the word. Without all of you, there is no way that I would be here right now. I can't possibly list every one, but I would like to give a very special thanks to Sandy Roman Borrero at *The Book Blog*, Christine Estevez at *Shh Mom's Reading*, Kayla Sunday at *My Book Muse*, Becca Manual at *Becca the Bibliophile*, Patricia Lee at *A Literary Perusal*, Nadine Colling and Tamara McRae at *Hook Me Up Book Blog*, and last but not at all least, Angie "Squeee" McKeon at *Angie's Dreamy Reads*.

Thank you to the following people who have come into my life and have made a lasting mark: Sandra Cortez, Michelle Finkle, Stephanie Sandra Brown, Shawna Vitale, Karina Anastazia, Crysti

Perry, LaStephanie Kannady-Foster, Dyann Tufts, Luisa Hansen, Sarah Lowe, Lizzy Henriquez, Ciara Martinez, Tessa Teevan, Fred LeBaron, and all my KBs!

And finally, to my family . . . I love you all and thank you all for your support over the years and hopefully many more to come!

ABOUT THE AUTHOR

Barbie Bohrman was born and raised in Miami, Florida, and ultimately moved to the Garden State, where she currently resides with her two children and fiancé. When she is not writing, you can find her trying to get through the 1000+ books on her Kindle or watching *Lost* or *Seinfeld*.

Connect with the author at:

Facebook:
https://www.facebook.com/pages/Barbie-Bohrman-Author/170019943145037?ref=hl

Goodreads:
https://www.goodreads.com/bbohrman1

Twitter:
@barbie_bohrman

Website/Blog:
www.barbiebohrmanbooks.com